TAMED BY A BILLIONAIRE

LOVECHILDE SAGA BOOK 2

J. J. SOREL

Line Edit &Proof - Red Adept

AUTHOR'S NOTE: This is a steamy romance with descriptive sex scenes.

CHAPTER 1

Mirabel

ETHAN'S WARM, MUSCULAR CHEST pressed against my back. His arms wrapped around me, holding me close, almost crushing me. His heart pounded in rhythm with mine.

He held me as though his life depended on us being attached, skin on skin. But how the hell was I meant to sleep with that huge erection poking my arse?

His breath tickled my neck, while his roaming fingers settled against my stomach before sliding down my back and making me tremble. As a wave of lust washed over me, I didn't want him to stop. Melting with desire, I sighed silently under his feathery caresses. An overwhelming ache screamed for his earlier hungry groping.

A thin piece of fabric was all that lay between us. I'd worn a T-shirt to bed, while he was naked. And now I could feel every inch of him. Arousal shivered down to my core. I was at the mercy of my hormones, and they knew exactly how they wanted this to end.

This was not meant to happen. *How did it get this far?*

I could barely think straight with his body spooning into mine and his teasing touches sizzling my skin. This was a friend in need, I had to remind myself, not that filthy-rich playboy I enjoyed poking fun at.

But would a friend in need have such a raging hard-on? And why did I forget to wear panties?

His warm breath on my neck made my flesh tingle. I could barely breathe in anticipation of what he might do to me.

How will this end? Me asleep? Or him asleep, and me playing with myself? Or me turning around and rubbing myself against him? Or me sucking him off?

I was meant to hate him—the womanizing heartbreaker, too gorgeous for his own good. But so many hot, sexy thoughts crushed my sanity as a deep, throbbing ache fired between my legs.

"Am I keeping you awake?" His rasp shot hot air into my ear.

I nearly laughed. *No, of course not. I always fall asleep with a throbbing dick poking at my bum.*

"Um. Well…" was my only response.

"It's not easy to sleep with all these curves rubbing against me. Hell, Mirabel, you're so fucking voluptuous. Almost to a fault."

"To a fault? You mean I'm overweight?" I had to ask. My ego remained strong as always.

"No. Just that you've got…" He ran his hands over my heavy breasts, and the lips of my slit palpitated in synch with my heartbeat. "Great tits. Full, soft, and real. You're a wet dream come true."

"And here I was thinking it was my raw creative talent, as you so eloquently put it, that had attracted you."

"Your song moved me to tears, whereas your body is turning my balls blue. I want to fuck you until I forget my name and hear you screaming mine."

I'd already forgotten my name.

His fingers slid over my legs and under my T-shirt to my naked arse. He released a heavy breath, and his dick twitched again. His teasing fingers left trails of sparks, leaving me breathless. His warm hand massaged my butt cheeks, so close to my vagina, it virtually wept. He spanked my arse gently then again with a little more force. But hotter. Sexier.

"You forgot your panties. Now I'm really going to have to fuck you."

I couldn't help but laugh. We'd always played little games. When we were kids, it was hidey around Chatting Wood. When we were teenagers, it was flirty, teenage-angsty games like the one that had led to *that* kiss. Now that we were adults, Ethan was spanking me.

"I'm wearing something."

He massaged my butt, and his finger hovered tantalizingly close to my swollen, engorged slit. Anticipation trapped air in my lungs.

"You feel fucking hot." He rubbed himself against me, and I gulped. My mouth went dry, and my tongue stuck to the roof of my mouth.

"Do you mind me doing this?" he asked.

A sticky "No" barely made it out of my mouth.

He fondled my breasts and released a groan.

That was the end of me.

We came face-to-face. His full lips brushed mine, and his tongue ran along the crease of my lips, still burning from that earlier kiss that had turned a cold night into a heatwave.

He crushed me with his smooth, firm body.

His stubble massaged my face while those moist, full lips devoured me. Groaning into my mouth, he kept touching my breasts. "My cock wants to drown in your cum."

The old me, the one convinced I would never let this man close let alone rub that huge erection against me, would have laughed in his face. But hot and seriously horny me dripped with readiness. I pressed into him as he pulled me close.

"Do you want my dick inside you?" He seemed to breathe fire on my nipples as he spoke before devouring them. "Can I taste you?"

I nearly laughed at that request. No-one had asked that before. I stammered, "Um... I guess so."

He parted my legs and burrowed his head between my thighs.

I nearly hit the roof as the tip of his tongue tickled my engorged bud.

He nibbled, licked, and drank me as though quenching a thirst until I couldn't take it anymore. I released clenched muscles and surrendered to a delicious cascade of stars.

"Please fuck me." I'd become a whimpering mess.

He came up for air.

As his gaze burned into mine, I'd become his slave. Raw primal lust had doused all reason.

I stared into those dark bedroom eyes and spread my legs to welcome him in. He entered me in one fiery hot thrust, and the burning, delicious stretch made me gasp.

"You're delectably wet," he breathed.

His slow, yet forceful thrusts made me feel so full, I didn't know where I ended, and he began.

"Fuck, Mirabel. You're even hotter than I imagined."

Friction intensified with each thrust, scraping nerve endings along the way, leaving me quivering.

I gripped his flexing toned arse as he plowed into me. His mouth moved from my lips, traveling to my neck and then sucking my nipples, sending me into a frenzy of sensory overload.

"I need you to come. Like soon." His breath was ragged. His sticky skin pressed against mine as his cock pumped into me, riding me hard. I went into the side splits to welcome every hard inch of him.

The slurp of my pussy and the thud of his balls slapping against my skin became urgent. Our dance turned fierce and greedy as our whimpers and moans thickened the air. My eyelids fluttered and my toes clenched.

"I need you to come." He groaned.

The muscles of his arse clenched and relaxed on my fingers as he moved faster. Grunting, groaning, and making all kinds of agonized sounds, Ethan had turned into an animal. A tall, muscular, well-endowed beast.

My breathy sighs turn into loud moans as a warm wave swallowed me up and tossed me around in a universe of stars and meteor showers. As his dick pulsed inside me, a volcanic eruption of hot seed gushed into me.

Heavy breathing mingled with my panting, as we clutched each other. Then I started to laugh.

After a moment or two, Ethan pulled away from my arms and frowned. "What's funny?"

"That was crazy."

A slow sexy smile grew on his flushed features. "Yeah. Insanely hot. I always sensed you'd be nice to fuck, but shit, I never imagined this."

I stared into his eyes. "What do you mean?"

"I just love the way you feel. And you've got this addictive flavor. Everything about you." He rubbed his head as though I'd stumped him.

Complimented, nevertheless, I couldn't even count to ten let alone make a sensible comment.

He took me into his arms and kissed me tenderly while stroking my hair. Feeling too many emotions to deal with, I wanted to cry. What he didn't know was that I'd never orgasmed while being penetrated. Ethan had opened me up, stirring something inside that I couldn't quite understand.

"This was not meant to happen," I said.

He frowned.

Looking at that just-fucked hair, dimples, chiseled jaw, and large brown eyes, I thought I was hallucinating. *How did this ridiculously good-looking man end up in my messy bed?*

"I'm glad it did."

The serious glint in his eye had me spellbound. I was searching for the version of him that rambled on about silly nonsense, with a hint of sex. Always sex. Although I called him a conceited prat, I secretly got off on his flirtatious banter.

His father just died. This is Ethan as you've never seen him before.

"I hope you don't think I took advantage of you," he added, caressing my arm. His lulling, feathery touches were too addictive to roll away from.

"No." I smiled meekly.

"You can hate me tomorrow," he said with a sad smile. "Remind me why again?"

He looked into my face. A line formed between his dark brows. Normally, he would chuckle at my little digs, but this was different. His fingers slid up my arm and over my shoulders, robbing me of sanity again.

"Um... You're spoiled and a womanizer and..."

His finger kept moving over my puckering skin. "Continue…"

"I can't think straight with you doing that."

"I like it too."

"You like touching me?"

"That too. But I meant I like it when you spit vitriol at me. It's kinda hot. Your eyes get this sexy spark."

I had to laugh at that.

He smiled tightly, and we held each other.

"I'm sorry. You're grieving. I shouldn't poke fun at you."

"Hey, I asked," he said then kissed my cheek tenderly. "Thanks."

"For what?"

"For being here for me."

We continued to hold each other, and I rocked him gently in my arms. A tear dropped onto my skin. Yes, he was heartbroken. Having lost my parents, I understood that grief only too well.

My heart ached for Ethan and the Lovechildes. His father was a good man. Despite our differences, I'd grown up around that powerful family and felt a connection of sorts with them.

CHAPTER 2

Ethan

EVERYTHING SEEMED A BLUR as people poured into the church, filling the pews. I'd struggled to even get out of bed, let alone face people. Smiling was out of the question. That was even more painful than trying to remember the names of family and friends I'd known since childhood.

Theadora close by his side, Declan stood at the church entrance, holding out his hand and welcoming people, while Savanah and my mother hid their faces behind black-veiled hats.

Everyone took their seats, and Theadora sat at the organ flooded by a kaleidoscope of beamed light.

To the sound of heavy, sorrowful notes, the service began.

As the priest began his sermon, I heard whispers and shuffling from the back of the church. I turned to see who'd arrived.

Illuminated by a shaft of blinding daylight, Mirabel stood at the arched entrance, dressed in black. Her long, wavy hair gave off a fiery red halo, and her presence added electricity and life to an otherwise-grim affair. Not that she would have intended it that way.

She'd become my most welcomed, if not guilty, distraction from this crushing sadness, the likes of which I'd never experienced before.

If I were being honest, I preferred losing myself to replays of that hot, steamy night over being consumed by dark, unsettling thoughts of my father's untimely death.

We hadn't seen each other after *that* night, one week ago. Not for lack of trying. I'd called her from London, where, as newly appointed CEO of Lovechilde Holdings, I'd been all week.

"Harry Lovechilde was loved by many within the Bridesmere community," the priest said. "He worked tirelessly to ensure no family went without, especially during crop failure and the devastating floods that swept through the region two years back."

I recalled that period. My mother had fought with my father over the suspension of farming rents, which added up to about one million pounds, or so she kept reminding him. For us, it was a no-brainer. Those families had been there forever.

So what does that now mean? That question had already come up more than once, but with my head buried in my hands, I was in no emotional state to think about the next hour, let alone the future of the surrounding farms.

The priest stepped away for Declan to take the podium. After clearing his throat, my brother spoke of our dad as a loving, nurturing parent. He shared sweet anecdotes, including the time our father tried to perform CPR on a duck who'd crashed to the ground. That charmingly absurd episode brought a few chuckles from the mourners.

No matter how much I tried, I couldn't muster a smile. Savanah squeezing the blood from my hand while crying her eyes out did nothing to improve my mood. I succumbed to endless contagious sobs that had me tasting my salty tears again. The only time I'd cried like this, although not for such a sustained period, was after the death of our pet dog when I was twelve.

Declan deserved a medal of bravery for standing at that lectern. I could never have done it. I'd barely uttered a coherent sentence all week.

My mother just sat there, blank-faced. Will was at her side, also emotionless. I couldn't figure that out. All I could do was think about the voluptuous local who reminded me that I was still alive and hot-blooded, despite this crippling sorrow.

We rose, knelt, then rose again as we recited prayers and sang a hymn accompanied by Theadora on the organ. Finally, the service came to an end. More hugging ensued, then I became one of six pallbearers.

To the strains of Bach, I took slow, careful strides, my eyes cast down as we carefully moved through the church, down the steps, and onto the grassy side of the cemetery where my grandparents, along with other Lovechildes, rested. Their cold and worn tombstones stood side by side. The grey-etched stone reflected the melancholic sky while circling ravens squawked overhead. We placed the casket down, and I took a step back.

"Ashes to ashes. Dust to dust," the priest orated, and we all tossed dirt over my father's coffin.

My sister fell into my arms, sniffling, and I patted her back. "I don't think I'll ever be the same again."

I knew how she felt. I was no longer that flippant man flitting from bar to bar. My father's death had sent me into a dark cave of introspection. A place I'd never visited before.

Is this what an epiphany feels like?

Declan and Theadora joined us.

"That was a stirring speech." I hugged my brother and kissed Theadora on the cheek.

"I don't know how you managed to keep it together," Savanah said, wiping her nose.

"Someone had to do it." He gave his wife a sad smile as she took his hand with love glowing in her eyes.

The shining light that beamed from their eyes in a show of touching affection tugged at my heartstrings. Seeing how close they were and the strength they drew from one another, especially at such a dark time, made me pine for what they had.

"That was a moving performance," I said to my new sister-in-law.

"Thanks. I spent all night practicing." She gave Declan an apologetic smile.

"One doesn't tire of Bach easily." Declan kissed her cheek and then turned to me. "So how was your first day with the staff in London?"

Although business was a far cry from my current thoughts, I welcomed the change of subject. "Good, I think."

"The board wants to impose cutbacks," Declan said. "That's the meeting you missed."

That was also the morning after that sleepless night with Mirabel. I didn't leave her flat until late after we'd spent the entire night and morning talking, fucking, drinking tea, and fucking.

"That meeting was called a little too soon for my tastes. Dad had only died three days before. Savanah didn't make it either."

He raised his palms in surrender. "Hey, I wasn't there either. For the same reason, I thought it in poor taste too. But I got the minutes. Didn't you?"

I rubbed my head. "I haven't read it yet. It's there on my laptop." I pulled a tight smile.

Possessing a sixth sense around discussions of business, my mother stepped in. "The hotel's running at a loss, I hear."

I turned to her. "Not for long, if I can help it. And must we discuss this now?"

As the new CEO, I knew I had difficult decisions to make. I wasn't so naïve to assume it would be smooth sailing. As all these commercial concerns restored me to the land of the living and what awaited me, I turned and spied Mirabel chatting to Sammy, one of the local farmhands.

Her gaze reached mine, and I raised my hand to acknowledge her. She touched Sammy's arm and headed my way just as my mother turned to speak to me.

"The new spa by the duck pond looks to be progressing nicely. I hear that you've signed off on the designs and that it's to expand to the Newman farm."

Just my luck, Mirabel arrived in time to hear everything my mother uttered.

Sudden frustrated anger shot out of me. "Not now. Dad's only just been buried."

As I turned to Mirabel, she looked at me as though I'd grown horns and my face had turned furnace red. Her brows knitted. "Newman's farm used to belong to my family."

I led her away from my mother's supersonic ears.

Mirabel spoke, but all I could see was her naked, my mouth on her nipples as she ran her hand over my throbbing dick. Pushing that lusty scene aside, I reminded myself this was hardly the time for such wicked thoughts.

I lost myself in those beautiful, angry green eyes, almost forgetting my name before an uncomfortable mix of grief, desire, and remorse shook me out of my haze.

"I just asked a question." She was back to her feisty best, and much to my guilt-ridden shock, my dick hardened. I couldn't have my pants tenting at my father's funeral.

"That's a community space for everyone in the adjoining properties," Mirabel persisted. "We played there as kids. Remember?"

I forced my mouth into a weak smile. "It's nice to see you, Mirabel. Thanks for coming. It means everything to me." I paused for a response, but my subterfuge must have taken her aback. "You didn't respond to my texts."

She was staring down at her feet, then her stunning green eyes rose and nearly bowled me over. "I've been busy." Despite her mouth twitching into a faint smile, her mood remained dark. "People are worried about what's going to happen now that your father's no longer alive."

"That's understandable. Can we talk about this over dinner? Like another time."

Her face softened. "You're right. I shouldn't've brought it up here. And again, I'm so sorry about your father."

I touched her soft, warm hand, which brought back memories of holding her in my arms. "Your presence here today means a lot." I sucked in a breath. "And don't worry, I'm going to rescind the project. First thing Monday."

She studied me, looking deep into my eyes as though sifting through bullshit.

It *was* bullshit. I'd signed a contract—one that came with a big price tag. The investor who owned part share was dead keen on the project. I couldn't imagine him budging, even if I offered double to buy him out.

What would I say? "Um... sorry can't go ahead, I want to fuck the woman opposed to this project."

"It's all good. Promise. I'll sort it out."

She nodded slowly. Those witchy eyes penetrated deeply. Whether angry or nice, Mirabel had this uncanny ability to lift the dark cloud hanging over me.

Was that a spark jumping between us? My heart seemed to feel it because I felt blood pumping through me again.

CHAPTER 3

Mirabel

ETHAN WORE DESIGNER. I wore charity shop or boho chic picked up on eBay and street markets. I used environmentally friendly essential oils, while he wore that expensive cologne that was probably going to rewire my DNA, even if it made me want to come on the spot. He was planning on destroying farmlands, whereas I fought to maintain our land's heritage.

Grr...

I kept berating myself for wanting to fuck him again. His constant texts made that desire worse. Despite the smile his persistent contact brought, I'd decided we were too different. Fiery sex or not, this would never work.

So get out now before my heart gets too invested.

I could have driven to London, but needing to economize, I'd caught the train instead. Dodging crowds, I tugged my suitcase along and made my way to Dalston junction.

A cacophony of car horns, excited voices, and general city noise jolted me out of the sexy reel playing in my head. I kept seeing Ethan's dark seductive gaze staring deeply into mine while he rode me hard and deep. I was sure I'd caught a glimpse of vulnerability.

Ethan's rawness was only natural, given his father's passing. But his unshifting gaze also seemed filled with searching as if he were trying to unravel my soul. I kept pushing those thoughts aside by reminding myself that Ethan was a natural heartbreaker.

Getting accustomed to the city after sleepy Bridesmere always took a moment. In many ways, I was still that country girl who loved roaming through the forest or reflecting on the ocean's ebb and flow. Nevertheless, the city was as necessary to a musician as the sea to a fisherman. And had I not been distracted by a certain billionaire, I would have bubbled with excitement. A gig at the trendy Green Room wasn't something to sneer at.

When in London, I always stayed with my cousin at her East London flat. Sheridan was a couple of years older than me and worked as a social worker.

When I arrived, I found her on the sofa in her pajamas, dark rings under her eyes, and sipping tea.

"Hey, Sherry." I popped down my guitar case. "You look like you've had a big night."

She stretched her arms and yawned. "You could say that. A big work function."

"Where's Bret?" I asked after her boyfriend.

"He's off on one of his primal masculinity weekends."

I laughed. "Let me guess—a bunch of men beating their chests and hunting wild boar?"

Rising from the couch, she set down her book. "More like a big piss-up. Let me get you some tea. You look like you can use one."

"I'd love one."

I followed her into the cramped kitchen—an extension of the living room partitioned by a laminated table.

Like me, Sheridan was a little untidy. That's why my staying there worked. We even looked alike. She had the same thick red hair, freckles, and green eyes as me.

"So you've scored a gig at the Green Room." She whistled. "Things are looking up."

The butterflies invading my stomach acted as a reminder that I needed to practice. Especially if I wanted to live up to the standard of artists who performed at that trendy venue.

She inclined her face. "Then why are you looking so down? Are you nervous?"

"No. But it's been a pretty eventful week back home."

She poured hot water into a cup, and I dropped in a teabag and jiggled it.

We settled on the couch with our hot drinks and biscuits. Outside the window, a parade of hip people bobbed along, dressed in mismatched colors, and oversized, worn clothes—hobo chic, as I called it. The flat sat close to the pavement, so we heard most of the street noise, which made sleeping tricky on weekends. When the pubs closed, people spilled noisily into the streets, singing, yelling, or fighting against a backdrop of police sirens.

"What's been happening, then?" She turned to face me.

"Ethan Lovechilde happened."

When we were growing up, Sheridan spent her summers on our farm. As a teenager, she would turn all giggly and silly whenever we crossed paths with the tall brothers like they belonged to a sexy boy band.

Her jaw dropped. "You finally hooked up with that dishy brother?"

I rolled my eyes. Why was that such a foregone conclusion? Had I made my guilty crush that obvious? I was meant to hate him.

I gritted my teeth. "Why would you say that?"

"Because you kissed that time when you were sixteen, remember?"

How could I forget? And now I could add tingly memories of those sanity-hijacking full lips roaming my breasts and beyond.

"His father died." I sighed. "He came to the Mariner and cried on my shoulder."

"Oh. That's so sad about his dad. He seemed like a nice man." She pulled a sad smile. "So you gave him a shoulder to cry on and then fucked?"

I flinched at her abridged version, which made me sound like one of those mothering types who milked up around needy men.

I gulped back my tea. "I've never seen him like that, to be honest. That shallow Casanova version was nowhere to be found. Instead, he was down to earth. He even recognized Nick Drake, for heaven's sake."

"Right…" Her eyebrows knitted. "So, you're telling me you jumped his bones because he liked Nick Drake? Or because he was sad? Or because the guy is fucking hot?" Her voice kept going up in pitch until she stated the bleeding obvious.

"We were only meant to sleep in the same bed so that he didn't have to be alone, but then…" A guilty smirk took over my mouth.

"And then you had shameless, dirty sex."

I splayed my hands. "It just happened. I can't even remember who initiated it, to be honest." A big smile grew on my face as I revisited Ethan spooning me.

"You make it sound like you played a game of chess. Was he a bad shag or something?"

My head moved continuously from side to side, like one of those wide-mouthed clowns at amusement parks. "No way. The absolute opposite. He was the shag of the century. In *every* way possible."

"Oh. He made you come?" Her face lit up with excitement as though she'd screamed through an orgasm herself.

"He did. I've…" A streak of heat flushed my cheeks. This was an embarrassing subject suddenly. "I've never orgasmed while penetrated before."

She looked at me as if I'd admitted to stuffing rats as a pastime.

"Okay. So I'm weird. I know."

"No, you're not," she sang. "I've never come with a dick before."

Now it was my turn to look at her strangely. "Really?"

"Hello, it's all about the clit."

I thought of Ethan's tongue and how he'd demanded I straddle his head after mutual animal attraction did away with formalities. That was the morning after.

"I sat on his face," I admitted, squirming.

Her jaw dropped, and a smile formed at the same time. She rose.

"Where are you going?" I needed her to sit and talk this out, especially now that I'd opened up about a night and morning that still had my raging ovaries partying at a non-stop bender.

"This calls for wine," she said.

I looked at the large clock on the mantle. "But it's only one thirty in the afternoon."

"You don't have to have one. I need it. The hair of the dog."

She settled down with a glass of red wine in her hands. "Okay. So you sat on his face. Oh my god. How cool is that? I'm jealous."

"You are?" *She should be.*

"I can't even get Bret to go down on me. We have to use a fucking vibrator." Her mouth turned down. "Anyway, enough of my dull sex life. Tell me more. So you sat on his face, and he fucked you with his tongue?"

A rush of swelling heat suddenly made me relive the moment I'd nearly bit the bedhead. I wondered about the scratches on those sinewy arms and shoulders of his. Not to mention the bite marks I'd left on his neck.

"It was one of many," I said coyly. After learning of Sheridan's dull sex life with her partner of five years, I didn't want to blow my trumpet about a night of sex that called for its own photo album. Those memories, I would cherish forever. That was if I ever got over the overwhelming need to see him again.

He's developing that hideous spa. Remember?

But he promised to rescind it.

My polarising halves were at it again.

Bad me wanted to massacre my credit card with an expensive skin-tight, woman-in-heat dress and seduce him, while good me demanded I march in carrying a placard with Ethan wearing horns and holding a pitchfork.

"You lucky girl. Tell me you didn't come with his dick too?"

And fucking how.

I nodded with a timid grin. "It was like nothing I've ever experienced. I've read about multiple orgasms but never believed it."

"Yeah, about as mythical as the second coming."

We looked at each other and laughed.

"Pun unintended," she added.

"I can now confirm that such a thing exists. I've had my share of guys. But absolutely nothing compared to this."

Her eyes widened with excitement like she was living her sex life vicariously through me. "Was he hung?"

My cheeks heated, as a smile grew on my face.

She lowered her voice. "Like how big?"

I demonstrated with my hands.

"Fuck, that's enormous... Was it thick?"

"Yep. It hurt, to be honest, but after a while..." I could have contracted my pussy and come on the spot. I'd already masturbated more than usual, reliving him holding that blue-red veiny cock in his hand before entering me.

"I'm all hot and bothered." She took a gulp of wine. "So why the fuck are you here? Shouldn't you be there? Like fucking him senseless?"

I sighed. "Because I now hate him."

Her face scrunched in utter shock. "How can you hate someone who's a fucking god in the sack? Those men are rare. Enjoy it. I would let him fuck me even if he admitted to killing my mother."

My face scrunched in horror. "Oh, Sherry, that's awful."

"I'm being ironic, silly. You know my black humor. So why is he your enemy?"

"He's a developer. A filthy rich, self-entitled prat." I exhaled in frustration at my conflicted self. "I just had a night off from hating him."

She frowned. "You're nuts." Her eyes lit up. "That's it. Tension makes for the best sex. Maybe that's what Bret and I are missing. He's so compliant. Even when I'm due and something like a stray knife with butter on the bench turns me into a raging psycho, he humors me."

I grimaced and chuckled at the same time.

"Has he tried calling you?" Sheridan asked.

I played with my fingers, and my lips curled at the thought of Ethan's constant texts. Messages that I hadn't deleted, and even scrolled on often as though trying to remind myself I had not imagined *that* night. "Quite a few times. Even at the funeral, Ethan wanted to talk. But then I overheard that he's about to tear down our old farm and turn it into a spa."

Sheridan furrowed her brow. "So? It's their land."

"Hello," I barked, frustrated by my cousin's blasé attitude that mirrored most people's. "Farmers need to make a living."

"Bel. You're nuts. You hate him because of that?"

I bit into a fingernail. There was a little more to it.

"We're on opposite sides." I kept my reason vague. Even to me.

"Forgive him. Have more hot sex. And then use that to cajole him. To turn him."

That was the best idea I'd heard all day. My body certainly liked it. My stubborn conscience, however, gave it a thumbs-down.

"Talking's helped. Thanks." I rose. "I need to get ready for a sound check. I'll go and have a shower, I think."

She followed me. "I better get dressed and face the day. I'm off to my mum's for tea."

"Are you coming tonight?" I asked.

"I wouldn't miss it for the world. And who knows? I might actually meet someone." She waggled her eyebrows. "After hearing all about your sexual adventures, I'm all hot and bothered."

"Bret's nice. You can't leave him."

"Yes, but nice doesn't exactly make for an exciting sex life."

I couldn't argue with that. I'd met so many nice guys, I could start a congregation for men willing to chop their balls off for a cause.

CHAPTER 4

Ethan

I WAVED AT THE concierge as I stepped out of the revolving door. Expensive fragrances wafted through the air as guests dressed in designer clothes glided past me, adding to the luxurious atmosphere of our family hotel.

Instead of Mayfair, I was now staying at the penthouse suite, where my father lived whenever he was in London. The private elevator deposited me straight into the living room decorated with Persian rugs, modern and classic art, and figurine lamps.

The bedroom, in burgundy accents, was decorated with canvases of minimalist art and nude male statuettes. A figurine of David with a very large erection reminded me of my father's homosexuality.

How did we not see it?

I made a mental note to bid for a female nude or two at my next visit to Sotheby's. I liked beautiful things, and it was a great place to pick up girls.

Pick up girls?

Maybe that was what I needed to become that cold-hearted developer who aimed to fuck his way into the Guinness Book of Records.

Is that what I want?

My phone vibrated, and putting the phone on speaker, I answered, "Andrew."

"You've been trying to reach me?"

I stretched out on the green Chesterfield. Through the windows, I stared at the spiky Westminster and London Bridges sprinkled with dots of humanity and traffic jams. "About the design of the spa."

"What about it? You signed off on them, and we've got the final drafts ready. It looks great. You didn't get the attachments?"

"I did. And I agree—they look great. Only can we go back to the original design?"

"You mean start again?" The note of surprise in his voice made me take a breath.

I scratched my prickly jaw, which cried for a visit to my favorite barber. I recalled Mirabel's throaty moans as I gently rubbed my face against her soft curvy thighs.

Focus!

"I'm having second thoughts on developing Newman's farm. Let's go with the original plans."

"Can't do that, mate. My investment was contingent on the expansion."

I took a sharp breath. "Right. I thought so much. How much to buy you out?"

"No way. Promised my wife. She's dying to get involved at the design level. You know—happy wife, happy life." He chuckled.

"Can we somehow avoid that farm?"

"It's happening. The tenants have received their orders to vacate by the end of the month. They agreed to the generous sum we offered without as much as an argument."

Mm... not if you're trying to make a local feisty girl happy.

"We'll speak at the end of the week." I ended the call.

I made a note to find an alternative for the Newmans. I thought of Declan's boot camp and his organic farm idea. I could suggest that the Newmans manage the farm. There was also room for livestock and even a home.

Good. That's the plan. Now I can move on.

I brought out my laptop and looked up Mirabel Storm's Facebook page. She wasn't taking my calls, so I decided to go and find her instead.

As I scrolled through Mirabel's pictures, I fell into those addictive green eyes. Aside from arousing lust, her beauty bowled me over. It always had.

I clicked on a video of her performing. With that sultry voice, she oozed sensuality, like she was being pleasured one moment then pouring her heart out with evocative poetry the next. Even the way her mouth parted reminded me of her sighs when I was deep inside her.

Rivetted, I went from watching her beautiful, expressive face to her undulating hips and breasts.

All hot and aroused, I unzipped my pants and fisted my dick. I played the video again. It didn't take me long to blow, jerking off not to porn, but to a folk singer.

Am I losing my mind?

After cleaning myself up, I clicked on her Facebook page and found that she was doing a gig tonight at the Green Room.

My phone buzzed, and I took the call. "Mother."

"There's a meeting at six sharp. The reading of the will."

"So soon?" I squirmed at the thought of complex family business affairs.

"It's been two weeks, Ethan."

"Any news on the forensic reports?"

"Your brother's been with the detective. Call him. I've got to go. Wear a suit. No ripped jeans."

I let out a deep breath. "Okay."

DECLAN WAITED FOR ME at a bar close to the solicitor's office. As I raised my arm to wave, I felt somewhat constricted by the tight jacket that the salesman had insisted fitted me like a glove. Perhaps I wasn't used to wearing suits. The trousers clung to my legs too. The young salesman carried on about the perfect fit, wearing stars in his eyes. The shirt also fitted snugly, as he went on about showing off my abs. All those hours pumping iron and sneaking a few sessions at Reboot's new gym had paid off.

"Dec?"

He nodded.

"Do you want another?" I pointed at his half-full pint.

He shook his head and stared down at his Rolex. "We've got to be there in half an hour. We have to make this quick."

The waitress arrived, and I ordered a beer. I unbuttoned my jacket and sat down.

"You're looking pretty smooth," he said. "I don't think I've ever seen you in a suit during the day."

I touched the slim lapel. "Mother insisted I suit up."

His mouth twitched into a half-smile before reverting to seriousness again as the waitress delivered our drinks. "I spoke to the police. The forensic report's in."

I sat up straight and took a long slug of my beer. "And?"

He stared at me for a moment without blinking and my spine chilled. "It's suspicious."

"Fuck." I stared into space for a moment, a million questions banking up. "What did they say exactly?"

"That he had drugs in his system."

"Okay. But maybe he was imbibing?"

"Rohypnol and whisky."

"Shit. Date rape drug," I said.

"He was strangled, as you know."

The beer gurgled among the knots in my stomach. "Someone did this on purpose? Or a date gone wrong? What's Luke's story in all of this?"

Declan exhaled. "Questions I asked that remain unanswered."

"Crisp," I said. "It's a no-fucking-brainer. Dad didn't want that development, and now they're moving ahead. Did you at least mention Crisp's interest?"

"His name came up straight away. The detective got back to me on that. The prick's got a fucking solid alibi."

"A hitman?"

"Probably," he said.

We sat in silence for a moment, my head swimming. "Does Savvie know?"

"Not yet. Let's keep it quiet for tonight."

"That's a sound plan." My fingers gripped my glass. "Crisp's not that stupid to stoop to a hitman."

"I don't know about that. If it's a sophisticated job, then it won't lead back to him, will it?"

"But everyone will guess. He'll be ostracised."

"You know that scene: once they develop and the glamour that comes with running a five-star resort, everyone will become his lap dog. They won't give a rat's arse about anything."

My body slumped in frustration. "We're not going to leave any fucking stone unturned, are we?"

He shook his head slowly. "No, we're not."

Three hours later, after hearing about the considerable portfolio of assets owned by the family, I jumped into a cab and headed for the Green Room, weighed down with an extra two billion pounds—money that I could either invest or flit away. I knew my father would want me to use this money to not only improve my financial situation but also to help others, starting with the Newmans.

The cab dropped me off on a busy strip, where colorful types bounced along, embracing their individuality. In my Armani suit, I probably looked like I'd ended up at the wrong end of town.

I stepped through a glossy green door, which was unattended by bouncers. From what I could see in the bar's mood lighting, everyone seemed friendly and probably unlikely to cause a drunken stir.

In the corner, a frameless piano stood as a sculpture, and the place smelt of stale beer, sweat, and cheap perfume.

I settled at the bar and removed my jacket, unbuttoning a couple of shirt buttons. A bass thump coming from recorded music made it to my ribcage as I ordered a drink.

I peered over at the stage, where I spotted Mirabel talking to a couple of guys. One looked like the sound guy, and the older one, in a purple suit, was virtually on top of her. He was flirting with her. I could tell by the way he smiled and the way she tilted her head and smirked. Putting aside the garish suit, he was tall and good-looking, boasting Nordic features.

He leaned in and whispered something, and she gave him one of her "Are you for real?" looks. I could only assume he'd propositioned her. I'd received that same look one drunken night after asking if she'd forgotten to wear a bra.

Alexander Skarsgard's double finally left the stage, and the spotlight came on.

Mirabel looked striking in a shimmery blue dress that showed off her curves. Her thick, waist-length hair cascaded over her full breasts and framed her milky complexion to perfection, as though arranged that way for a photograph. She always looked beautiful. It didn't matter where I saw her. Whether on the street without makeup, on stage, or standing at the cliffs with the wind blowing through her fiery hair, Mirabel always took my breath away.

Her fingers ran with ease over her guitar strings. I envied her skill. I'd learned piano as a child but was always too distracted to practice.

Her voice carried echoes of the crashing sea at night—at times filled with rage, sadness, and despair, then also smoky and sensual like a balmy summery night somewhere exotic. Just like her spellbinding performance at the Mariner, I was taken on a journey. Captivated by her art, I lost track of time and had to remind myself that I was in a bar and not some magical forest, frolicking with a sexy nymph.

Rapturous applause soon roused me from my dream. She'd been performing for forty minutes, but it only seemed like a few moments. After taking a bow, she stepped off the stage, and with a graceful glide and subtle sway of hips, she moved with the natural confidence of a siren. She seemed oblivious to all the attention she generated, mainly from males, who looked like I felt—awestruck.

Her gaze landed on mine, and her brows knitted as though I were the last person she'd expected to see. I rose from the barstool and kissed her on the cheek, breathing in her honey-and-wildflower scent.

Her eyes traveled over my body, more with a look of "What the fuck are you wearing?" than of the flirty kind. She didn't do flirty anyway.

At last, she asked, "What brings you here?"

"I came to hear you play. And I'm glad I did. That was crazy good."

Her suspicious frown, an expression she often wore around me, faded into an appreciative smile. "Thanks. I'm glad you enjoyed it. No tears this time, though?"

I sniffed. "No. I've manned up. No more crying in public."

She smiled sympathetically. "You're all dressed up."

"I didn't have time to go scouring for vintage 70s like that guy coming onto you on stage earlier."

"That's Orson. He runs the venue."

"He looks close." *Like he wants to gorge himself on your tits.*

She scrutinized me as though trying to extract meaning from my words.

"Can I buy you a drink?" Just as I asked, Orson turned up and put his arm around her.

His eyes had that "I want to suck your nipples" shine. I knew it well because that's how mine would have looked if I weren't performing the Mr. Cool-guy act.

He appeared a little drunk too. Stepping away from him, Mirabel didn't seem very interested.

"Let me get you a drink," he persisted.

"I'm all right for now," she said.

"Oh, come on"—his arm curled around her waist, drawing her against his tall, skinny frame—"I was looking forward to us hanging out." His eyebrow arched.

Mm... a euphemism for fucking, you mean?

"I'm not up for a big night," she said.

"Come on." This time, he took her arm.

She shrugged out of it. "No, Orson."

I stepped between them, removing his hand. "You heard her. She doesn't want a drink."

He retaliated with a dismissive smirk and returned his attention to Mirabel, ignoring me entirely.

"There's a great jazz venue up the road," he said. "A friend of mine's running it. They're thinking of having a blues night. Maybe we can drop in later?"

"Maybe not tonight." She forced a strained, friendly smile and then returned her attention to me.

"She's with me." I decided to take a stance. Either that or punch him in the nose.

Her eyes widened.

But after he kept at her, I stood between them. "Are you low on hearing?"

His mouth curled into a sheepish smirk, and he looked at Mirabel, who nodded ever so slightly.

After he walked away, I asked, "Can I buy you a drink?"

Her brow furrowed as she mulled over my proposition. She took a deep breath and let it out slowly. "I'm shitty with you, remember?"

"How can I forget?" I opened out my hands. "I'm here to make amends of sorts. Just have a drink with me. It can't harm. Can it?"

"I suppose it can't." Her brows pinched.

"That Orson strikes me as thick-skinned." I inclined my head towards him. "He seems to have started to chat up another girl, anyway."

She smiled and shook her head. "That's about right. He's a serious womanizer."

I bought her a drink. As I passed it to her, our fingers touched, sending a spark through me. Electricity seemed to bounce between us.

Her eyes rose slowly and met mine, falling into my unblinking gaze before looking away.

She took a sip. "Orson's pretty pushy. I think that's why he gave me the gig."

I frowned. "Really?"

"Hey, don't look so surprised. That 'I'll scratch your back if you fondle my penis has been happening since the cavemen."

I laughed at her blunt but honest view of men's deplorable treatment of women. "I know that, but you don't need him. Your talent speaks for itself. You're sensational. Maybe get yourself a manager who doesn't want to sleep with you."

She nodded. "It's on my to-do list."

Speaking of men who want to sleep with you... "You haven't answered my calls."

"I've been busy. And look, Ethan..." She sipped her drink.

The music went up, and I had to lean in. "Is there somewhere quieter we can talk?"

She took a moment to respond. Her face wore a question again. I could see my being there had thrown her.

I got it—she hated me. Or thought she did.

"There's the backroom, I suppose, and I've got to pack up my gear."

As soon as Mirabel opened the door to the band room a thick haze of smoke hit me in the face.

One of the pair sharing a spliff looked up. "Hey, man."

I raised my hand to greet them.

He passed the joint to Mirabel, and I watched those pretty lips sucking on it and wishing it was my cock.

CHAPTER 5

Mirabel

IN THAT SNUG DESIGNER suit, Ethan had billionaire playboy written all over him. The jacket looked stitched on, cut to show off his broad shoulders, his lean waist, and the perfect swell of his upper arms. His crisp white shirt accentuated his tanned features, giving him that sexy Mediterranean look, especially with those big dark eyes.

Smoke hit the back of my throat as I sucked back the weed to help ease my nerves. It normally made me paranoid, which was why I smoked on rare occasions.

With Ethan looking like he belonged on the cover of *Sexy Billionaire Monthly*, I needed something to help me chill. His shirt seemed close to bursting, especially during that tomcat act around Orson.

How could I turn away from him when he looked like that? And he'd come to see me. Then there were all his messages.

I bent over to pick up my guitar and nearly ripped a seam. I'd bought a stretchy 80s dress, which was tighter than my normal floatier outfits, from a local vintage shop. My hormones must have done the choosing, given how sexy the dress made me feel.

Ethan's gaze roamed from my face to my nipples, which had started to poke through the stretchy fabric.

I clipped shut my guitar case and waited for him to say something since he'd asked to speak to me. He hovered about looking uneasy instead.

What have you done with that easy-going, strut-through-life version of Ethan Lovechilde?

Dirty thoughts buzzed around in my head, like letting him fuck me senseless before spitting abuse for being a greedy developer.

Pushing that guilty urge aside, I didn't fuck billionaires. Particularly ones about to decimate significant pastoral land.

He pointed at my guitar case. "Can I carry that for you?"

I shook my head. "I'm good."

We stood at the back of the venue, shifting about and looking uncertain. It wasn't usually this difficult for me to communicate.

"I actually should go back and sell some CDs," I said, shifting my weight again.

Suddenly, we were awkward teenagers, stealing glances at each other while pretending to play it cool.

He ran his hand over his dark-brown hair.

"Why don't we go somewhere quiet? Dinner?" He gave that uncertain half smile again that was new for him, then added, "I'll buy the lot."

I frowned. "You'll buy all my CDs so you can have dinner with me?"

He rubbed his thumb over his plump lower lip. "I mean, I'd like one for me. And I'm sure Declan, Theadora, and Savvie would each love one."

I hesitated before answering. My mind went blank as I watched him lick his lips. All I could think about was how much I wanted him to do that to me. "I can't be bought, Ethan. Now, if you'll excuse me."

I headed to the door, but then he touched my arm, and sparks sizzled through me. An awkward gap of time swallowed my thoughts. I couldn't think straight. Why was I allowing this man to affect me this way? I wanted to scream.

"Hey. No. I didn't mean that." He wouldn't break eye contact with me, and the same inner conflict I felt seemed to reflect back at me. I wondered if the hurt of losing his father had deepened him. He'd already proven he wasn't as shallow as I'd always assumed.

I was fucked. At least when I'd seen him as a vain, empty-headed player, giving him the middle finger was easy. Now that I'd had a taste—well, okay, a banquet—I'd grown attached to him. Maybe it was just that beautiful dick and what he did with it.

So what does that make me? Shallow and driven by sex. Just like him.

He ran his tongue over his lips again, and I had to lean against the wall to hold myself up. *Talk about pussy teasing.*

Losing all sense of time, I couldn't tell how long we'd been standing in that dark hallway with our eyes locked.

His was more a sizzling eye fuck. I imagined mine was more that of the stunned-animal-caught-in-lights look.

"I'm meant to hate you. I mean, I *do* hate you." The exasperation in my tone reflected the brewing frustration between my head and my vagina.

He pulled me towards him, his eyes devouring me. "Then fuck me and hate me afterward." His mouth grew into a smile. "The more you abuse me, the harder my dick gets."

My entire body went limp as I fell into his arms. His smell, a mix of cologne and testosterone, made me lightheaded. His lips were soft as they brushed against mine, and an electric current seemed to sizzle between us. I surrendered to that kiss like someone starved of passion.

He pushed me gently onto the wall, his body on mine. I could feel his hard cock on my stomach and my core flooded with need as the crotch of my panties dampened. He rubbed his bulge against me as though to provoke me. "See how fucking hard you make me? Don't you want to feel every inch of my cock inside of you?"

I was lost to the heat of the moment when the clearing of a throat snapped me out of a lusty daze. Smiling at me was the pair of weed smokers from earlier.

"The band room's empty," one of them said, arching a brow.

Powerless to resist Ethan, I cocked my head. "Let's go somewhere, then." I guided him to the back-door entrance.

We stepped into the alleyway, where people sold drugs and all kinds of shady characters gathered. If one ignored them; they were harmless enough. Some of them were buskers or street people whose main crime was poverty.

I climbed into the taxi as he held open the door for me. He got in, his shoulder against mine.

His hand stroked my palm as we rode through London, while pulsing lights and endless crowds blurred into an abstract painting. Adjusting his slacks, he touched his dick, which made my breath hitch. Anticipation tingled down to my sticky panties.

We arrived at Lovechilde Hotel, a nineteenth-century work of beauty. I'd always been a sucker for historical architecture, which made London so fascinating. The hotel, with its white façade, layered with columns and sculptured embellishments didn't disappoint. Particularly at night, bathed in red light, it made for an aesthetic spectacle.

"I've got the penthouse suite," he said casually.

We stepped onto the red carpet and climbed marbled stairs bordered by golden rope. A concierge greeted Ethan with a nod, as we stepped into the glossy entrance with glittering crystal chandeliers. In one corner was a moody piano bar, where guests talked quietly under Tiffany lamps. Astounded by an overload of opulence, I felt like Alice visiting the queen's residence.

"I must look so out of place." I tugged at my dress.

He smiled. "You look stunning. That dress suits you."

"That's because it's seriously tight."

"Yeah. Nice." He smirked. "But, hey, don't worry about what people think. I never do."

I paused. "You don't have to."

He shrugged. "It works both ways. I felt like a fish out of water at the Green Room."

I chuckled. "You did look like you'd fallen from another dimension. Just like I do here."

He pressed the elevator button, and in we went. As soon as the doors shut, his hands were all over me, squeezing my arse, and his hard body pressed against me. His hot mouth was wide, moist, and impatient.

He ran his hand under my dress.

I pulled away. "Hey someone might enter."

"It's a private elevator." His hot breath on my face. "I can't wait to see you dance on my cock."

A stuttered breath left my mouth. I couldn't wait to dance on his cock either.

The doors slid apart, and with our bodies tightly bound in an embrace, we stumbled into a massive space.

Leather sofas. More original gilded art. Sea-green walls. Marble male figures scattered about artfully.

"Oh my god. How lavish."

Ethan scratched his shadowed jaw. "My father lived here for a while. It belongs to the family. But as I'm now the CEO of the hotel, it's my pad for a while."

"Pad?" I turned around, soaking in the aesthetic room. "More like a palace."

Beyond the wall of windows, London swarmed with life, as thousands bustled over the bridge. Beneath them, the murky Thames flowed through the city like a dark rippling sheet of satin.

He removed his jacket. "A drink?"

"Sure."

"Champagne?"

I nodded. I wanted the full treatment. Expensive bubbly tingling on my tongue. Him ripping my clothes with his teeth. His hot breath on my clit. Us having hungry sex with his dick burning orgasms through me.

He peered into the fridge. "Damn." He reached for the phone. "Forgot to remind the maid to stock the fridge. Easily rectified." He dialed before I could say I didn't mind what we had.

"Mindy. Yes, I'm good. Could you bring up some Moet? One minute..." He covered the phone. "Moet okay?"

I rolled my eyes and, with a posh accent, said, "Oh, it will have to do, I guess."

He ended the call and pounced on me. A knock came at the door just as his fingers were hooking into my panties, making me forget to breathe.

He opened the door to a gorgeous blonde girl. She sashayed in, wearing a short skirt and a fitted white shirt.

"Ethan, when did you return?" She sounded very familiar.

"Today." He pointed. "Just put it here." He lifted the bottles off the trolley.

"Oh, you're planning on a big one? Do you need someone to help you finish those? My shift ends soon."

She mustn't have seen me, but I could see her in the mirror. My instincts were to show myself, but for some reason, I remained in hiding. I think I wanted to hear his response.

"No. I'm good."

"Oh... you can't drink alone. You didn't the other night."

What? The other night? Was this after us or before?

Us?

"Mindy. Not now."

She pouted and sashayed off.

After she left, he popped the champagne and filled our glasses. He handed me my drink as though nothing had happened.

"Thanks," I said coolly.

He studied me. "Is there something wrong?"

"Well, I'm wondering if you've been bonking the maid this week."

He raked his fingers through his hair, messing it up in a sexy high wave. "Nope. The last woman I made love to was this very sexy, curvy singer I met at my local."

That made my lips curl. "So why did you come tonight?"

"To hear your music and buy a CD." He moved up close to me on the couch.

I propped my legs up on a velvet-covered footrest. "Not because you wanted to fuck me?"

A slow sexy smile grew on his lips. "Mm... ah... yes. What do you think?"

"So have you fucked her?"

"Who?" His hand settled on my thigh.

"The maid."

"Maybe once."

I had to remove his hand in order to think straight. "And she swans in here offering herself again? Would you have fucked her if I wasn't here?"

He puffed out a breath. "I probably wouldn't have ordered champagne to start with. And no. I'm not that attracted."

"But yet you fucked her?"

"Well, I am, I mean, *was* single at the time."

"Was?"

He turned to me. "And what about Mr. Purple Wanker?"

I had to laugh, despite him side-stepping my question. "No. We haven't fucked. He's married."

"Jerk. And he's all over you. That's plain fucking wrong." He tilted his head, and his mouth curled at one end. "I guess he has nice blue eyes. Or is it some kind of daddy fascination?"

I walked over to the window and peered down at the convoy of taxis banked up and people pouring in and out. "Daddy fascination? I don't have one of those." I turned to face him again. "I prefer dark-eyed, sleazy rich boys."

"Oh, do you just?'" He rearranged his tight slacks, making room for his dick, an action that I found seriously erotic. "Then that counts me out."

I laughed. "Going on that scenario with the maid, I'd say you well and truly fit that description."

"I'm not him anymore." His smile had faded, and a serious expression shone in his eyes.

I ran my finger along a smooth marble statue, turning my back to him. "Do you know the color of my eyes?"

"Silly question. They're a deep green and almond-shaped. In the light, they're bluey green, which robs me of speech. One of your best features."

"One of my best features?" I joined him on the couch again.

He walked his finger along my face, stroked my hair, then traced my breasts making my nipples stand at attention.

I held my breath as his finger slithered down to my thighs. By this stage, my panties were drenched. I fell into his arms. Who he'd fucked before me mattered little.

"You're perfect all over."

"I'm a lot chubbier than her," I added. I'd never really worried about my body until I met Ethan.

He nuzzled into my neck. "Deliciously so. I love your body. Love curves. Love your curves." His hands traced my waist and beyond.

I gave into lust, my hand settling on his very hard dick. "And I love your dick."

"Good, because he's pretty crazy about you too."

We sipped champagne, then at his request, I did a very slow striptease as he held that heavy, engorged cock in his hand.

CHAPTER 6

Ethan

MIRABEL FUCKED ME SENSELESS. My orgasm was so explosive, stars shot before me, and I cried out.

It was like I'd fallen under a spell.

I pulled away to look at her pretty face. "I came too quickly. I didn't make you come." I stroked her rosy cheek. "Just give me a while, and I'll be better next time. Promise."

"You made me come with your tongue." She nuzzled into my neck, and the fit was cozy and comfortable.

For the first time in weeks, my body felt light, and I fell asleep with a smile.

I'm not sure how long I'd slept, but her warm breath on my neck roused me from a dream, and still half asleep, I entered her deeply.

The fit was perfect. Tight and agile. Gyrating and rocking her hips, she had all moves to make me burn.

The hairs on the back of my neck spiked, and drunk on her pussy, I roared through another mind-bending climax, pouring everything I had into her.

We fell on our backs, panting.

"Sorry, did I wake you?" I asked.

She giggled. "Your dick did. But, hey, give me multiple orgasms over sleep any day."

"You've got a very nice pussy."

"And you've got a very nice dick."

I wrapped my arms around her and sucked in her musky scent as I would an expensive cologne.

I couldn't take my hands off her. I must have gotten around an hour of sleep, so when my phone alarm went off, I reached to turn it off. Then it dawned on me that I had a meeting with Declan and Savvie at Merivale.

I stepped into the bathroom, and Mirabel entered, crossing her arms.

"Are you cold?" I asked.

"No." She smiled shyly. "It's just so bright in here."

For someone I'd always considered strong, Mirabel had started to show a fragile side to her nature. I did my best to remind her how gorgeous she was, but I sensed it went deeper.

I tested the water. "It's warm enough. Don't worry. I've seen your tits before. They're pretty hard to forget."

She stepped into the shower. "This shower's big enough for ten people."

I smiled meekly.

"You've had an orgy in here, haven't you?" She tilted her head.

"Not as such." I pulled her under the jets, which came from every direction.

"Oh." Her mouth fell open. "It's like a massage. One could get used to this."

I squirted some body wash onto a sponge and rubbed it all over her.

"Don't look too close."

"Hey. You've got a stunning body." I ran my hands between her soft thighs, and my cock stiffened. It hardly went down around her.

"I don't go to the gym. I tried hot yoga the other night and nearly suffocated. Never doing that again."

I laughed. Her eyes had a sardonic twinkle like she rolled her eyes at life.

She got down on her knees and took my dick into my mouth. After fucking all night, it was a little sore, but it soon went steel hard squashed between her fleshy lips. Her tongue flicked teasingly over my creamy head. I leaned against the glass wall to hold myself up. Her eyes looking up at me, she took me in deep.

"You've done this before," I said.

Her eyes smiled up at me.

"Hey, I'm about to come," I warned.

She seemed determined to take it all the way until I blew to the back of her throat. Then drinking me dry, she wiped her pretty mouth and gave me that "How was that?" look.

I took her into her arms. "That was sensational."

ALL THAT SEX HAD given me a raging appetite, and I was pleased to have arranged for breakfast to be delivered.

Dressed in a bathrobe, Mirabel padded around barefoot, rubbing her wet hair with a towel.

"One could get used to this." She chuckled. "The heated floor alone is insane."

I was glad when it was a male server who wheeled in our breakfast. Mirabel had already guessed that I'd fucked half of the pretty female staff. Not something I was proud of. I made a mental note to ask the female staff about not being so flirty. Perhaps I could tell them I'd become devoutly religious and turned celibate.

Mm... as if.

The aroma of fried eggs and bacon had my stomach rumbling.

"That smells delicious," she said, licking her lips.

"I forgot to ask if you were a vegan." I led her into the dining area.

"No. I'm a carnivore. I used to be, but I lacked energy." She patted her stomach. "I love my food. Unfortunately."

I smiled. "I think that's healthy, myself. Take a seat."

The server placed the teapot and a rack of toast with softened butter onto a dish.

Mirabel shook her head. "Do you eat like this every day?"

I poured the tea into two cups. "Depends. If I've got a lot on, I pick something up at a café."

"This is nicer than breakfast cereal." She spread avocado on her toast.

"I've got to head back to Bridesmere this morning." The thought of dealing with all the issues back home doused my otherwise upbeat mood.

"I'm here all week. I'm recording a few songs with Orson." She bit into her toast.

That left a strange feeling. "Oh?"

"He's a very talented producer, among other things."

"Among other things? By that, you mean him being a poseur and a sleaze?"

She laughed. "Poseur? Yes, I guess he is. Orson seems to think he's living in the seventies. He often laments that he was born a decade too late. Sleazy? Mm... He's just hot-blooded." She paused to study me. "Why are you frowning?"

"I would never have expected you to defend someone's overt bad behavior."

"Was I doing that?" She thought about it and shrugged. "Are you jealous?" Her pretty eyes sparkled as she tilted her head.

"I don't do jealousy."

Her eyes held mine. "Then you're unique. And he's not that bad."

"The last time I looked, he didn't exactly take no for an answer."

"I can handle him. He's just frisky. He's giving me free recording time at his house."

My eyebrows contracted. "At his house. Alone?"

"He's got a wife. Although I think she's his ex. It's hard to keep up with Orson. They're on and off. That's why we never went past a kiss. I'm not into affairs."

"No. Not good." A knot formed in my stomach at the thought of her alone in that player's home.

They kissed...?

Mirabel rose from the table and went to her bag on the sofa. She stopped and looked at me. "I'm sensing something here."

I shrugged. "It's nothing. Just that I don't think you should be together alone. I can read a player from a mile away."

"And you should know, right?" She grinned.

I scratched my prickly jaw. "I'm not that guy anymore."

After a staring competition, she blinked first and said at last, "I'm just going to get changed."

Mirabel had one of those expressive faces that made it difficult not to stare. The more I looked at her, the more beautiful she grew.

Mirabel returned, tugging at her dress. "I don't know what possessed me to wear this. It's so out there."

"It suits you." I ran my hand over her indented waist. "You look sexy."

"But not on the tube."

"I'll give you a lift. Don't worry about that."

"Really, you don't have to." She wore a sweet smile that made me want to call everything off and keep her there all day and night.

"I want to." I pulled her onto my lap and kissed her.

She giggled. "I'm crushing you."

"No, you're not." I ran my hand up her leg and discovered her naked pussy. "No panties?"

"Um, you ripped them off. Remember?" She laughed.

"Mm... I did." I fingered her, and she was all snug, wet, and hot.

I readjusted her, undid my bathrobe, then slowly had her lower onto my hard cock. I lifted her up and down as she rode me, taking me very deep. So deep, my eyes rolled to the back of my head. "Holy fuck, Mirabel. You're hot. Like, really hot."

She bounced up and down over my dick, my hands groping her bouncing tits, my mouth on hers. Her moans turned into groans as her creamy release drenched my thighs.

"Good girl," I breathed before grunting through another mind-blowing orgasm.

She fell into my arms, and we remained in a tight embrace.

"I think I need to go home and sleep all day. I've never had so much sex." She laughed.

"Nor I. Not in one night, that is."

She pulled away and gave me her signature questioning look. "So do you fuck a different woman every night?"

Despite that personal question, Mirabel wasn't half as intrusive as other girls I'd dated.

Are we dating?

"I don't. I used to get around a bit more." I raised a brow. "But since turning thirty, I've slowed down."

More like every second night. Until I met you. Hm...

"Have you fucked someone since me? Do I need to get an STD check?"

I shook my head. "No. I haven't. Just you. I haven't even looked at another woman."

She studied me. "Are you going to develop the spa?"

I took a deep breath. She was back to her intense best. I headed to the bathroom. "I couldn't wiggle out of the contract, I'm afraid."

Mirabel's face scrunched in dismay. "But you promised."

"I tried." I held out my hands.

She placed her hands on her hips. "It's going to ruin that area. The Newmans will be gutted."

"I've offered them work at the spa."

She ran her hands through her tousled hair. Her eyes were wild and back to the woman with a cause, who loved to remind me that I was morally bankrupt. "Are you kidding? They're farmers."

Mirabel grabbed her bag and her guitar. "You know what? I think I'll catch the tube. This wasn't a good idea. The Newmans are like family. I thought you'd at least leave their farm."

I combed my hair with my fingers. "Let me drive you."

My phone rang, and seeing it was Declan, I picked it up. "Hey, I'm on my way to Merivale."

"We've got to talk about Dad's murder."

I released a tight breath. *Fun and games ahead.*

Mirabel pressed the elevator button.

"I'll see you soon. Got to run." I ended the call. "Hey, please let me drive you home at least."

"No. This was a bad idea. You're a bad idea." And just like that she jumped into the elevator and was gone.

I stood there gobsmacked. *Fuck.*

Was it that she wouldn't speak to me again? Fuck me again? Or simply that she saw me as evil for kicking out a family who'd been on the land for a decade?

All of that.

CHAPTER 7

Mirabel

I FOUND MY COUSIN in the kitchen, frying an omelet. The smell of eggs filled the room, and despite my low mood, hunger still rumbled in my stomach.

Unlike most of the population, the edgier I got, the hungrier I became.

"Hello, you," she said, looking up from the frying pan.

I went to the fridge and grabbed the carton of juice. "Do you want some?" I poured orange juice into a glass.

She shook her head.

"Have you eaten?" she asked, turning off the stove.

"I had some toast for breakfast. Don't worry about me."

"There's plenty. I made enough."

Feeling low, I forced a smile. *How could I allow myself to get emotionally attached to Ethan? It was meant to be sex. Hot sex. And nothing else. But here I am, feeling heavy and bleak.*

Sheridan cleared the table of newspapers, books, and bills and set our plates down.

"So what happened to you last night?" I asked.

"I fell asleep." She flipped the omelet onto a plate. "Sorry. I so wanted to come. Was it good?"

"People responded well to my songs."

"You didn't come home." Her eyebrows rose.

"Ethan was there." I toyed with my food. "I ended up at Lovechilde's. In his penthouse suite."

Her face lit up. "You don't say. I bet that was pretty swish."

Sipping tea, I nodded slowly.

"So why do you look so dark?"

"It's all so fucking confusing. I slept with the devil." I sighed.

"Mm... great sex, though. I mean the devil would be a better shag than the other one."

My brows gathered, and I grimaced. "Jesus? Ew. That's so uncouth."

She laughed. "You're agnostic, so it shouldn't offend, should it?"

"No." I sighed. "I guess not." I took a forkful of omelet, placed it on my bread, and took a bite. "This is nice, by the way."

"Thanks. Why are you pissed off?"

"Ethan's an unethical developer. He's on the wrong side of everything I believe in. I just wish he wasn't so fucking good in bed."

She laughed. "Just go with it, Bel. You can't change the world."

I released a breath. "No. I can't. But I can at least try to do the right thing."

"By not shagging hot billionaires?"

My phone beeped, and I went to look.

It was a message from Ethan. *I had a great night. Love your music. Bridesmere doesn't look the same without you.*

I smiled, and Sheridan asked, "From your hot billionaire?"

I nodded and put my phone away without returning a message.

"You're not going to respond?" Her eyes widened.

"Nope." I squared my shoulders. We were too different. It was nice sex. Okay, not nice, astounding. But I had to be realistic. Men like Ethan did not stick around. And if I allowed myself, I would fall in deep and lose my heart to him.

I was already drowning in a sea of emotion, telling myself it was just hot sex when in reality, I couldn't stop thinking about how he kissed me softly, held me while we slept, and stroked my hair or his soft fingertips and that gentle, almost shy smile he gave me whenever our eyes collided. If it was just hot sex, why the tenderness?

My eyes pricked with tears. I'd already grown attached. And it wasn't just from all those multiple orgasms.

I ate my meal with Sheridan staring at me as though I'd lost my senses. I suspected she wanted more stories about Ethan to cozy up to like one does a romance novel with that foregone conclusion of eternal love. This was real life, though, and women like me did not end up with men like Ethan Lovechilde.

"So are you at least going to see him again?" she asked.

"I'm sure we'll run into each other. We live in the same village."

She shook her head. "You're fucking nuts. I mean, what have you got to fear?"

I shrugged. "I hate how I've lost part of myself to him already. And it's only been twice. Two nights spent together, and I can't think straight." My voice choked up. *Oh no. Not tears. I'm stronger than this.*

"That's called love."

"I don't think so." I turned away before I lost the plot. Having developed a habit of denial, I put on a brave face and suppressed further thoughts about Ethan. "I've got to go and change. I have a recording session this afternoon."

ORSON OPENED THE RED door to this two-story Chelsea home and greeted me with a kiss on the cheek.

I followed him down the long hallway, where framed 70s record albums of Bowie, T Rex, Lou Reed, and others hung on the walls.

"Are your family here?" I asked after his two children, who normally ran wildly throughout the house.

"No. They're with their mother."

I studied him. "You're separated?"

He nodded slowly. "I told you that."

I followed him into his kitchen, which looked out to an overgrown garden.

"Tea?" he asked.

"Sure." I set down my guitar and backpack.

"You performed well last night." He poured the tea from a pot.

"Thanks." I smiled.

After a bit more small talk, we headed into his studio, our cups of tea in hand.

Orson lived and breathed music in all its many aspects. A gifted musician himself, he was more into nurturing talent by working as a producer and manager, as well as running the Green Room.

"Ethan Lovechilde?" He looked up from his console behind a glass window.

"We grew up together." I tried to keep it cool while tuning my guitar.

He adjusted some of the dials on his sound desk. "He seemed pretty hot for you. Can't say I blame him."

Looking up at me, he shot me a suggestive smile. Orson was a charmer who attracted lots of women. I couldn't even believe he'd stayed married for as long as he had.

"So I was thinking we should lead in with the vocal line first," he said, getting down to business.

I liked that about him. Professional first, sleaze second.

We worked solidly for two hours. Time just slid away when I was engrossed in music. And after three takes, I nailed my favorite tune titled "Song of the Sea."

He nodded. "That's the one. What do you think of the ambient ocean sound washing over the vocal fade?"

We listened again. "I like it. You don't think it's too 'Riders on the Storm'?"

"Maybe a little." He opened his hands. "But hey, why not? Nice to have that atmospheric vibe. Don't you think?"

I had to agree. Having the howl of wind and roar of the ocean did add a certain depth to the song.

He stretched his arms, stood up, and pulled out a joint. "Feel like a smoke?"

Putting away my dog-eared notebook filled with poetry and lyrics, I shook my head. "I'm pretty tired."

He grabbed himself a bottle of beer from a bar fridge and offered me one.

Opting for water instead, I declined.

"A big night with your hot-shot rich guy?" He chuckled as I followed him out into a courtyard.

"You could say that." I'd known Orson long enough not to play the coy card.

"Why do you look so sad, then?" He pulled a clownish downturned smile.

I stifled a yawn by covering my mouth. "I'm good. I'm just tired." Drained after a long session of playing, all I could think of was going to sleep.

"What about tonight? There's a great gig I'd love you to see. Interested?"

He sucked back on his joint, and for some reason, my focus settled on his lips. Yes. He was a hot, talented man with important contacts in the music industry. If ambition burned through me, that would have worked. I didn't even know if I wanted to be a musician forever, though, at least from a commercial point of view.

This was a moment in time when creativity had taken hold, but I hadn't given a lot of thought to my future as an artist.

Thanks to a small inheritance, I owned my flat, and I had a slush fund that was going down fast. Up to now, busking and selling CDs had brought in the same money as waitressing or cleaning, and on that front, playing music seemed like the more enjoyable option.

"Maybe," I said. "I'll see how I am at ten o'clock. I need to have a siesta, though."

He looked at his psychedelic watch. "At five o'clock?"

I shrugged. "I'm stuffed."

"Have a sleep here. Relax. Have a bath. Make yourself at home." He puffed out a plume of smoke.

"Maybe a sleep." I held up my finger. "Which doesn't mean you hitting on me."

His blue eyes twinkled as he chuckled. "I prefer it when the pleasure is mutual."

"You were pretty insistent last night," I said, sitting down on the wooden bench among pots of lavender and roses.

"I'd been drinking. Sorry about that." He stubbed out his spliff in an ashtray with a Hilton logo. "I think that was a good session today. We've got down three tunes."

I nodded. "Thanks so much for this."

"I'm in for my cut—you know that."

I thought of the contract I'd signed with him. Orson was a business-man at the end of the day. I hoped I'd managed to get it right.

I lifted my tired, sore body. "That bath's looking nice. The door locks?"

"Yes." He shook his head. "God, Bel, you don't half trust me, do you?"

"Let me get back to you on that." I smirked.

Orson was very slim, unlike buff Ethan, who fitted into my body like a glove. Even without Ethan invading my every waking thought, I wouldn't have been that attracted to Orson, despite his talent and good looks.

I just had to keep reminding myself that Ethan Lovechilde was very wrong, like a guilty, late-night sugary snack that leaves a taste of regret.

CHAPTER 8

Ethan

MY BRAND-NEW WHITE TRAINERS sank in the mud as I tramped over puddles to the Newman farm. It had been a while since I'd visited the adjoining lands. and I'd forgotten how soggy it got.

I found John Newman in the shed, watching a vet treat an unwell cow. The poor creature looked up at me with a doleful look, and I experienced a twist of guilt after that steak sandwich I'd gobbled down on my way back to Bridesmere.

Despite looking much older, the dairy farmer would have been around my father's age. Like most people who worked the land, they were up at the crack of dawn. My privileged existence meant that I was often up until dawn but never up at dawn—unless pressed against Mirabel's voluptuous body. The thought of her produced a silent sigh.

I needed a repeat performance or two. Or more. How could I get her to forgive me?

That's why you're here staring at that poor cow.

He wiped his hands on a rag, and I followed him outside the barn.

"Thanks for seeing me. I'm sorry to have caught you during a bad time."

He rubbed his neck. "Yeah. That's the third cow this week."

I nodded sympathetically. "Can it be saved?"

He shrugged. "Not sure."

"Look, um... I'm sorry about the order. I... we..." Coming unprepared, I felt nervous all of a sudden. I squared my shoulders and took a deep breath. "I have a proposition for you."

Declan liked my idea of offering the organic farm contract to the Newmans, which came as a great relief. The deal was that they'd end up with a few farmhands who happened to have records. A small price, I thought.

"Anyway, there's an acre of land on offer. There'll be a house built for you and your family."

His eyes slowly looked up from the ground. In his tired eyes, I caught a spark of interest.

I looked over his shoulder at their old mudbrick house. While it boasted a certain rustic charm, I imagined it being draughty and damp. I made a mental note to ensure their new home enjoyed all the comforts of modern living.

"The same rent?" he asked.

"Rent-free for the first year while you settle and find your feet."

His brows moved ever so slightly. "Where?"

"On the northside of Chatting Wood."

"Is that by that boot camp?"

I nodded. "There are a couple of stipulations."

"Them being?"

"Organic farming. Best practice. The land's been cleared. No hazardous topsoil. It has a certificate."

He nodded slowly. "Jenkins is getting good money on his milk production from going organic. I just wouldn't know where to start."

"I will talk to my brother about introducing you to an expert."

"And the other condition?" he asked in a deep guttural tone.

I took a moment to consider my words. "That land had been earmarked for an organic farm all along. And when this opportunity came up..."

"You mean when you decided to boot us out?" He stared me square in the face.

I smiled weakly. "My brother's vision for the farm was that some of the lads from the boot camp work as farmhands."

"Work with drug addicts and troublemakers? I don't think so." He removed a pouch of tobacco and rolled himself a cigarette.

He lit it up, and as the smoke billowed toward me, I almost asked for one.

"They're not all like that. And he's only going to employ boys that are proving to be reliable. And on top of that, you will not have to pay them."

He studied me closely. "That's a bonus, I suppose." He puffed on his cigarette pensively. "When do you need an answer?"

I shrugged. "Whenever you can. The house is being laid down as we speak. It should be habitable within two months."

"Two months? But we have to be out of here in a month," he said.

"I'll cover your rent if need be. But first, I'll see if we can delay the spa build so that you can stay here until the house is built. I think he'll be amenable. That's if your livestock can handle all the comings and goings."

"Let me talk to the missus and get back to you," he said.

"That would be good."

He was about to walk away when he paused and turned. "Why?"

I frowned as he scrutinized me closely. "Because it's the right thing to do. This area's been farmed for hundreds of years. I want to ensure you keep farming. At least with organic certification, you will get good prices for your produce."

He nodded slowly. "And what about all the others?"

"The others? Oh, you mean the resort?"

"Yep. Word has it that now that your good father has passed, they plan to send three farms packing."

I nodded thoughtfully. "I'm not up to speed on that. I'm sorry. So much has happened lately."

"Your father would be appalled. He was a good man."

I swallowed back welling emotions, knowing how close my dad was with the farmers.

"Declan's trying to talk our mother out of it."

"Word has it he was knocked off." He scratched his cheek.

I shook my head. I couldn't do this now. "We're looking into it. Anyway, Mr. Newman..."

"John," he said.

"John, it's been good chatting. Let me know as soon as you can, and we'll arrange everything for you." I held out my hand, and he took it. "Good luck with your heifer."

He nodded and lumbered off.

I headed back to Merivale, checking my phone for a response from Mirabel. Nothing.

Despite my motives related to wooing her back into my bed, another part of me wanted to help the Newmans. I got a kick from seeing how his eyes lit up with a glimmer of hope after I mentioned a new house and free rent for a year.

I MET DECLAN IN the yellow room. He listened with interest as I filled him in on my meeting with John Newman.

He gazed pensively into the oval gilded mirror above the mantelpiece, and I could see the gravity in his eyes. "I met with the detective today. They questioned Mother and Will."

I headed over to the decanter of single malt. "I think I need a drink. You?"

He shook his head.

"And?" I settled into a green velvet armchair with my drink.

"You know about him being drugged." He turned around to stare me grimly in the face. "They found Rohypnol in his bathroom cabinet."

"Right?" My brows knitted. "Why would he have those? Or was it a plant?"

He shook his head. "The detective told me that Father had a script. He had problems sleeping."

"But isn't that a date rape drug?"

"According to the detective, Father's doctor revealed that Dad suffered from severe insomnia, and after trying other sedatives, he prescribed those."

I walked around the room and then stood at the window, staring absently at the forest in the distance. My eyes settled on a circling raven in the sky. I stretched my fingers out of my clenched fists. Dissecting our father's personal life challenged me. I preferred to think of him as that affectionate father who didn't engage in kinky practices. Family secrets were best kept hidden. Despite my curious nature, snooping around was not in my DNA.

"So what else?" I asked.

"There was another man there for sure." He paused. "He'd partaken in some form of sexual activity because they found DNA on him."

"One of those weird sex acts using strangulation?" I gritted my teeth.

He ran his hands over his face. "Maybe."

"But why take a sedative?" I shook my head.

"The visitor called the ambulance. But they only found Father. The caller didn't leave any details, and the phone was untraceable."

"That proves he had something to hide," I said, walking to the decanter for another shot. "Isn't there any CCTV footage?"

He shook his head. "It wasn't working."

"That's suspicious, isn't it?" I asked.

He exhaled. "The detective seems to think so. They didn't find anything on Father's phone to suggest a booking."

"By 'booking,' you mean with a prostitute?"

"I'm not sure what to think, to be honest." He rubbed his neck.

When Theadora walked in, his face brightened. "How did you go?"

I rose and kissed my sister-in-law, and she smiled before turning to Declan. "I passed."

"Theadora's just got her teaching degree." Pride flickered in Declan's eyes. He draped his arm around her shoulder and kissed her.

"Well done," I said, genuinely pleased for Theadora, if not a little sympathetic, considering my mother's cold reception towards her.

After learning of their marriage, my mother claimed that since he'd "married down," I would have to marry up.

In defense of my new sister-in-law, I said, "Thea's a talented musician. Think of the good-looking babies."

"You have to stop this new-girl-a-night lothario act," she persisted.

"I don't do that anymore." I thought of Mirabel. My mother would love her. Not.

I returned my attention to Declan. "What do you make of Dad's murder?"

My mother walked in just as Declan opened his mouth.

She paused, raised her chin almost dismissively at Thea, and I felt for the poor girl. "You're all here."

"Where's Savvie?" I asked Declan.

"She's in London. She's hiring a PI." He turned to our mother.

"Why?" Her forehead creased.

"Why?" My head lurched back in disbelief. "Hello. Dad was murdered. We need to know who's responsible so that the arsehole gets what's coming to him."

Declan nodded in agreement.

Mother winced at my tone. "You look awful. You haven't shaved for days. And I smell smoke. Have you been smoking again?"

I became that little boy again. Gulping down my drink, I shook my head. "I've been with John Newman. He mentioned that you're moving on with that resort. You didn't waste time."

"Yes, we're moving forward."

"We? You and Crisp, you mean?" Declan asked with ice coating his words.

"He's my partner, yes." She got a bit fidgety and walked off.

"So, what about Luke?" I asked, trying to make sense of our father's investigation.

Declan joined his wife on the floral sofa by the window. "Dad left him twenty million He was running in the red just before father died."

"Could he have had something to do with it?" I asked.

"Luke has a rock-solid alibi. He was with another person, which has been corroborated."

My eyebrows squeezed. "But wasn't Luke Dad's partner?"

"Apparently, they had a loose arrangement." Declan tented his fingers. "It might just have been one of those freak accidents."

I looked Declan in the eyes for a moment. "Do you believe that?"

He shook his head slowly then shrugged. "I don't know."

I left them, lost in a million thoughts when my phone rang. I saw Mirabel's name and picked up.

"Hey, gorgeous," I said, smiling for the first time in hours.

There was no response, just muffled voices. She'd obviously pressed on her phone by accident.

I heard, "No. Orson. No."

I called out her name, but she didn't respond.

CHAPTER 9

Mirabel

SLOUCHED ON THE COUCH with Sheridan, watching yet another Hugh Grant movie, I jumped when I heard the knock on the door at midnight.

"Are you expecting someone?" I asked. I'd just returned from Orson's house and agreed to a glass of Chardonnay.

"I don't know who that could be." She frowned as she headed for the door.

A moment later, Ethan strolled in, and I froze like a lump on the couch. I felt winded, as though I'd been punched in the stomach.

I was wearing the crappiest pajama bottoms known to mankind—baggy, with the crotch somewhere halfway down my legs. Adding to this sexy ensemble, I wore fluffy dog-faced slippers.

My heart raced like a car careering down a hill without brakes, and Ethan, shifting from leg to leg, looked as comfortable as he would naked in a church.

"What are you doing here?" I asked as Sheridan gestured for Ethan to take a seat.

He dropped his head while rubbing his neck and wearing an awkward smile. "I tried calling, but you didn't respond."

Sheridan stretched her arms and yawned. "I was just about to go to bed."

She wasn't, but I appreciated her giving us space.

I remained on the couch, my face burning.

Wearing a burgundy blazer and black designer jeans that showed off his long, well-toned legs, Ethan looked incongruous on that worn armchair. He glanced over at the TV. "He looks young there."

"Sheridan's a Hugh Grant tragic," I said.

"I don't mind him either. I find his bumbling uncertainty rather endearing." He looked down at my feet and pointed. "They're cute."

I turned my feet inwards, as though willing my childish footwear to disappear.

I rose. "Tea?"

He nodded. "That would be nice." He followed me into the kitchen. "Sexy PJs."

I turned sharply to face him. We were enemies, I had to remind myself. "What the fuck are you doing here, Ethan?"

He leaned against the bench, rubbing his jaw, looking bashful even. "I came because I was worried about you. You weren't answering my calls or texts."

As he held my stare, I found myself drowning in his chocolate eyes, searching for that playful glint. Instead, his gaze reflected genuine concern.

I took a second to get my thoughts together before I spoke. "My phone's on charge." Despite my determination to hate him, I couldn't stop the cascade of warmth rippling through me. He'd come all this way to see me.

I poured water from the tap into a kettle. "Why would you be worried?"

"You must have pressed on your phone and called me without knowing it. I heard you yelling, 'No, Orson,' and I got worried that he might be hurting you. So I rushed into town."

While pouring hot water into a cup, I repeated, "You rushed into town?"

"Hey. Watch it," he said, pointing at the cup just as water spilled everywhere.

"Shit." I got a tea towel and wiped up the water. "You heard me and Orson?"

He nodded. "I thought you were calling me. It kind of made my night."

I looked up at him, still holding the dripping tea bag. The simple act of tea making had suddenly turned complicated as I tried to process Ethan's extraordinary excuse for his presence in that dingy kitchen, fiddling with his hair.

"And you came from Bridesmere? Tonight?" An intense frown made my head pound.

Wearing a faltering smile, he nodded. "It's probably an overreaction, but I was worried. You were yelling, for God's sake."

He slicked back his hair with his hand, and my focus zeroed in on his high cheekbones and perfectly proportioned face. When his tongue licked those well-defined lips, I wanted to pounce on him, tear open his fitted shirt, and rub myself against him. But also on a deeper level, I just wanted to cuddle him.

Horniness, I could probably handle, but my heart was another story. I had to keep my distance. If I were being entirely honest with myself, I was using the spa development as an excuse to hate him. I hated myself for being so spineless. But men like Ethan Lovechilde didn't stick around.

"I recorded a few songs, and I was so tired after last night"—I raised a brow in reference to our sexathon—"that I just crashed on his bed."

Ethan took the cup that I handed him. "Right. Well, I guess that was an invitation of sorts."

"An invitation?" I frowned again. "We didn't fuck."

I envisioned Orson snuggling up to me. The phone was in my jeans pockets, and when he went to hold me, I wriggled out of his arms.

"He tried. He always tries. But he's also quick to get the message, and he's never forced himself on me. That's why I've maintained our professional relationship."

"Then it *was* a serious overreaction on my part." His mouth stretched into a grimace. "Sorry."

I tilted my head with a sad smile. "That's nice of you to worry about me. I'm just sorry to have dragged you here this late. I should have checked my phone. Silly me."

He shrugged. "It's all good. And it's nice to see you anyhow." Again, his gaze lingered, and my body went to liquid.

Clutching his cup, he sat on the couch and stretched out his long legs. "It's okay. I've got a meeting with the head of staff at the hotel tomorrow. So it's not a wasted trip."

I sat next to him. "I look terrible."

He regarded my striped pajamas. "I don't know. I mean, a negligee will always win the day." He chuckled.

Back to randy Ethan. "I still hate you, you know."

"Hate's a bit harsh." He raised his hands. His smirk was replaced by an uncertain flicker in his eyes. The air between us thickened, and the longer the silence, the more intense my emotions grew.

"What do I have to do to win you over?" He spread his well-manicured hands.

I searched his face for his normal playfulness, but he'd become hard to read. "Don't build that spa."

"It's going to happen, Mirabel. I can't reverse it."

I released a frustrated breath.

He kept looking at me, and I had to turn away, stonewalling him.

"Oh well. I best be off, then." He smiled tightly. "Glad you're okay. That's what counts."

Our eyes locked, and again, time stood still. It felt like he was waiting for me to say something.

I opened the door and practically pushed him out. When he left, my heart barely pumped. A moment earlier, just standing close to him had made it palpitate in my ears.

I went to the fridge and grabbed the Chardonnay.

Sheridan came to join me as I shuffled around in the kitchen looking for clean glasses. "Oh, you're still up?"

"You look miserable," she said.

I shrugged. "I'm okay."

"Why aren't you having hot sex with that very sexy billionaire?"

Just hearing her say that made me laugh. "That sounds so ludicrous."

"I know. It's amazing. This is the kind of romance scene I love to read about. And you throw him out?" Her voice went up in shrill disbelief.

I gulped down my wine solemnly and nodded.

Her red bob wobbled from side to side as she shook her head repeatedly. "You're fucking mad. Do you know how boring monogamy is? The same guy every night. Farting. Making a mess. Smelling the bathroom out. Boring missionary sex that lasts five minutes at most."

I had to laugh. That was Sheridan—always complaining about Bret. "Then dump him and date different guys for a while."

She sighed. "Maybe. He's good to have around for company. He's great at fixing things, and we laugh."

I nodded slowly, wondering if Ethan was good at fixing things. The only thing I imagined was fixing a drink.

"So why was he here? That burgundy jacket. Woo. Sexy."

"Yep. He's stylish, all right." I sighed. "He was worried about me." I told her what had happened with the phone and Orson hitting on me.

"Shit. That's major, Bel. He came all this way, and you kicked him out? You're nuts."

I puffed. "He's about to evict a family friend. He's developing an important part of our history. It would be like sleeping with the enemy."

"I'm sure you can enjoy the sex and keep it casual. Not everyone needs to know."

I tangled my fingers and looked abstractedly at the Picasso dove print on the wall.

"Hey. Why do I get this feeling it's more than the farms?" she persisted.

I smiled sadly, my eyes burning with tears. She could read me well. "I'm falling for him."

She sat closer and put her arm around me.

I grabbed a tissue from the coffee table and blew my nose. "It is about the Newmans, but it's also about this." I tapped my heart, and my voice thickened with emotion.

"You're worried he'll hurt you." Sheridan's soft tone filled with understanding.

I nodded slowly. "After our first night together, I kind of fell for him. Even earlier than that when I was sixteen, I fell for him. And that was only after kissing him."

"Love at first sight?" Sheridan wore a dreamy smile.

"More like love at first fight." I chuckled.

Sheridan laughed. "Good title for an enemies-to-lovers romance."

"That's what this is kind of. Only we're no longer lovers." A tear ran down my cheek.

"You're just frightened, sweetie."

"I'm terrified of how I feel. When we were together nothing mattered. I flew. It was insane how I was able to transcend the mundane. I abandoned myself to lust."

"I love the sound of that," she said, filling our glasses.

"You're just a wild romantic." I sniffed.

"And so are you, Bel."

I sighed. "Even the other night at his penthouse it was like I'd been transported into a world of opulence and unimaginable luxuries. I mean, the floor was heated, and the shower—oh my god, that shower had massage jets washing every part. One even positioned right on my vag."

Her mouth fell open with glee. "Oh, that would do it, wouldn't it? One could come from that."

I laughed. "You've got orgasms on the brain."

"Well, after hearing about you and your multiples, I'm feeling a little envious. This brings us back to the beginning. Why the fuck aren't you fucking him right now?" She pulled a pained grimace.

"I'm scared."

My voice cracked. I hated myself. *What happened to me barrelling fearlessly through life?*

"That's not like you. You're the one that fucked first and thought later. I admired that in you when we were discovering ourselves."

"I know, and I have the scars to show for it." I thought of all those reckless drunk fests when I would hook up with some vaguely attractive guy, and the ones that ended up stalking me. "I haven't exactly gotten it right."

"Ethan's classy and sexy, and at least he doesn't wear his womanizing on his designer sleeve."

"I might go off men for a while and try organizing my life a bit better. Make a recording then perhaps think about getting a real job."

"Music's your life," Sheridan protested. "You can't become one of us. You're too interesting for that."

I smiled sadly. "I'd like to be boring for a while. It seems like an easier life. You know, someone who isn't looking for her next thrill at every corner. I kind of envy those people who are happy sipping tea and chatting about the weather. They seem to smile through their simple lives."

"And lose their minds to dementia."

Her dry tone made me laugh despite the dark nature of that topic. But dark humor seemed to help us get a handle on life.

My phone pinged. I read: *I never thought old men's PJs could look so sexy. That's become my latest fantasy.*

I laughed and responded. *You're a dick.*

The three balls bounced. *Yep. Guilty as charged. BTW just found your ripped panties.*

My face burned from shock and humor combined. *Ew. Toss them out. Like now.*

Are you kidding? He wrote. *That's never going to happen.*

You're a sicko.

A horny sicko.

There's always that blonde maid, I wrote, despite a prick of jealousy digging into my belly.

Why would I settle for artificial sweetener after savoring delicious nectar? Natural and free-flowing?

My core thickened with desire at the memory of his tongue on my swollen clit, and how, after relaxing my muscles, I'd drowned him in orgasms.

You can toss my panties away, I said.

Sleep tight, he wrote.

You too.

See you at Bridesmere?

I guess you will. I kept it cool, despite my inner tiger roaring for action.

The conversation ended, and after letting Sheridan read it because she would never have let up, I crawled off to bed.

I pulled out my trusty vibrator and visualized Ethan dangling my ripped panties in one hand while holding his dick.

Mm... nothing like a dirty fantasy to come hard. It would never match the real thing, though.

CHAPTER 10

Ethan

THE BOOT CAMP WAS in full swing. Some boys dug while others crouched down, popping seeds into the dirt as a gardener stood close and instructed.

"The garden's coming along," I said, joining Declan and Carson.

"Things are moving along quickly," Declan responded. "The boys are happy doing it."

"They're getting paid. That's why," Carson said in his deep voice. I studied the burly guy. I would want him on my side if faced with violent thugs.

"You've turned this into a functioning unit," I said, watching the boys lift crates off a truck.

"You've been spotted after hours in the gym," Carson said.

I nodded. "I love the equipment, and Drake's a talented personal trainer."

"Drake's a good lad when he wants to be," Carson said.

"He guided me well. I must say, Dec, you've gone state of the art with that gym."

Declan looked pleased. "I'm glad you're making good use of it. Maybe you can convince Mum one of these days about Reboot's value to the community."

"I already have. She heard me discussing the workouts with Savvie. You know Mother—she thinks gyms should only be for weightlifters or gymnasts."

Drake approached us. Tall and muscular, with black hair and bright blue eyes, he was the kind of guy I could easily imagine the girls liking. "We've finished planting the cabbages." He wiped his forehead and then greeted me with a nod.

"Have a break. I'll be there in a minute." Declan turned to me and cocked his head. "Come with me."

We headed to the back of the boot camp, where the foundations were being laid for Newman's new house.

"So he's keen?" he asked after John Newman.

I nodded. "He signed the contract for five years. He's happy to train three of the boys."

"He knows it won't be ready for another two months?" Declan asked as we walked through Chatting Wood.

Being late afternoon, the sun-sprinkled leaves shimmered. That forest always charmed me. As children, we were convinced wizards and witches lived in the trees.

"He knows," I said, thinking of John Newman and how he lost years off his face when I'd offered him a holiday in Spain and then arranged for them to stay in a village cottage while the house was being built.

"His wife's expressed interest in working at the spa."

"But that's a month away, isn't it?" Declan asked as we traversed the path onto the back laneway to Merivale.

"It is." My back ached from the thought of all the work I still needed to do. Between the hotel and the spa, I had a packed itinerary.

SAVANAH WANTED TO CELEBRATE her twenty-eighth birthday at The Rabbit Hole, one of her favorite West End bars, filled with "*our* people," as my mother would have it. I couldn't say whether I connected that deeply with that trendy bar with its rib-thumping dance music and wall-to-wall people in designer, downing shots and talking loudly. I liked the scene at the Thirsty Mariner just as much.

Dressed in an orange dress with purple splashes, my sister always went for the craziest designs she could find.

I pointed at her outfit. "This is out there."

"Vivien Westwood. I love her. Matches her hair color." She giggled.

Sienna, my sister's party girlfriend, looked like she'd been squeezed into a skin-colored dress. Her fake-tanned shoulder touched mine as she joined us. We'd had a *thing* that had lasted a few nights, and she was again in flirty mode.

"I thought you were naked, from a distance as I walked in. I had to do a double take," I said.

She giggled. "I think that's the idea. Get men all hot and bothered imagining us in the flesh."

"Oh, we don't need a skin-colored dress to heat up," I said, recalling Mirabel in her own fitted number that hugged those perfect curves. "I prefer color myself."

She touched the lapel of my jacket. "This is quaint. Houndstooth. Reminds me of my grandfather's jackets. It suits you, though."

"I picked it up in Scotland. I'm rather fond of Harris Tweed. The process is rather staggering. They dye their wool from local plant life."

She smoothed down her super-straight blonde hair. "I wouldn't have picked you for a nature-loving type."

"That's me through and through. My city persona's just a front."

Declan and Theadora stepped through the door and made their way through the noisy crowd, which seemed to double in size due to all the mirrored surfaces.

"Ah, there's big brother and sister-in-law," Savanah said, holding a bottle of beer in one hand and a shot glass in the other.

It was fair to say that my sister liked to party.

"I thought Mummy was about to have a heart attack when she saw that ring on Declan's finger." My sister chuckled.

I nodded, recalling how the blood had drained from my mother's face. "I'm happy for them."

"Yeah. So am I. Thea's such a talented musician."

"You could have practiced your scales as Mother hounded you to do."

"I'm too distracted to practice anything, I'm afraid." Savanah pulled a sad smile. Despite her skipping carefree through life, there were moments when that façade cracked, and I caught a glimpse of a fragile girl who hadn't quite grown up.

Savanah hugged Declan, followed by Theadora, who then placed a gift-wrapped present in her hand.

"It's not much. We didn't know what to get you," Theadora said.

Savanah unwrapped the present, and a chunky necklace dangled from her hands. The purple baubles went perfectly with her outfit.

"It's something I picked up at a vintage shop. Mary Quant, I believe. They have a whole lot of designer stuff from the 60s, 70s, and 80s." Theadora smiled, while Declan, wearing stars in his eyes, had his arm draped around her waist.

They were very much in love. Enviably so.

Do I want that? I wasn't meant to.

On that confirmed bachelor inner note, I noticed Alex, a drinking mate and wingman, sauntering towards us. He was known to carry me out, or more like us carrying each other out, after many big nights of partying.

"Hey, you," he said.

"We're celebrating my sister's birthday. You know Savvie?" I asked.

He smiled and saluted her.

"Join us." I made space for Alex.

"I would, but there's this girl." He cocked his head towards a leggy blonde by the bar. "She's coming on strong." His eyebrow arched. "What about you? I haven't seen you for weeks."

"I've been busy, what with running the hotel. I'm also overseeing a spa project back home. I haven't felt like random hook-ups either."

His face scrunched in disbelief. It even surprised me to hear myself admit that.

"Have you met someone?"

"Sort of. But she's not interested."

His face lit up in surprise as though I'd spoken of having my chest hair plucked. One excruciating strand at a time.

Mirabel hadn't returned my texts after my visit to her cousin's flat, which had me shuffling off with a bruised ego.

Sienna turned to look at me, her tongue running over her pumped lips.

Alex noticed. He noticed everything to do with women. The man was addicted to the chase. The girls liked him, too, with those eyes that twinkled, "Let's party."

I guess we made a good pair. Drinks. Pick up a girl. Compare notes. And repeat.

Years later, I was left with a head full of interchangeable names and faces. I certainly didn't miss having to scrub lipstick off my dick every morning.

"She's nice. Great mouth." He wore the bright smile of a man without a care in the world.

I shrugged. "That's if one feels like a collagen-filled gob around one's nob."

He laughed. "Yep. Sign me up."

"Talking about pouts, your girl looks like she's pining for you," I said, staring at the tall woman dressed like every other woman at that bar. Tight. Synthetic. Glittery. Spiky-heeled shoes that could double as weapons.

I thought of Mirabel in her earthy dresses worn over boots. She didn't even wear lipstick. I'd forgotten what naked lips tasted like. Organic. Healthy. Fucking nice.

He nodded. "I better get back there. See you soon."

"You will." I joined Declan. "Any news from the detectives?"

He shook his head. "They haven't found the visitor yet."

"Do you think we'll ever know?"

Savanah joined us. "Are you talking about Daddy's murder?" Her voice cracked. "I still can't believe he's gone."

I put my arm around her shoulders. "Hey. Try not to go there. It's your birthday. Dad would've wanted you to have a great time."

"I feel his presence sometimes, you know," she said with a pained look in her eyes. "I wish I'd told him I loved him."

I tightened my arm around her shoulders. "Me too." A knot curled in my chest. "I'm staying in his penthouse. He's everywhere."

"I'll have to drop in."

"Hey, stay there whenever. I'm going to be spending the next few days at Merivale."

"Mummy's got the bulldozers moving in already for the resort. That tosser Crisp's hanging around like a bad smell. I'm still going to help with the interior designs." She looked over my shoulder, and her eyes sparked.

I turned to see what had lifted her mood and saw a heavily tattooed guy lumbering towards us.

"Oh, here's Dusty," she sang, her face bright and back to party mode. "He's come from Bridesmere." She looked from me to Declan.

Dusty joined us, and we were introduced. The ink plastered all over his neck, hands, and fingers made me assume his whole body was covered—a kind of scrawled testimony of his lawless, probably dark existence. His neck was as thick as his head. I didn't get the allure. But he was attractive, judging by how some of the women checked him out. That brutish, caveman appeal, I could only guess.

I pictured skinny Orson, asking myself if that was more Mirabel's type. Then I recalled how she'd run her soft fingers over my six-pack while releasing a breathy moan.

Watching Savanah follow Dusty to the bar, I turned to Declan. "I see our sister's appetite for street fighters hasn't abated."

He shook his head. "He looks like a fucking dickhead."

I had to agree there. "Yeah. A fucking heavily built one that I'd prefer to have on my side."

"She's sniffing around Carson. He's too much of a softy for our sister, though."

My eyebrows flung up. "A softy? He could take on six Dustys in one go."

"I've seen him wipe out a gang on his own." He grinned. "But Carson's got a deep side to him for sure. I saw tears in his eyes while Theadora played the piano at the boot camp. She was teaching one of the boys, and they ended up doing a duet." He turned to his wife and put his arm around her, drawing her into him. His eyes filled with love. "I think it pulled on his heartstrings seeing that boy, normally a troublemaker, lost in the music. Afterward, the boy was as docile as a lamb." He turned to Theadora.

"He has a ton of raw talent," she said.

There was so much happening, I hadn't even thought to ask about my new sister-in-law's musical progress. "How's the music coming along?"

She nodded. "It's good, thanks. I've set up a space to teach from home, as well as teaching one day a week at a local primary. And now at the boot camp, it seems." She tossed Declan a look, and he leaned in and kissed her. "I've also got a gig at the Mariner with Mirabel tomorrow night."

My ears warmed to that. I looked at Declan, and he had stars in his eyes. "Your wife will be touring soon."

He shook his head slowly and drew her in close again as a reminder that she was part of him.

"He doesn't want me touring. He's jealous of the male groupies." Theadora giggled.

"I've got cause to," Declan said.

I thought of Mirabel and how men ogled her on stage. Why wouldn't they? She was a goddess.

Theadora smiled. "I'm not that ambitious. I just like Mirabel's music, and when she asked if I could play a few tunes, I agreed. I'm also playing on her new song. I was there at Orson's house today for the recording."

"She was with him today?" I frowned.

"You know him?" She looked surprised.

"I have had the unfortunate pleasure of meeting him. He's all over her. That much, I do know."

She gave Declan a side glance. "Right? Um... I don't know. I mean, he seemed a bit close to her, I guess."

Declan inclined his head. "You're still sweet on her?" He turned to his wife. "Ethan and Mirabel have a history."

I clutched my glass tightly and shifted my weight. "She's not talking to me at the moment. The spa's got her back up."

"Does she know about the Newmans moving and how you're paying for their house?" Declan asked.

I sucked back a breath. "Nope."

"You should tell her. John Newman looked pretty chuffed when he was walking around the new farm with the architect."

"That's good," I said, recalling how the farmer had called me just fifteen minutes after my proposal to accept my offer.

That's why I tried calling Mirabel, but when she refused to pick up, I gave up. I could have texted, but I didn't want to come across as desperate. She would find out soon, I imagined. Whether that was enough to have her naked and in my arms, I couldn't say. I'd stopped taking anything for granted.

CHAPTER 11

Mirabel

THEADORA ROSE FROM HER piano stool, and the applause grew. I always enjoyed performing at the Thirsty Mariner. My local pub had the same warm, accepting atmosphere as a family home. It was also great for trying out new material.

Looking like he'd just come off a movie set, Ethan leaned against the bar. Dressed in a blue-check sports jacket and jeans that fitted him in all the right places, he oozed the confidence of a man who owned the world. With that inviting smile, he seemed comfortable with anyone. If only he were arrogant, it would be easier to hate him.

A pretty blonde whispered in his ear as he continued to gaze my way. I could almost feel the heat from those bedroom eyes making a pathway to me, causing me to fumble and drop things.

"Hey, that was super," I said to Theadora as she stepped away from the piano.

"It was nice to play a tuned piano. Unlike the last gig. This poor old thing was in such a desperately bad state." She tapped the piano that was scratched and worn.

Although married life suited her, she was still down-to-earth and real.

"That was such a generous gesture. Jimmy must have loved you for tuning that old thing," I said.

"At first, he thought I wanted him to pay." She laughed.

Winding a lead around my arm, I grimaced. "He doesn't like spending money. But he's a good guy, and I'd hate him to sell out."

"He's not going to?"

Her look of horror made me smile. "No, The Mariner's been in his family for hundreds of years."

After I closed my guitar case and tucked away my leads, I ran my hands down my clingy dress to make sure it hadn't ridden up again.

I followed Theadora, who joined Declan. His eyes lit up with pride and love as he placed his arm around her shoulders and kissed her.

"That was sensational. You both sound great together." He shot me an appreciative smile.

"Thanks," I said. "The recording's come along nicely. Theadora performed Bach-like passages, and it just works so well."

Declan kissed Theadora on the cheek again. They were such a beautiful couple. Not just physically. They radiated such warm, inclusive vibes. Like their inner light shone outward and their hearts were big enough to hold the world.

"You both have such a loved-up aura," I said.

Declan's eyes slid to his wife. "If you're saying we look madly in love, then yes, I'm madly in love with my beautiful wife."

Ethan squeezed into our huddle and stuck his finger in his mouth. "Will you two stop it? Have a fucking argument. Do something normal, will you?"

I had to laugh, despite my determination to avoid eye contact. He regarded me as he would any friend, almost as though we hadn't fucked in positions that would have impressed yoga masters.

"We have our moments," Theadora said. "Like jam all over the butter. Or leaving the seat up in the loo."

I let out an exaggerated hiss and added jokingly, "Oh, that's bad."

"That's why God invented bathrooms in the plural," Ethan retorted.

I was about to respond when a blonde girl, who was screaming with laughter over something Savanah said, hooked her slim arm through Ethan's.

I turned away sharply like someone had slapped my face, praying Ethan didn't notice that visceral reaction. After excusing myself, I stepped outside for a cigarette, my first in a week. Ethan Lovechilde was a bad influence on not only my sanity but also my health.

Just as I was lighting my cigarette, I saw a shadow and pivoted to find Ethan wearing an infectious honeyed smile. One couldn't deny the man anything when he looked like that.

"Do you mind if I have one?" His eyebrow raised. "Again."

The last time I gave him a cigarette, we'd shared more than just tobacco.

I persisted with my Ms. Cool act. "Sure. But I'm not talking to you. Remember?"

He spread his hands out. "Why are you punishing me?"

I studied his face for a hint of that playful smirk, but he'd turned deadpan.

"I just don't want to turn this into a thing between us. We're too different. And you're going to keep doing awful things like inappropriate developments. I'll end up carving an effigy of you and tossing it in boiling oil."

His face scrunched in shock. "Ouch. That's pretty severe." His dark chuckle dragged me along. It was a crazy thing to say, and I had to laugh at myself. Reverting to straight-faced, he huffed, as though frustrated by something. "I'm not interested in Sienna, by the way."

My jittery fingers made rolling that cigarette difficult. I licked the paper and passed it to him. "It's none of my business."

I lit his cigarette, and his eyes scanned mine as though looking for some hidden meaning behind my words.

A plume of smoke exited his mouth. "I just wanted you to know that."

I shrugged one shoulder. "Whatever."

We smoked in uncomfortable silence, then he butted his cigarette and left.

His sudden departure felt like a punch in the gut. I wanted him to keep trying. Or win me over with his cute gestures.

He paused and swirled. "You're the best fuck I've ever had." He then walked off.

My eyes nearly popped out of my head. What gave me the edge over all those beautiful women who breathed down his neck?

He's probably only just saying that... Then why did those brown eyes shine with depth?

As I tried to make sense of Ethan's jaw-dropping admission, I went back inside and got caught up in a crowd of friends, who invited me onto their table. Grateful for the distraction, I joined the farmers and their girlfriends.

Steve, who worked on a farm next to the Newmans', bought me a drink and sat next to me. We'd grown up together. He was my age and had always liked me. I wasn't into him that way, and he knew it. So now when we caught up, it was more a sibling connection rather than flirtatious. Unlike Ethan. Even before we'd hooked up, Ethan flirted openly with me, which I secretly enjoyed.

Speaking of the devil, across the bar, Ethan kept stealing glances, rattling my nerves, despite the warmth in my chest.

Who doesn't like to hear they're the best fuck ever?

My inner nag, however, was convinced he'd only said that to get me into bed again. But why would he need me when he had that pretty girl in designer virtually sucking on his earlobe? I imagined she would offer herself at the end of the night. Ethan was way too horny to knock back a gorgeous girl.

Jealousy twisted me into knots, and my head nearly dislocated from my neck as I watched them leave. Together.

Just as he was about to step through the door, he turned and waved at me. Talk about rubbing it in.

A sudden surge of frustration hit me. Why did I have to scale the slippery slope of morality when I could just wade in that blissful morass of apathy?

Or was it that on a deeper level, as I'd admitted to Sheridan, I was trying to protect myself from heartbreak?

Men like Ethan Lovechilde didn't marry girls like me.

Marry?

Since when, did I want to marry?

I thought about my parents, who were very much in love until their lives came to a heart-shattering end from a car accident.

They were *also* very different. My father came from wealth, despite my grandfather gambling it away, and my mother from a farming background.

Steve waved back at Ethan.

"Ethan's a good guy underneath those designer jackets." He chuckled.

"Really?" I scrunched my brow. "He's about to knock down your livelihood."

"That's Caroline Lovechilde."

"What about that spa? The Newmans are about to lose everything."

"Not from what I've heard." He pointed at my empty glass. "Another?"

I shook my head. "What do you mean?"

After Steve told me about Ethan paying for the Newmans' relocation and a holiday they couldn't normally afford, I sprang off my chair like I'd been bitten on the bum. I had to find Ethan before that girl's puffy lips squelched on his dick.

"Are you okay?" Steve asked.

"I'm fine." I kissed him on the cheek and raced out the door, without getting my pay or saying goodbye to Theadora and Declan, who were making a night of it.

I stepped outside, and on spotting Ethan's red sportscar, I sprinted. My heart thumped in my ears.

Just as I got there, I noticed a blonde head down near his crotch.

Oh shit, she's blowing him.

My heart turned the size of a pea, and my legs buckled. Then he saw me. I probably looked like I'd walked in on a lewd act—and I had. Only why did it have to be the man who'd stolen my heart?

CHAPTER 12

Ethan

I PUSHED SIENNA AWAY. My dick slept—a first for my once-restless member. Had those steamy nights with Mirabel drained my body of testosterone? Or something a little less clinical and deeper? So deep that I no longer recognized myself?

Now she probably *really* hated me. The way her eyes went from warm and playful to shock and horror within a blink made me want to yell.

I wasn't even into Sienna. All I did was offer her a lift back to Merivale, and she'd pounced on me, her teeth yanking at my fly. She was meant to be hanging with my sister, but Savanah had left earlier with Dusty.

We drove through the iron gates of Merivale. At night, the columned façade resembled a concrete chameleon with an array of changing colors beaming over its white walls.

"You've got a thing with that singer?" Sienna asked. "She seemed pretty upset. Sorry if I messed that up."

"We *had* a bit of thing. It's really nothing, I guess. But I do like her." I chewed on my bottom lip, trying to make sense of this "thing" between Mirabel and me.

I couldn't work out why someone identifying as a free spirit could be wound so tightly when it came to me. Okay, there was that little detail of my developing land that should have remained untouched.

Even I regretted that decision, but it was too late now.

"She looked pretty freaked out. I can tell her nothing happened, if you like," Sienna said while playing with her long, blue fingernails.

Guilt hit me hard again. How many girls had I hurt? All those calls I hadn't returned. Not to mention the face-to-face confrontations after being caught hiding or doing a quick getaway.

I'd always thought we were having sex just for fun, but certain people had a way of seeping into your pores. I'd never thought that possible. Until now. Maybe it was the loss of my father, but I no longer identified with that brash guy looking for the next party.

"Hey, I didn't mean to lead you on. That wasn't my intention."

She smiled. "It's cool. I'm the one that offered to blow you. Remember?"

I smiled at her raw honesty. "Come on, let's go in. And look, I'm tired. So..."

She opened out her hands. "I get it. You like someone else. It's sweet. She's a lucky girl. Although she looked seriously pissed off with you."

I wasn't about to contradict her. I *was* sweet on Mirabel.

While I couldn't disagree with Mirabel in describing us as being different, we were also very similar. And she knew more about me than any other woman I'd dated, which was probably why I wasn't unclasping her bra that minute.

Sienna and I walked up the lit path, which cast shadows over the garden, almost animating the sculptures that, as a boy, I'd convinced myself came alive at night.

I wished I could be him again and start afresh. I wouldn't waste my time chasing girls, but instead pursue science or something more satisfying than carving up old land.

I was never the bookish type. I liked making money, and I'd learned how to do that under the guidance of old college friends who played the money market. Figures came naturally to me, and I found maths a breeze. Had I not horsed around as much, I might have gone into complex mathematics.

We entered the great hall, which under the lamplights, resembled a museum. Marble statues and valuable vases sat among classical somber paintings and contemporary acquisitions. Everything in its perfect place.

"Okay, then," I said. "The kitchen's always open for snacks and drinks." I crooked my finger. "Here, let me show you. You know where the guest room is?"

She giggled. "I've been here heaps of times, Ethan. But that's so nice of you. I might grab some munchies, though." She rubbed her belly, and I smiled.

I liked her. My dick, however, wasn't so into it. But then my dick was suddenly in conference with my brain and heart. They'd decided that they all needed to be part of the action from now on. That made Mirabel a hard act to follow. She had brains, beauty, and depth.

I saluted Sienna and trundled off to bed. I went to my room and yawned. I had an early start the next morning.

I sent Mirabel a message. *Nothing happened with Sienna. She was looking for her eyelashes.*

A few minutes later, she replied, *Pull the other one.*

I had to laugh. Of course, she wouldn't believe me. *We didn't do anything. She wanted to, but I wasn't keen. I'm here all alone at home, pining for that beautiful woman I watched gyrating on stage earlier tonight.*

She replied, *I don't gyrate.*

Oh yes, you do. And how.

Why didn't you tell me you were building a home for the Newmans?

I wanted to, but I always forget things when I'm around you.

Crosswords.

Huh?

Sounds like you're suffering from memory lapse.

I typed, *That's because when you're around all I can think of is getting you naked.*

She responded, *In your dreams.*

Dinner?

I've eaten.

I mean tomorrow night.

I'm going to London to record.

With Mr. Purple?

Yep.

Dinner afterward? I need to drive in later for a meeting at the hotel. Maybe.

I'll call you. Sweet dreams.

You too.

Pleased that the call ended on a civil note, I put away my phone. I fell asleep and dreamt of a red-haired beauty rolling around with me naked by the duck pond. I woke with a raging hard-on.

ALTHOUGH MERIVALE HAD A gym, I preferred Reboot. Plus, the walk getting there put me in a chilled headspace.

When I arrived, Drake was clowning around with a tall, skinny red-haired boy.

Seeing me enter, he nodded.

I stretched my arms and then went over to a set of weights.

Drake strolled over to me. "Hey, do you need a hand with those?" The weights I was about to lift were way beyond my normal range. This new resolve to do better had suddenly translated into pushing myself at the gym.

"Sure," I said.

"You might want to start with something lighter, though. As a warm-up." He pointed at the assortment of dumbbells on a shelf.

"Why don't you take me through the course, like the other day? That was awesome. I felt great afterward. And I had no pain the next day. Unlike when I'm left alone."

He nodded slowly. "I remember. You were about to do some damage."

The gangly red-haired boy joined us.

Drake knocked his friend playfully in the ribs, and they laughed. "This is Billy. He talks too much."

"Get fucked. You're the one that never shuts up."

I laughed at the cheek in his eyes. With that Irish accent, he made it sound like life was to be laughed at.

The lads joined me, Billy trying to outperform Drake, but never getting there. Drake was an impressive specimen and ran rings around the both of us. But I was stronger than I was the other day. I'd made progress and had moved up to heavier weights.

Although Billy was skinny, he showed impressive strength. His face turned red from determination to keep up with his friend. Then he got bored and pummelled a punching bag instead.

"Billy's training to box," Drake said. "He's really good. All those street fights are paying off."

Billy raised his chin. "I can always swap this for ya ugly head if ya like."

"Nuh. I might knock out those girly teeth."

"Fock off," Billy said, punching away.

"He's always brushing his fucking teeth," Drake told me.

I had to laugh. I liked them.

Drake's eyes darkened, and I turned to look at the boy who'd just burst in, dressed in Nike, head to toe, which made me wonder if he dealt drugs.

"Who's he?" I asked.

"That's Bailey. He's a fucking tosser."

Bailey regarded us and then looked over at Billy. "If it isn't the orangutang."

"Shut the fuck up, you Tory cunt," Billy said, punching more furiously.

My head pushed back, and I had to remind myself these boys had done prison time. They weren't about to share a respectful conversation about some Miss Marple mystery on TV.

Drake rolled his eyes. "He's fucking trouble. He just turned up, like two days ago. A rich arsehole. Thinks he owns the place."

Although muscular, which suggested he worked out, Bailey sat on the press bench and went through the motions in a perfunctory fashion. He struck me as uncommitted. After a few repetitions, he walked over to Billy and whispered something. Billy, who was already red in the face from his fierce thumping, headbutted him.

Bailey fell onto his arse. He scrambled to his feet and pulled a fist, but Billy ducked and was about to pounce on him when Drake raced over. The blonde toff would have come off second best, I conjectured, as I watched what had gone from some friendly ribbing to a full-on fight in a matter of minutes.

"Don't you know if you get caught again, you're back in?" Drake berated Billy.

Billy wiped his forehead with the back of his hand. "Then tell that turd to fuck off. He started it."

Bailey laughed. "He can't help it if his mother's a spaz."

Billy flattened Bailey, while Drake yelled at him to stop.

Carson ran in and separated them as one would a couple of warring puppies. "Not you two again." He let out an angry groan, then pointed into the Irish boy's face. "You've already been warned."

"He fucking started it," Billy appealed.

Drake nodded to corroborate his mate's appeal.

"I was watching," I said, joining them. I pointed my chin towards Bailey. "He came in looking for trouble. I'm sure."

Carson scratched his chin. "Just get out. Now."

They all left. He turned to Drake. "Go with them. Watch over them."

Drake nodded and left.

"How are you?" I asked Carson.

"I was good until I stepped in here. He's fucking trouble, that Bailey."

"Why don't you throw him out?" I unscrewed my water bottle and took a swallow.

"Can't. He's someone's rich son. I don't know. Something doesn't quite make sense, to be honest. We had him lumped on us. He hasn't been locked up or anything. Although he should be. We were asked to turn him around or else."

"Or else what?" I asked.

"We're on notice. Any trouble, we lose our license." He handled a weight Drake had left lying about and picked it up like it was a blanket.

"This place gets shut down, you mean?" I asked.

"We can keep the commercial side of things going." He scratched his bearded jaw. "The boot camp's getting a lot of interest. Mainly from the corporate scene. But I'm here to help the boys. They're all good lads. I've grown fond of them. Until he turned up the other day. He's on Billy's back. Keeps making fun of his mother, who's in a wheelchair."

"You're kidding." I shook my head in disgust. "No wonder he wanted to punch him out. That dickhead was sledging Billy about his disabled mother."

"Yep. A rich son of a bitch. Can't stand him. I'm going to have a word with Declan."

"I will too. Billy strikes me as someone who can hold his own. But I'd hate to see him jailed for defending his mother. But, boy, I've never seen anyone punch into a bag like that."

Carson nodded. "He's talented, all right. We're bringing in a boxing master. Maybe a ring."

"Hey, that's a great idea. Boxing's a very popular sport."

"As a pacifist, I hate it."

I studied Carson, and my eyebrows rose. "Right." He didn't have the body of a man who hated fighting. It was like someone with perfect pitch hating music.

"Billy's a shit-stirrer, but he's a good kid."

"What got him locked up?" I asked.

"Hit someone on a boozy night. The victim lost an eye."

I screwed my face. "Shit."

"He's paid for it. I read the counselor's notes. He cries himself to sleep virtually every night. He's also really close to his mother, always making sure she's okay when she visits. He's got a big heart, that boy."

I nodded slowly. Being there had been a big eye-opener.

After the gym, I dropped into the hall for a coffee before my meeting at the spa. I found Declan arguing with our mother in the library.

"Hey what's up now?" I asked.

My mother rolled her eyes. "Your brother disapproves of the boundary for the resort."

"You bet I do. You said three farms. Now you're encroaching on a fourth?"

She tapped her pen on her desk.

"I disagree on principle." Declan turned to me, looking for my opinion.

I opened out my hands. "I haven't seen the plans."

"That's because you weren't at the board meeting," my mother said dryly.

"I've got to go," Declan said.

"The soiree. Will your wife perform Debussy, as promised?" she asked.

Declan puffed. "Theadora has agreed, despite my misgivings."

Her eyebrows drew in. "Why would you not wish to parade her talent? We need all the support we can get over this marriage of yours."

He pointed at her. "She's not an object for show."

"This will be a formal introduction for your wife. An important step forward. Wouldn't you agree?"

"She's agreed to do it. Just treat her a little more warmly. Up to now, you've done nothing but give her the cold shoulder."

Her mouth twitched into a faint smile. "I'm always cordial. You know my feelings about this marriage. I'm only just getting over the shock of my eldest son marrying below him."

"She's my equal, Mother. Get over it."

I turned to Declan, puzzled. "What soiree?"

He regarded our mother. "Perhaps you can explain."

"I thought it would be a nice touch to host a recital in the ballroom." She smiled.

"That should prove to be a fun night."

My brother's mouth curved slightly at my wry remark, as I followed Declan out.

"Hey, look, I've just been at Reboot, where I met Drake and Billy. They strike me as good people. Anyway, this arsehole Bailey showed up and caused all kinds of trouble."

"I know. He's a dickhead." He rubbed his face. "Bailey's the son of one of Mother's acquaintances."

"If you need me to testify against him."

"I think he's a plant, myself." He inclined his head towards my mother's office.

My jaw dropped. "She designed it?"

He shrugged. "Or Crisp. If there's any trouble, Reboot gets shut down."

"I'll be there as support."

I followed him into the kitchen, where we were greeted by the staff, who busied themselves preparing food. A baking aroma made my stomach rumble.

"Some lunch?" Janet asked us.

Declan looked at me, and I nodded.

"We'll take it outside. It's a nice day," he told Janet.

We settled in the courtyard overlooking the pool area.

"Have you been swimming much?" I asked.

"I prefer the sea. But yes, I have," he said, stretching out his legs.

"I might take a dip later. It's warm today." I wiped a trickle of sweat from my brow. "However, the pool might need a good clean. I accidentally stumbled on Savanah and her latest boy. I'll have to remind her to keep her sex life behind closed doors."

"She was in the pool at night again?" he asked.

"Yeah. I imagine there's some foreign DNA floating around."

His face scrunched. "She lives dangerously, our sister. Mother sleeps early, so I guess she assumes she won't be seen."

Janet delivered our steak-and-kidney pies with salad, and my mouth salivated. The fragrance brought back warm memories of family dinners. That was why I loved being at Merivale—the food, the fond memories, and positioned between the sea and forest, the sheer beauty of my childhood home.

She placed the dishes down, and I returned a grateful smile. After that workout earlier, my appetite was strong.

"How's married life, then?" I placed a forkful of pie into my mouth, savoring the taste of the meaty gravy on my tongue.

"It's wonderful. I've never been happier. And it gets better all the time."

His eyes reflected that rare glow of deep satisfaction. I envied him for finding his center at last. I was still scrambling about in the dark, looking for mine.

"Crisp's now Mother's official business partner." He shook his head in disgust. "Savanah's hired a computer hacker, I believe."

"That's going down the criminal path." I wiped my mouth with a cloth napkin. "You still suspect that it wasn't an accident?"

He took a sip of water. "Mother and Crisp haven't wasted time, have they?"

The resort and how fast it was moving *did* disturb me because there was also one other clear suspect in all of this. Our mother.

CHAPTER 13

Mirabel

AFTER A WEEK OF recording in London, I was back in Bridesmere, and seeing that my cupboards were bare, I headed off to the supermarket. While strolling along the aisles at the local grocery store, I ran into Theadora.

"Hey you," she said, hugging me.

"I'm so glad I saw you. I was going to call you about doing a gig in London for the release of my CD."

Rather than blocking the aisle, we stepped aside to let people pass.

Her frown faded, and her face lit up. "I know. A swap of sorts."

I gave her a quizzical look.

"I'm performing tomorrow night at Merivale. Perhaps you could join me? They're hosting a soiree, of all things."

That piqued my curiosity. What I wanted to ask was whether Ethan would be there. "That's not surprising. Caroline Lovechilde likes to parade as a woman of culture."

She rolled her eyes. "Doesn't she."

Her cool tone wasn't lost on me. "I'm sensing you're not close."

"She hates me. A former maid marrying her darling son." She chuckled. "Nothing I can't handle. I'm well-practiced at cold, domineering mother figures."

My eyebrows rose at that loaded comment. "That sounds intense."

"I don't let it get to me." She wore a strained smile.

We paid for our goods, and I followed her out to the street.

"Let's walk over to the pier so that I can buy some fresh fish," she said. "That's if you've got the time."

I placed my backpack over my shoulders, and we crossed the road.

The tide was high, as unrelenting waves crashed against the pier, splashing froth in the air. Seaspray spritzed our faces as we walked to the fishmonger's shop.

"I suppose your mother likes Declan?" I asked.

"She hasn't met him."

I stopped walking. "Really?"

"She keeps ringing for an invite. She's dying to visit Merivale."

Theadora told me what had happened to her, and I shook my head in shock. She was surprisingly deadpan and unaffected as she described her hideous upbringing.

She smiled at my look of horror. "Hey, I'm good. We've only got ourselves in the end. And I would never have met Declan. I would go through it all again just for that."

I nodded slowly, thinking about Theadora being drugged. "And this Crisp character, who's part of the mother's inner circle, will he be at the soiree?"

We stepped out of the path of a fisherman wheeling a cart. I tasted salt on my lips as I wiped my face with the back of my hand.

"Probably." She shrugged. "Declan's already punched him in the nose." She raised her eyebrows. "I've moved on, even though I don't trust him."

"I can't blame you."

We stood in line at the fish van with the catch of the day on offer.

"So now your mother wants to be part of your life?" I asked.

"She does. I told her that when that monster husband of hers was no longer around, I might allow a visit." She stared out to sea. "It's funny how the roles have reversed. I'm the one that's now pushing her away. Just like she treated me. I don't forgive easily." Her face brightened suddenly. "Hey, why don't we perform together at Merivale? It would be a hoot."

That sudden shift in subject jarred me. I took a moment to process her suggestion. Other than his cute text, I hadn't spoken to Ethan since the gig at the Mariner. That dinner in the city never happened because I was busy recording while fighting off Orson's advances.

That was a week ago. Ethan had called a few times. I just hadn't returned his calls. I was still stuck in that we're-too-different camp.

"Won't I be unwelcomed?" I asked.

Theadora's mouth curled slowly. "Yes, enjoyably so."

I responded with a shocked laugh. "Are you using me to stir things up with Caroline Lovechilde?"

Her eyes sparkled with a hint of mischief. "Maybe. But hey, it will be fun. And it will give you some exposure, won't it?"

It came to our turn, and I waited as Theadora made her order. After she paid and received her parcel, we headed back to the street.

"What about Ethan?"

"What about him?" she asked. "He's smitten, by the way."

I stopped walking and whipped my head around to stare her in the face. "Has he spoken about me?"

She removed her bike from the stand. "Ethan always asks after you. So, do you want to do it?"

Questions banged into each other. I was gobsmacked. I shrugged. "Why not?"

"Yay." She looked excited like we were fifteen-year-olds breaking rules for a bit of fun.

"What are you wearing?" I asked.

"I've got this Spanish costume I picked up in London. It's amazing. You should see it."

"That sounds colorful."

She nodded. "Although I'm performing a Debussy piece, my costume has inspired me to perform a piece from *Carmen*."

"That sounds passionate. Now I'm worried about what I'm going to wear. And what will I sing?"

"'Song for the Sea.' I love that song." Her eyes lit up. "I've got an idea. Do you have time to come over today for a rehearsal?"

"I guess so."

"I just had this idea." Theadora's infectious burst of enthusiasm made me smile. "I'm playing 'Clair de Lune.' I'm sure I can find a smooth segue into your song. It will work for sure."

"Okay."

Her eyes remained on me. I sensed her mind ticking away. "Do you think you could learn a song by tomorrow?"

I bit into my cheek. "Like someone else's?"

She nodded. "A Bizet song from *Carmen*."

Theadora hummed the song she had in mind.

"I love that song," I said.

"'La Habanera.' Very sexy." She shimmied her shoulders and giggled.

My mind swirled with all kinds of possibilities. "Do you think I could sing it? I'm not a soprano."

"But that's better still. Sing it with that husky voice of yours. Make it your own."

My face hurt from smiling, as anticipation pumped through me. "I'll go home right now and download it." Adjusting my backpack, I asked, "Who else is performing? It's a soiree you say?"

"Poetry recitals and other musical numbers, I believe. Old-fashioned and stuffy."

I laughed. "There's nothing wrong with poetry."

Her thoughts were somewhere else. I could see Theadora creating a performance piece on the spot. I didn't mind. I welcomed my creative juices flowing again. Recording my song had been so mechanical, with all those repeated takes, that it was a chore.

"There's a market in Trentham tomorrow morning. We can go there and find something for you to wear. Something slinky."

I shook my head. "I think you've missed your calling as a director."

She giggled. "I'm all excited suddenly. I'm so glad I ran into you. With you there, we can have some fun."

"Okay, then. I've got a song to learn. And we're off to market in the morning for a slinky dress." I frowned. "Will I find one there?"

"There are so many stalls of vintage designer. I'm sure there'll be something interesting and sexy."

"I can't wait," I said. "Text me the rehearsal time."

"How about four?"

I nodded slowly. "I'll hurry back now and get cracking. I may not have the words down today. But I've got until tomorrow night."

I waved as she rode off on her bike.

CHAPTER 14

Ethan

WHEN THE WORD *ARROGANCE* was invented, they had Reynard Crisp in mind. Dressed in a blue velvet dinner jacket, he owned his wealthy pedigree like a dictator who'd bludgeoned his way to power. He wore that signature insipid smile, which never quite reached his eyes, while he stood with a stiff posture, engaging in social niceties with the guests.

I'd never had anything against him. Until now.

Declan and Savanah joined me.

"Do you think he's had Botox?" I slanted my head towards the man we'd placed at the top of our murder-suspect list.

"Probably." Declan's curt response startled me. If anyone should have been making a fuss about that prick's presence, it was him.

"Why are you taking this so easily?" I asked.

Savanah interjected. "I agree. I can't stand him. I told Mummy, and she just told me to like it or leave."

My eyebrows hit my hairline. "She told you to leave Merivale?"

Her mouth turned down. "I got caught having sex in the pool with Dusty."

"Oh." I slid my eyes to my brother, who gave her a stony look.

She knitted her fingers. "We're no longer together. Okay." Her edgy tone revealed something hurting in my sister. I'd noticed her darker moods since our father's passing. I made a mental note to spend some time with her.

"If you want to talk ever. You know I'm always there for you," I said.

Her mouth curved into a faint smile. "Thanks, Eth. I'm good, though. But I need a drink. Where's that waiter?"

Savanah walked off and left me with my brother. "You haven't said much about Crisp being here."

"I hate him. We all do. But we're stuck with the bastard. Savvie mentioned something about a hacker earlier. Let's see if they bring something up."

I frowned, worried about my sister and her impetuous choices, not only in men but underground activities. "That could get her arrested."

"If Crisp organized a hit, that's all we've got."

"But if evidence is gained by illegal means, won't that be inadmissible in court?"

"Mm... true." Declan rubbed the back of his neck. "I might have a chat with the family lawyer."

"You'd think she'd want to know, wouldn't you?" I puffed out a breath. Then, seeing the waiter, I grabbed a glass. I looked at Declan, and he nodded, so I took two.

Handing him a glass, I asked, "So where's your lovely wife?"

"Warming up, I believe. I've been out all day, dealing with an issue at Reboot, but when I got home, she acted all coy. I'm not sure what she's planning, but I get this feeling it's a surprise of some sort. My wife has a dark edge to her. In a good way." His eyebrow arched. "Mum's acted deplorably towards her. So if Theadora feels like performing punk rock or something just as radical, I'll be the first to applaud."

"Punk rock on the piano?" I chuckled. "Anything will be better than sitting through a poetry reading."

Dressed in a cream-colored dinner jacket, Will stepped out of the shadows, where he normally lurked at these social events, embracing his new role as lord of the manor.

"Will and Mother have come out as a couple."

Declan nodded pensively. "A bit too soon for my taste."

The butler rang the bell, and it was time for us to take our seats in the ballroom.

This was one of many soirees at Merivale we'd attended. The ball-room, with its high domed ceiling, lent itself to a makeshift recital hall. Seats were arranged in tiers facing a shiny black grand piano positioned in front of burgundy velvet curtains with dimly lit lamps for mood.

As always, I sat between Declan and Savanah. As kids, we'd poked fun at some of the more tedious performances. For a while there, my mother had a thing for Shakespearian actors. A friend of hers from Oxford was a director, and we would sit through long, convoluted monologues while pulling faces at each other.

After an exhausting poetry reading that went for twenty verses too long, Theadora came out draped in an embroidered shawl, wearing a costume with a ruffled train.

"She's gone all flamenco," Savvie said.

Whispers and little comments floated through the air.

"Is she about to stomp her feet?" I asked Declan.

He had stars in his eyes as he watched his striking wife with justifiable pride.

"Is she going to dance?" Savanah asked Declan.

He shrugged.

I glanced over at my mother, who fixed her unblinking gaze on Theadora. It surprised me that she'd even asked her to perform. At least my sister-in-law, in that vibrant theatrical outfit, had brought some welcomed color to that normally stodgy affair.

She sat down, flicked her long dark hair over her shoulder, then commenced her piece. Her fingers glided across the keys like they were made of air. I was transported to a French garden reminiscent of Monet, sitting on a stone bench, the late afternoon sun warming my skin, and jasmine making me light-headed.

"She's so talented," Savanah gushed.

Declan sat with his arms crossed. Admiration and adoration seemed to pour out of him. I'd never seen my brother so in love before.

A figure entered through the side door, and all eyes turned to her. My jaw dropped. Mirabel, in a slinky green gown, wore her lustrous burgundy hair waving over her curves.

I sucked back a breath and forgot to release it.

"Oh my god, it's Mirabel. She looks gorgeous," Savanah said.

Mirabel's voice harmonized with the strains of the piano, melancholic and deep. Once again, she transported me on a mystical journey over a stormy sea.

She pressed herself against the curvature of the piano and opened her heart and soul to us. Her sultry dreamy vocals had the entire audience under her spell. Not a fidget or sound could be heard in that room of about one hundred guests.

Now, this was poetry, especially with that subtle sway of hips and the way her chest moved with each breath.

When the song came to an end, I was about to clap, then Mirabel continued to sing. I'd been to enough opera to recognize *Carmen*'s 'Habanera,' which Mirabel took somewhere else with her sexy rasp. My pulse raced. Music had never aroused me like that before.

Her hips swayed flirtatiously, as Mirabel sang with all her soul, while Theadora accompanied with fitting passion. They'd made that classic song their own. Her lips curving into a teasing smile, Mirabel tossed her head back as she moved with the grace and fire of Carmen.

I went to liquid. I swear I heard some of the males groaning. *Or was that me?*

My mother turned and looked at Declan with a question in her eyes. I smiled. I could imagine her response to this classic tune turned into a contemporary R&B tune. I wanted to download it. Put it on my playlist. Have sex to it. With the singer.

The song ended, and the applause nearly lifted the roof off. "Bravo" flew through the air like we were at a concert hall. That reaction should have put a smile on my mother's face since she always aimed to please.

I turned to Declan, who kept applauding. "That was incredible."

"It was wicked. I filmed it on my phone," Savanah said.

My mother tapped Declan on the arm. "Why is that farmer's daughter here? These soirees are 'invite only.' And I'm the curator."

"Oh, get over it, Mum. It was fantastic. The guests are happy." Declan rose, and as Theadora joined us, he held her. "You were superb. I love this." He touched her dress.

"I loved it too. And that dress," Savanah said. "You were great."

Theadora looked at my mother, who returned a cool smile.

"Did you enjoy it, Caroline?" Theadora asked with a grin. I had to hand it to my sister-in-law. She had cheek. Just what the family needed—some originality to shake things up.

"I enjoyed the first number, but after that, you lost me." My mother walked off.

I pulled a sympathetic smile. "That was so unique. You were both fabulous." I scanned the room, which was awash with women in glitzy gowns and men in tuxedos and colorful jackets chatting loudly. "Where's Mirabel?"

"She left. She said something about catching up with a friend." Theadora studied me. "I don't think she wanted to see you."

"Why?" I frowned.

"She likes you."

That little revelation slapped me with a sunny smile. "Did she say that?"

She nodded slowly. "Don't tell her I told you. She just thinks you're a player and that she'll get hurt."

I shook my head. "For a courageous artist, she doesn't quite treat her private life the same."

"She's just sensitive. Like most artists."

"But she's a self-confessed relationship-phobe," I said.

"That's just her not wanting to open herself up."

"Has she told you about Orson?" I asked, taking advantage of Theadora's candor.

"He actually called her when we were at the market. I think she likes him, but I get the vibe it's her way of getting over you."

All I heard was that Mirabel liked Orson, flashing like a neon sign in my brain. "Has she slept with him?"

Theadora's eyebrows flung up. "I think you should ask her."

I leaned in, kissed her cheek, then left in search of Mirabel.

CHAPTER 15

Mirabel

AMBLING ALONG, I IMBIBED the pretty surroundings, pausing now and then to take in the breathtaking beauty of Merivale at night. Rippling beams of everchanging color cast a magical glow on the sculptures and hedges. Beyond the magic garden, the moon beamed over the silvery sea.

I was so caught in the spectacle that the sudden sound of a deep voice made me jump. "That was some performance you gave."

I turned, and a tall red-haired man who might have been in his early fifties pierced me with a cool, penetrating gaze. He sucked on a large cigar, looking like some wealthy baron.

"Thanks." I looked up at him. "That's if you meant it as a compliment."

"I'm rather fond of opera. I have a particular soft spot for Bizet's *Carmen*. The other tune was an original, I take it."

"One of mine."

"You've got talent." His eyes traveled up and down my body like cold, unwelcome fingers sliding over me. Feeling naked, I shivered. "Although it was probably better suited to a hipster bar than Merivale." He smirked, and I felt an instant dislike towards him.

From a distance, I noticed someone heading our way. I looked over the tall man's shoulder and saw Ethan.

He turned to the man. "I hope you're not making a pass at our guest artist." Ethan remained serious.

"We were just chatting about her tantalizing performance. No harm." He showed his palms in defense and walked off.

Ethan stepped closer to me, and my body buzzed just from a whiff of his herbal cologne. "I hope Crisp wasn't inappropriate."

"Oh, that was him," I said, recalling Theadora's harrowing story.

"I gather you've heard he's a nasty piece of shit?"

I nodded. "He struck me as pompous. But then the rich can be like that."

"I'm rich, and I'm not." A faint smile touched his lips. "You're safe. You're probably too old for him."

My mouth twisted into a scowl. "Gee, thanks." I turned to walk off.

"Hey, I didn't mean it like that."

I stopped and met his handsome face close to mine. He'd stepped in towards me as though trying to block me from moving. My insides turned over. I wanted to run away, but my heart anchored me there. I tried to speak but couldn't get the words out.

The weight of his gaze and the turbulent emotion his intense almost-black eyes evoked made him unreadable. I reached into my bag for my tobacco. All this intensity made me want to smoke.

He watched me rolling one, and without asking, I handed it over to him.

"Thanks. I'll have to buy you a packet."

"I'm still trying to give up," I said.

I lit his cigarette, and as he blew out smoke, he said, "What I meant was that Reynard Crisp likes his victims young. There's speculation he drugged Theadora the night Declan saved her."

"Theadora told me about that. Why's he even here?"

"Ask my mother. She's in thick with him."

"I won't be asking her anything." I scrunched my face. "She's the reason I left in a hurry."

His forehead creased. "Did she say something?"

"She asked me who I was and how I came to be there. I reminded her that I used to play here when we were kids."

He rolled his eyes. "I'm sorry. She's not the easiest person."

"She *is* kind of scary. The one you don't want to cross."

He chuckled. "You got that right."

His eyes locked into mine. It was like a man was trying to burst out of his younger, playful version. Or it could have just been whenever I lowered my guard, I related to Ethan as that boy I'd climbed trees with growing up.

My body, however, had discovered a man. My skin prickled the longer he gazed at me, and my breasts felt full. I drew in a breath and tasted desire in the dewy air. His woodsy scent was intoxicating.

Time stood still. Even after we stubbed our cigarettes, we didn't move. All I could see was conflict in his eyes as they swept over me.

Is that longing? Or does he just want me naked? That thought alone sent a shiver of desire up my thighs.

"Why don't you come in and have a few drinks and something to eat?"

The alternative option of going back to my messy flat and drinking cheap wine was nowhere near as attractive.

"But what about your mother? She practically kicked me out."

"You're my guest. I live here." He smiled and reverted to his playful self, which I welcomed.

It was an out-of-body experience as we walked along that magical path. "I still can't believe you live here."

"Remember when we used to play in the labyrinth?"

I stopped walking. "How can I forget? You tried to touch my breasts."

"You let me kiss you though." He wore that lazy smile that made me want to have dirty sex with him.

"You were horny then like you are now. Not much has changed."

"I haven't been with anyone since... us." His mouth tugged up at one end.

This sudden shift from playful to serious left me speechless. I just pointed at the columned mansion's entrance. "Show the way, then."

What could I say? That I slept with Orson and hated it? Why do the hell did I do that?

I'd been drinking and convinced myself that Ethan was a bad idea. Orson gave me a nice neck rub. Then before I knew it, his hands were crushing my tits, and I surrendered my body and principles.

I entered the hall to a room of lively, colorful guests. The women in their stitched-on designer dresses were indistinguishable—all beautiful, svelte, and eyeing Ethan, the latest eligible billionaire, with their hungry gazes.

As I made my way through the throng, people stopped chatting and stared. The older guests gave me a nod, and the odd "Well done," while others looked me up and down then looked away.

Their narrow-minded pretentiousness didn't bother me. If anything, it made me want to laugh—as did the rich princesses, sticking up their pert noses at me. What did worry me, however, was Caroline Lovechilde. She looked at me like I was about to open fire on her collection of wealthy friends.

I smiled at her and kept moving.

Disregarding his mother's obvious hostility, Ethan took my hand. She zeroed in on our clasped hands, turning sudden tingles into ice. Recalling Theadora's experience with the Lovechilde matriarch, I held my head high, refusing to be intimidated.

We entered a yellow room with all the extraordinary embellishments that made it difficult to know where to look. The walls, filled with original gilt-framed art, were a banquet for the eyes.

"Your mother's not going to be happy," I said.

Ethan took a plate and passed it to me. "I couldn't give a shit, to be honest. She's far from perfect."

"It sounds like you don't like her much."

"I know she's my mum, but she's not exactly my favorite person at the moment." He selected some food from the vast spread of offerings.

I accepted a plate of canapes. "Why don't you move?"

"Despite spending more time in London, I'm looking around for a place here." He took a bite of a mini quiche.

"Oh, you are?"

Chewing, he nodded. "My mother's becoming increasingly difficult to live with. I hate how she is with the staff and how she just treated you."

I frowned. "You can't have women here?"

He swallowed his food and blotted his lips with a serviette. "Well, I haven't exactly been living the life of a monk." His thin chuckle sounded apologetic. "If it wasn't for the spa, I'd probably live in London." He looked me in the eyes. "I hope you're not going to race out on me for mentioning the spa."

My stomach sank at how ridiculously petulant my charging out of the hotel that morning now looked.

I sighed. "I probably overreacted. And at least the duck pond is still accessible to everyone."

"That was never going to be part of the design. We all used to play there as kids. And one day, my..." He bit into a cracker.

"Your children, you mean?" I had to ask.

"Not mine, but nephews and nieces. I'm sure Declan and Theadora will have a brood."

"You don't like children?" I tilted my head.

"I do like them. But they come with a lot of responsibility. What about you?"

"Maybe. One day." This wasn't an easy subject. Deep down inside, I wanted to become a mother. That desire had intensified with age. "Anyway, about the spa, I like the rock wall façade. It harmonizes with the natural surroundings. Your architects have done well. I would have hated one of those steel-and-glass box buildings."

He laughed. "I had you in mind when I met with the architect."

My head lurched back. "Really? No. You're just pulling my leg."

"I really did." A smile touched his face. "Although..."

I shook my head. "What?"

His hand stroked my palm, and my nipples tightened.

I laughed. "You did that to get into my panties?"

He kept smiling. "It might surprise you to know that I like natural materials," he added, shifting the subject away from the bedroom. "I think a building should blend with its environment and not clash, like some of the city monstrosities."

Is he trying to impress me? "I would have thought all those hard edges and asymmetry your thing."

He pulled a face. "Hello, I grew up here."

"But you're young, rich, and modern."

"Sure." He shrugged. "But I am allowed to love classic designs. In saying that, I'm not opposed to modernity. I appreciate Calatrava or Lloyd Wright-inspired structures like any admirer of fine architecture might."

My eyes widened. "You do? That's a surprise. Although I have no idea who they are."

"I'm not just a pretty face."

I rolled my eyes. "Back to vanity again."

"Is that how you see me?" When his gaze collided with mine, he'd turned dead serious again.

Taking a sip of champagne, I considered my answer. "You do come across as super confident."

"But that doesn't mean I have a high opinion of myself."

"You used to come across as cocky, I suppose." I knitted my fingers. "But since I've gotten to know you, there's a kind heart in there. And, as I'm discovering, a creative spirit too."

His frown ironed out into a faint smile. "That gives me hope."

I tipped my head to the side. "You're sounding a bit down on yourself."

He played with his glass. "I recognize my flaws probably better than anyone. I have regrets, and I want to do better."

"Then you're deeper than you make out."

He held my gaze for a moment. "I'll take that as a backhand compliment."

"You should. I relate entirely to how you described yourself because that's me too."

"Then we've got a lot in common." His mouth curled up at one end in what looked more like a shy smile than an expression of vindication.

Whenever I dropped my guard, just like that first night in my flat, I felt a deep connection with him.

I slid a cracker over the pâté and took a bite, indulging in its deliciously seasoned flavor.

"I saw John Newman, and he's over the moon," I said. "That's a great gesture. And you've offered his wife work at the spa."

"We need a workforce, and why not? Do you want a job there?"

That suggestion took me by surprise. It did have some merit, though. Busking was becoming increasingly tiresome. "Hey, I might take you up on it. I could use the extra money. And I do like living here. London exhausts me."

We finished snacking, and Ethan directed me to the pool area, where we shared a cigarette.

"I'm glad you're here," he said, smoke pouring between his sculptured lips. "I've been wanting to see you for two weeks."

"I've been busy." I smoked silently for a moment. my head buzzing with all kinds of colliding thoughts. Fighting the burning need to feel his lips on mine, I kept searching for a reason to hate him. Before I could process that thought any further, I clutched my bag. "I guess I should go."

He shook his head. "Please stay."

"I can't stay here. Your mother creeps me out."

"Well then, why not invite me back to yours?" He stepped closer to me.

I felt his heat and fell under the spell of his hooded gaze. A primal surge of desire overpowered me as I succumbed to his magnetic pull and melted into his strong arms. His lips brushed mine softly before they crushed me with desperate passion.

"I want you." His breath tickled my tongue as he spoke into my mouth.

I heard someone, and we broke apart. Dizzy from that kiss, I had to hold on to a chair for support. Savanah appeared with Dusty.

"What's he doing here?" Ethan sounded like a protective older brother.

"He's just dropped in." Savanah looked at me. "That was awesome, by the way." Her eyes slid from me to her brother. "Are you two together?"

Ethan took my hand. "Yep."

I looked at him, and he shook his head. "What?"

"Well, we're not *really* together."

Savanah turned to Dusty, who had just lit a spliff. "You should do that around the back."

He nodded and walked off, and she waved us goodbye.

"Savvie," Ethan called out.

"What?"

"Be fucking careful."

She fluttered her hand, and off she went.

He rolled his eyes and exhaled. "She worries me. He's fucking trouble."

I smiled sympathetically. "I'm sure she'll figure that out soon enough."

"Yes, but will she be alive?"

Ethan's concern for his sister was touching. The more I got to know him, the more I began to realize that a thoughtful, caring person lived inside him.

"Now, where were we?" His gaze trapped mine again, and as he touched me, goose pimples puckered my skin. My nipples ached for his lips as his finger moved slowly into the crease of my arm.

"Would you like to see my bedroom? It's got a great view of the sea." Shameless playfulness shone in his eyes, back to his wanton best. But that *was* him: raw, animal, and seriously arousing.

Flushed by a surge of hormones, I took a moment to respond. "What about your mother?"

"Don't worry about her. This is a huge house. My room's miles away from hers."

With that fiery kiss still stinging my lips, I floated by his side to the back of the estate—through an entrance away from prying eyes. My body was now in the driving seat. My heart sat in the front, and I locked my brain away in the boot.

CHAPTER 16

Ethan

SOON AS WE ENTERED my room, I grabbed her hands and drew her against me, our mouths in a crush of lust. As I devoured her soft lips, an overwhelming need made me lose my head. I wanted to consume her.

Groping each other, we tore at our clothes. My fingers slid up to her lacy bra, teasing her hardened nipples. She pulled me against her, grinding her now free breasts against me.

After undoing my fly, she freed my throbbing dick. Our tongues met in a hungry tangle. Taking control, she pushed me onto the bed and then slid down the bed, taking my throbbing cock in her hand.

I dropped my head back in bliss as she swallowed me deeply. She twisted her tongue around the underside of my head and sucked gently. Her mouth did things to me that made it hard to speak, let alone think. I was helpless to stop her.

I clenched the sheets as a flood of pleasure gushed out of me and into the back of her throat. She licked her lips like a sated pussycat, her cheeks aglow.

I entered her slit with my finger, and she was so wet. I groaned. "You seem to get off on sucking my dick."

Gloriously naked, she lay back on the bed like an enchantress, and now it was my turn to return the favor. Her warm curves at my fingertips, I sucked on her nipples.

I moved down to her pussy and spread her legs. I breathed her in like I would an erotic fragrance. I grasped her arse, ravaging her until she cried out for me to stop.

She dripped cum all over my tongue, and I milked her release as she trembled in my hands while I sucked her juices. Blood had drained from my brain and engorged my dick.

"Do you see how hard you make me?" I whispered into her ear and licked it.

She moaned sweetly, like she sang, her voice husky and dreamy. We rocked in rhythm. Her soft curves rubbed against my pelvic thrusts as I entered her, soaking up her juices and her tight muscles clenching me.

I placed her legs up on my shoulders, filling her deeper. "Your so fucking snug and creamy."

Her groans grew as her pussy walls spasmed and squeezed my dick to the point of no return.

"I need you to... come," I stammered.

The friction intensified as our sticky bodies moved in a fierce rhythm. She scratched and bit me for what was exquisite pain. Sweat dripped off me as I pounded into her until I erupted into a fireball, coming like it was my first time. Molten red flames jumped before my eyes.

I stroked her tenderly and kissed her hot cheek. "Can we keep doing this?"

"We'll have to wait a while, though, won't we?" She giggled.

"That's not what I meant."

She untangled herself from my arms and looked at me with a puzzled frown. "Like a relationship? Us going exclusive?"

I played with her fingers. It did sound like I was asking Mirabel to be my girlfriend. Her green eyes gleamed with curiosity and something deeper. She had one of those faces that always offered something new.

"I haven't felt like fucking anyone since we hooked up," I admitted.

Her eyes narrowed slightly like she was searching for blackheads on my face. "I guess so."

"Don't sound so certain." I stroked her arm.

"I'd like to keep doing this." Her mouth curled at one end.

"You look like you're being asked to jump out of a plane."

She laughed. "Huh. Good analogy. It feels like that a bit. Not sure where the hell this will land. Impaled on a fence or rolling in a field of soft clover."

"There's only one kind of impaling going on here." I ran my fingers up her thigh.

Her chuckle helped tension drain from my shoulders.

"Does that mean you'll answer my calls and texts?" I asked, with a faint smile.

"Maybe." She looked up at me with a challenging twinkle in her eyes. "I'm not sure how to do this. I've spent the past decade or so thinking of you as a prat."

I scanned her face for a smile, but she remained serious. "Right. Well, maybe with time you'll see me as a generous prat who's got the serious hots for you."

Her lips curled into a slow smile.

"That's better." I took her into my arms. "From one prat to another."

Her laughter vibrated through my chest.

A WEEK AFTER THE soiree, my mother called me into the library. Will hovered about, as usual. I nodded to him in greeting. He was like a piece of furniture passed down from generation to generation—quiet, understated, and always in the same spot.

My mother, on the other hand, was like that priceless antique that drew all the attention. Dressed in red skyscraper heels and a pink dress that revealed an hourglass figure, my mother made looking glamorous effortless. She could have passed as someone twenty years younger. With her long red fingernail, she pointed to an image for Will to examine from a selection of mock-ups.

"Are those for the resort?" I asked, joining them.

She nodded. "We're hoping to open within twelve months." She tapped her gold fountain pen, which had been passed down from my grandfather. "We had a walk around the spa yesterday." She glanced up at Will, as though I needed reminding that he was part of the family. "It's rather bucolic with that stone wall finish. I thought you would have gone for a modern design." She rose from her desk and navigated the room, settling by the etched marble fireplace, where the bust of a stern Lovechilde ancestor sat.

"It blends in with its surrounds," I said. "Burnt-out city types like the rustic feel. They're surrounded by slick, clean lines. People like contrasts."

"Is that why you're seeing that folk singer?"

Her acidic tone made my spine stiffen. "It's none of your business."

Eyeliner accentuated her large dark eyes, capable of freezing with just one glance. "Oh, but it is, sweetheart. While you live under my roof, you play by my rules, which have always been pretty loose." Her dark, well-shaped eyebrow raised. "I've turned a blind eye to the many women you've entertained. Women from good families, whom I hoped you might've proposed to by now."

I shifted my weight and rolled my eyes.

"What is it with all of you?" She sighed. "Declan married that maid. Your sister and those detestable tattooed thugs, and now you with a farmer's daughter-slash-pagan." She scowled like she'd swallowed something rotten. "What next? You prancing naked around a fire under a full moon?"

I had to laugh at the ridiculous image. "I'm not that religious ritual type of person, Mother. And Mirabel's not into witchcraft. She's intelligent, talented, and she gets me."

Disbelief spread over her face as she glanced over at Will, who sat quietly absorbed, as though watching a performance. I'd never heard him express any opinion other than a nod.

"She gets you?" My mother scoffed. "We sent you to the best schools, and that's how you define this unfortunate and incomprehensible attraction?"

"We haven't exactly been exposed to great role models." I looked up from the globe on the desk and stared her in the eyes.

My mother wrung her hands. "What happened with your father was unfortunate." Her mouth formed a tight line. "It wasn't by my design. He married me that way, without ever telling me."

My stomach sank at the mention of my father. It wasn't an easy subject. And as my eyes settled on my mother's, I noticed a hint of sadness.

My heart knotted. She was my mother, and deep down, I wanted her to be happy, regardless of her toughness towards us and her inability to show maternal warmth.

"I understand that wouldn't've been easy," I said at last. "But you were together. I mean, he was our father." That came out as a statement, despite a question still lurking in the shadows.

"He was definitely your father. You keep asking. I might have made a few bad calls in my life, but cheating on my husband was not one of them." Her gaze shifted over my shoulder, and I turned to look at Will, who returned an awkward smile.

I understood their closeness and appreciated Will being our mother's stabilizer. Her brittle, some would say fragile, nerves needed a calming influence like Will.

"I like Mirabel. We grew up together. She's part of my history."

Her eyebrows drew in. "That's why you like her?"

I couldn't exactly tell my mother that Mirabel made me hot and insatiable, that I craved her being in my bed, even just to hold. She was great to fall asleep with, her body in my arms, all soft and warm. "We have good chemistry."

"Darling, this family needs someone with a peerage and money."

"We're seriously rich. I'm rich in my own right."

"I mean powerfully rich, darling. Powerfully."

"That sounds overly ambitious and tiring. In any case, you can buy peerages these days."

"I'm old-fashioned. I believe in inheriting it by marriage." She sat down on the floral couch, picked up a copy of *Vogue*, and flicked through it absently. "She's not to stay here again. I won't have that woman here."

"Fine. I'll move, then." I walked out of the room before she could respond.

CHAPTER 17

Mirabel

ORSON GLANCED UP FROM his console. "What do you think?"

"The transition between the piano and vocal works well."

Orson had a great ear, and for someone as indecisive as me, his input had been invaluable. High on something, Orson bounced around his music room, turning off equipment, popping cords into boxes, and opening doors covered in soundproofing foam. Like many in the music industry, his love of sniff was no secret. Orson wore a long-sleeved Marc Bolan T-shirt over orange jeans. His dirty-blonde hair with streaks of grey was scruffy in that carefully disheveled way that made certain males attractive.

His jerky movements made me jumpy. Now that our session was over, I'd become edgy. We hadn't spoken about *that* night yet.

I wasn't sure if I would ever forgive myself for sleeping with him. Orson had this charming way of making me feel special and desired. I'd always been a sucker for a compliment.

Regret sucks. If only I could press rewind.

Sheridan kept reminding me that Ethan and I weren't together and that men did it all the time, so why couldn't women? That was a reasonable argument. But I still felt like shit about it.

After I packed up my stuff, I joined Orson in his kitchen. He offered me a bottle of beer, which I took gladly. I needed something to drain the tension out of my body. As I sipped the cool bitter liquid, his playful blue eyes met mine. My cheeks flushed, and I turned away, unable to maintain eye contact.

I gulped down a third of the contents and then cleared my throat. "Orson, what happened between us…" I paused to find the right words. "I was drunk, and well, it can't happen again. Ethan wants us to be exclusive."

Just saying that made the bottle shake in my hands. *Are we really doing this?*

I could be with Ethan as easily as breathing. But could I keep him happy?

Kinky sex, I could do. I liked it. But would that be enough? Would he want threesomes? Jealous to a fault, I could never agree to that.

He pulled a mournful, sad-clown face. "I'm broken-hearted."

"Don't make fun. I mean it." My voice cracked.

"I'll get over it." His cocky smirk made me want to slap him.

"You know me." He chuckled. "I'm not a one-woman man. Monogamy's an outmoded institution."

He pulled a box of crackers from a cupboard and dipped his hand into it. "There's this young singer I met the other night at Blue."

"I'm happy for you," I replied coolly. "So today was good." I shifted the gear back to business. "I think it turned out well."

He offered me a cracker.

"No thanks," I said, leaning against the kitchen table scattered with newspapers, magazines, cups, and glasses.

"I think it's a good album, Bel." He crunched on a cracker, as streaming sun through the kitchen windows highlighted the wrinkles around his eyes. "My lawyer will email the contract. I'll be taking fifty percent of royalties, as discussed."

Orson was a professional over and above everything, and when it came to his time, he didn't do anything for free. I respected that.

"Fine." I rose and released a breath that helped untangle the nerves in my chest. The queasiness I arrived with had finally settled.

I was relieved that our session had ended. Even his smell, which pierced my nostrils when he hugged me, repelled me. Ethan's scent, on the other hand, sent a warm tingly wave through my body.

I placed my guitar in a backpack case. "I need to go."

"Ethan Lovechilde?" He walked me to the door.

"It's a little crazy, I know. We grew up together."

"He's a party boy and a womanizer, methinks. Don't let your heart get too invested." The patronizing tilt of his head made me want to stamp on his foot.

"Gee. Thanks for the advice."

He chuckled. "Only looking after you. Although heartbreak does write the best songs."

"Fuck off, Orson," I said.

He leaned in and kissed my cheek. "Love you too."

My mouth tugged up at one side. I left him at his door, waving at me. I stepped onto the Chelsea pavement and glanced over at the manicured park with its velvet lawns and uniform trees. Everything looked clean and in its place. A far cry from my life.

What does this mean for me now? Will I have to shop at Harrods and blend in with everyone else in that posh scene?

When I first visited Ethan at Mayfair, in my mismatched floral skirt and checked shirt, I looked like I'd been beamed down onto that spotless street by the TARDIS.

I climbed into the black taxi with Orson's words ringing in my head. He'd sewn doubt in me again—something easy to do, given the entrenched self-doubt that nagged at me.

ETHAN OPENED THE RED door to a three-story Edwardian home that oozed aesthetic charm, just like everything around him. He hugged me warmly like we hadn't seen each other for a while, though I'd woken up in his ridiculously large bed that morning.

We'd been in London all week, staying together in Mayfair. Sheridan kept calling me to make sure I was okay. I think she missed my Ethan stories. I explained that we would catch up soon, and I would tell her all about Mayfair and its jaw-dropping antiquities and amazing art collection.

"It's that sexy trophy boyfriend I'm more interested in. Not their art collection," she'd replied.

Trophy boyfriend?

I thought of how his mother looked at me as though I was a terrorist about to blast their comfortable lives into smithereens.

How the fuck can this work?

I could only be that girl who, from an early age, spent hours strumming her guitar and staring out the window, living in a dream world of possibilities. That was still me—fragile at times, boisterous, and bursting with inspiration at others.

But what about the ordinary me? I was her most of the time. Ethan was anything but ordinary. But he was also a great listener.

As kids, he would listen to me playing the guitar in the forest or by the duck pond. He used to sit there quietly for a while then toss a twig at me. He would turn into that wild boy and coax me into playing hide-and-seek or paddling around in his little red boat, where he'd pretend to be Mr. Toad from *The Wind in the Willows*.

We'd often go down to the cliffs and watch the ships in the distance. Ethan would tell me lots of stories, like how a distant Lovechilde, part of Lord Nelson's admiralty, thwarted Napoleon. Or we would spin in circles with the wind roaring around us—dangerous little games that might have seen us tumble over the steep cliffs.

We entered the living room with sky-colored walls looking out over the park. I loved lazing on the window seat with velvet cushions.

His phone buzzed just as we entered. "I need to take this." He looked apologetic as he touched my arm, something he often did.

Ethan was very tactile. He expressed himself through gentle touches, which always left a warm imprint on not just my skin, but also my heart.

I was less so, mainly due to insecurity. If I opened my heart complete-ly, I might never stop, like one of those doting mothers who incessantly hugged their children.

I figured that call was about the spa, as he paced about holding the phone to his ear. Barefoot, he wore distressed jeans and a moth-eaten T-shirt with Tate Gallery faded onto it. The type of clothes that once only those living rough might have worn had become a staple for the superrich. I didn't get that. But he did look sexy, especially with that rip below that arse that I loved to clutch as he thrust deeply into me.

I'd become an orgasm junkie around this man. Maybe that's all this was: a sex feast. I just needed my heart to stay out of the picture, so that I could enjoy unbridled pleasure without paranoid thoughts of heartbreak stealing the show.

With those hard, sinewy biceps, which seemed to grow bigger each time I looked, Ethan raked and pulled at his hair as he spoke on the phone, leaving a sexy mess.

He must have noticed me ogling because his eyes landed on mine, and he smiled in that heavy-lidded, "let's get naked" way.

To calm my racing pulse, I distracted myself by lifting a heavy mod-ern art book from the glass-topped table and flicked absently through its satiny pages.

Ethan returned and squeezed my shoulder affectionately. "Sorry about that." His extended sigh wasn't lost on me.

"You look ruffled." I placed the book back.

"That was Declan. They've closed Reboot." He shook his head, look-ing disturbed, which surprised me. I hadn't realized how important that project was for Ethan.

That was equally disappointing for me. I admired Declan for what he was doing. "Oh? Why?"

"It's still open for business. It's become quite popular with city corporates looking for some weekend punishment." His dark chuckle made me smile. "The boys are being shipped out. There's been a bur-glary at Merivale. A ruby necklace handed down from our grandmoth-er. Worth around half a million or even more."

I whistled. "And they're sure that it was one of the boys at Reboot?"

"They've got footage of someone loitering on the grounds. I've met him. He's an Irish boy. I like him." He ran his hands over his face.

"That's a pretty radical response, sending the boys packing."

"That was part of the agreement. Should any crime happen, the estate of Merivale would sue."

I rose from the couch and took a walk around the circular room. The sun splashed bright light everywhere. I paused at the bay window overlooking Grosvenor Square, where I'd taken a selfie in front of the enchanting statue of rabbit-headed lovers straddling a horse for my Instagram page.

He came to join me and put his arm around me. We remained there, close and comfortable, tender and sweet. We'd had plenty of those moments between bursts of explosive sex.

"I have to go back tomorrow." He kissed my hair, and his herbal-infused scent rushed through me.

I stared him in the face and soaked up his beauty before speaking. "I wouldn't mind a lift back. All my work here is done for now."

"Oh, sorry. I didn't ask. How did it go?" His sweet smile made me want to get down on my knees and suck him off again.

I'd never liked blowing men before. I avoided it. But I loved Ethan's dick and how it grew steel-hard in my mouth.

I'd almost forgotten what we were talking about. I couldn't look at Ethan and not think of sex. "Orson will bring in a publicist, and off we go."

He slanted his head. "Are you tired?"

"No. I'm just a little burnt-out, I think." I frowned. "Does it show?"

He laced his fingers in mine, and suddenly, it was pure affection, like my well-being meant everything to him. "No. You're gorgeous. I like seeing you look tired. It's a good excuse to go to bed." His brow arched, and I smiled.

Yep, we're both sex mad.

I allowed him to play with my fingers, the gentle massage tingling through me caressingly. "I think I need a break from music. I'm thinking of doing something else for a while."

"Really?" A line formed between his brows. "I thought you loved it. And you're so talented." His eyes shone like he meant it.

I smiled. "Thanks. Just a break from gigs and recording for now. I'm sure I'll spring back after a few weeks."

His phone rang again, and he flinched.

"Take it. You've got a lot on."

I sat on a blue velvet armchair by the window and allowed my mind to take a stroll around the park over the road. I felt tired, all right. And a little nauseous too. I'd missed my period, which had me worried. Six weeks ago, I had sex with Orson, then a few days later, I had sex with Ethan. Scattered from all the crazy shit going on in my life, I might have forgotten to take my pill; sometimes I did. However, Orson had used a condom.

Am I ready for motherhood? To be a single mother? My stomach contracted, and I raced to the bathroom.

Later that evening, I hoped Ethan hadn't noticed me picking at my food. The house came with an excellent cook, and it was like eating at a five-star restaurant every night. I couldn't take advantage of it, though, because of this sudden nausea. Perhaps it was nerves, I told myself. That made sense, considering how edgy I'd become between rounds of hot sex and endless orgasms.

THE NEXT DAY, ETHAN dropped me off at my flat in Bridesmere.

He turned and asked, "Can I stay here tonight?"

Now that was like him asking if he could swap his opulent Mayfair home for a council flat, where it was drug dealers and not some butler with a plum in his mouth standing at the entrance.

My eyebrows met. "Sure. It's not exactly luxurious."

Playing with a strand of my hair, he smiled at my perplexed response. "My mother won't let you stay. I'm sorry. While I'm here, I might find another place. Would you be interested?"

I bit into my cheek. "Like us live together?"

He chewed on his lower lip, something he often did when searching for an answer. "I'm not here all the time, as you know. Or it can be your place, and I can stay whenever I'm here." His face brightened, as though he'd finally solved a complex puzzle. "What do you think?"

"Like I move?" I repeated.

He smiled. "You look bewildered."

I am. Just a little. Independent to a fault, I fidgeted. A ton of scenes flashed before me, like a computer game on steroids. "It's a big thing for me to give up my flat."

"Don't worry." He shrugged, looking cool and unfazed. "It was just a suggestion." He leaned in and kissed me. "We'll catch up later?"

I nodded and jumped out of his SUV. As I entered my tiny flat, I dropped my backpack on the sofa covered with a blanket to hide the holes. I buried my head in my hands. I should have been elated, but instead, I wanted to cry.

His mother hated me. I'd fucked Orson. I could be pregnant. And now Ethan had offered to upgrade my living arrangements.

Nausea returned with a vengeance. I'd dropped into a chemist on our way back and bought two tests. When Ethan asked if I was okay, I told him I needed female products, which wasn't entirely false.

CHAPTER 18

Ethan

Is *that horror or shock on Mirabel's face?*

I'd even surprised myself because that suggestion had come out of nowhere like some otherworldly force had taken possession of me. I didn't want to just catch up when we were in London, and her flat, with that shower, which went cold after a minute, wasn't going to work for me.

Perhaps I could sneak her into Merivale. Mother sleeps early... but do I want to keep doing that?

I knew I wanted to keep seeing her. The more I tasted, the more I wanted. I just couldn't take my hands off her. I'd become greedy for her body. I loved her feminine scent and how she felt when I was buried deep inside her.

Then there was that cute, confounded smile she pulled whenever I talked shit. And I just loved looking at her gorgeous face. Little things like the way she'd flick that thick, silky hair away from her face. Those magnetic emerald eyes that I always managed to lose myself in. Even when I was a boy, she would transport me to places just with her eyes.

When I arrived home, I found my mother talking to a new staff member. I walked up to them and introduced myself.

"This is Bethany," my mother said. "She's taking over from Amy."

"Oh, Amy's gone?" I wasn't surprised. I thought my mother would have fired the talkative maid long ago.

She held up her hand for me to wait before returning her attention to the new maid. "For now, she can stay. But only on the weekends. You should have told me. I don't take kindly to anyone staying at Merivale without my knowledge."

Somewhat cold and aloof, Bethany didn't strike me as contrite, as she responded with a terse nod.

When the new maid had left us, I asked, "What's wrong?"

She shook her head. "Good staff are so hard to find these days." She sighed. "She's a single mother, and she's got an eighteen-year-old daughter who's been staying here without my knowledge."

"Give the daughter a job. Bethany has a right to have her daughter close."

My mother studied me. "You're sounding more like your brother every day. We're not social security. I already employ ten staff. And soon, we'll be recruiting at least a hundred staff for the resort."

I shrugged. "Then offer the daughter a gig until that opens."

"I did." She exhaled. "But she's a training beautician who's looking for an apprenticeship."

A lightbulb went off in my head. "The spa. We need staff. We're recruiting. It opens in two months."

She nodded slowly. "I'll tell Bethany to have her daughter apply. In the meantime, I suppose I can offer her the odd job for some of our weekend functions." She crooked her finger. "Come with me."

I followed her into the library. "Where's Will?"

"He's meeting with the resort architects."

"Has this resort got a name?"

"Elysium by the Sea."

"That sounds overused."

"Perhaps. But it works." She settled down at her large desk. "Will arranged market research on the building design. While I'm more inclined to window-walled, super-modern chic, it seems that the groups favored a more bucolic experience for their resort getaway."

"That figures." I grew an inch for making that call on the spa design—Mirabel inspired of course.

"Therefore, we'd like to connect with your architects and perhaps for them to form a partnership with our team."

"Sure. Can do. I'll give Will the details." I rose and stretched my arms.

"I haven't finished."

Her stern command made my shoulder blades tense.

"You're still seeing that hippy, I take it?"

"She's not a hippy, Mother."

"Whatever. She's fornicating her manager, you realize."

My mother and her antiquated words—*fucking* had not made it into her vocabulary.

Would that have made it better, hearing that?

I wanted to use an expletive or two at my mother for meddling. It wasn't just that, though. Something else slapped me hard—Mirabel had denied sleeping with Orson. In any case, I didn't do jealousy. I'd never had cause to. *Then what's that knot in my chest?*

I played my cool card. "That's Orson. I've met him. He's producing her latest song."

"He's sleeping with her." She tapped her long fingernails over the pad in front of her.

It suddenly dawned on me that my mother had sent someone to spy on Mirabel. "Now look, you're completely out of line, Mother."

With that full face of makeup, like she was off to an important function, my mother's face barely moved.

"From what I hear, theirs is a professional relationship. He's just a womanizer who likes to swing his dick around," I said.

She winced. "Don't be crass."

I couldn't tell what pissed me off more: the spying, discussing my personal life, or that Mirabel had slept with Orson.

All of it.

"I know you men can't keep it in your trousers." Her red-painted mouth curled into a patronizing smile. She leaned back on her high-backed leather chair. Her top bun, without a strand out of place, looked sculpted onto her head.

"We don't ask you about your personal life with a much younger man, who I might add you were sleeping with while married to our father."

"Orson has been going around telling whoever asks that he always sleeps with his proteges. And when asked about Mirabel, he wore it like a badge of honor."

"Then it's before we became exclusive."

A crease appeared on her face, her eyes wide with disbelief. Her guard had crumbled, and I finally got a reaction from her, which I preferred to her cold indifference. "Oh, please don't tell me she's become your actual girlfriend?"

"I like her." I sighed. "In any case, I don't have to explain myself to you or anyone for that matter."

"What happened to all the well-dressed girls you used to consort with?"

"Consort with? I'm not a criminal." I sniffed.

"Stop playing with my meanings."

"Those girls who you described as dressing like common streetwalkers?" I challenged.

Her mouth twitched into a cool smile. "I prefer that to someone in hand-me-downs."

"You're just being elitist." I headed for the door. "I have to go to a meeting at the spa."

"You haven't heard the last of it," she said waving a pen in the air.

I smiled sweetly, and just as I was leaving, Declan arrived, looking dark. I touched his shoulder. "Are you all right?"

He shook his head while glaring at our expressionless mother. "He didn't do it." Declan leaned on her desk. "He's been falsely accused."

"Then let the police decide," she responded coldly.

I remained at the door, only because I wanted to speak to Declan, but I could see he was about to explode. That boot camp meant the world to him.

"The boys have been sent away." His voice trembled.

"Good. Then I can sleep comfortably again. I saw a tattooed brute loitering around the pool the other night and was too frightened to even step out of my own house."

"That's Dusty," I said. "Savvie's new boy."

Declan pointed. "See. Nothing to do with the boot camp. It wasn't Billy. How the hell would he have gotten into your bedroom? You're always here."

She stonewalled him with silence, and he stormed out.

I followed him. "So all the boys have been sent away?"

"Nope. Drake's running the gym. And there are three boys on Newman's farm, helping the builders, as arranged."

"I'm sorry for Billy. He seemed like a good kid," I said.

Declan nodded. "They're all good kids. They just needed some direction. This is bullshit." He shook his head.

I patted him on the shoulder. "Whatever I can do. Just let me know."

He nodded. "Thanks."

The new maid entered the front room, and I turned to acknowledge her. "Declan this is Bethany. She's new here."

She nodded without a smile.

He smiled at her before turning back to me. "I'm off, then. Come over later for dinner. Bring Mirabel if you like."

That suggestion took me by surprise. "You've heard that we're seeing each other?"

"Theadora mentioned something."

I nodded slowly as I processed this new situation in my life. I was seeing Mirabel. This was family, and I liked the idea of us being seen together. "Mother's fuming."

Declan rolled his eyes. "I bet. Not just one son, but both. And Savvie's not exactly hanging out with royalty."

I chuckled. "Catch you later, then."

After Declan left, I approached Bethany as she wiped down a gilded oval mirror. "I hear your daughter is training to be a beautician."

"Yes, she is." Her eyes narrowed slightly.

"I'm opening a spa in eight weeks. We're recruiting. If you like, I can give you the details for her to apply."

Her cool eyes warmed slightly. "That would be good."

"Is she in London?"

"She is. But I want her here with me."

"That's understandable. I'll see if I can arrange for her to stay here in the servants' quarters."

Her face warmed slightly. "I'd appreciate that."

"I'll get back to you with the recruiter's details."

She nodded then went back to polishing.

As I walked to my car, I decided to call Mirabel. I couldn't shake off that conversation with my mother and the fact that Mirabel could be sleeping with Orson.

"Oh, Ethan." She sounded surprised.

"Have I called at a bad time?"

"Um, no."

"Can I pop in for a cup of tea? I need to ask you something."

"Okay." Her voice wavered.

"Are you sure you're okay?"

"Are you coming now?" she asked.

"I am. Just for a moment. I've got a few things on the go. I'm about to invest in a social housing development in London."

"Oh really."

"I just procured an old warehouse that will be converted into low-rent studio apartments."

"That sounds wonderful." Her bright voice brought a smile to my face.

"See you in a minute. Hope you're not wearing much." My dick thickened. It didn't take a lot to get me hot around Mirabel. Even her breathy voice on the phone set me off.

"I'll see what I can do."

I closed the call and jumped into my MG convertible. The day was warm, and I loved driving without a roof.

A few minutes later, I arrived in the village and parked on the main street. Mirabel lived at the back of a shop. And while her flat was detached and private, I still managed to get a few looks as I walked down the laneway.

Everyone knew everything in that village. I waved at an old lady, who looked at me as though I'd fallen out of the sky.

Do I look that different? I didn't wear gold. My jeans, despite being ridiculously expensive, looked like they'd been worn during a hundred years of toil. They were pretentious, I knew, but airy and comfortable.

Mirabel answered the door in a long, loose T-shirt and nothing else. Unable to contain myself, I pushed her against the wall and smothered her lips with mine. My tongue entered her deeply like I was claiming her. I ran my hands beneath her T-shirt and slid my fingers over her warm, naked curves. Lust shivered through me, and my cock thickened.

I couldn't get enough of her. Even her sandalwood scent did things to me. Her silky red hair fell on my face as I ran my fingers over her puckering nipples.

"You feel nice."

She removed herself from my arms. "I made you a cup of tea."

That abrupt breakaway was jarring. She was right, though—I'd come to talk not ravish her. But I had to ask, "Too much sex for one day?"

She rolled her luscious lips, shaking her head. "I thought you wanted to talk about something."

I took a breath. She was right. Was that me trying to fuck my way out of an awkward conversation?

I raked through my hair and followed her to the windowless kitchen, which was the size of a cupboard, and the sagging shelves looked about to snap at any minute.

I need to get on to that realtor for something better than this.

As she passed me a cup, I touched her hand and looked into her eyes for clues as to her feelings. Mirabel wasn't easy to read. "I'm sensing that something's wrong."

She bit her lip. "Nothing. Really."

Maybe she was about to tell me about Orson herself, and that was guilt I was reading. She did seem a bit jittery.

After we'd taken our cups into the living room, I stood against the mantlepiece, where a picture of her mother and father sat among books, candles, and other knickknacks.

I sipped my tea and then barrelled right in. "Have you slept with Orson?" It just came out. Normally, I would skim around the edges, but curiosity gnawed away at me.

Mirabel was a mystery to me. So far, I'd learned that she didn't trust me like she expected me to hurt her. Only now, the shoe was on the other foot.

Am I hurt? The gut-wrenching sensation was new.

She twirled a strand of hair around her finger, which sat seductively over her large chest. Even in that old T-shirt, she made my heart skip a beat.

"So you have?" I finally asked.

"Why are you asking me this?" Her voice trembled.

"Because my mother had you investigated, and when questioned, Orson boasted how he'd slept with you as he does with all his proteges." I sniffed. "Waving his dick around with pride."

She looked at me without blinking, her face draining of blood. "You're fucking kidding me? Your mother had me investigated? That's seriously fucked."

"I wasn't too happy about it myself." I studied her closely. "So is it true?"

She stared down at her feet. "I'd been drinking. It was when I wasn't seeing you. In between."

"When you pushed me away because you thought I'd fuck around?"

She winced at my cutting tone. "Look, Ethan, this is so weird. Us. And you could do so much better than me."

I frowned. "I'll decide who's right for me. It might come as a shock to hear that I like you. Always have." I waited for a moment, but she remained silent, looking at me as though she'd woken from a bad dream.

I continued, "In these past weeks, I've grown attached." I took a deep breath. Talking about my emotions wasn't something I did well. "So you push me away because you think I'll cheat on you, and then you go and fuck your manager."

"It's not like that." She shook her head repeatedly as though I'd accused her of murder. "I'm really into you too. I was hooked after our first night, which terrified me in many ways. I'm sure you could tell." A shy smile spread across her rosebud lips. "And now with your mother hating me and having me investigated, it seems so fucking difficult." She buried her face in her hands.

I wasn't sure whether to comfort her or storm out. My ego had been bruised. She'd slept with another man.

I thought of Stephanie, a girl who'd grown attached after we'd fucked a few times, and how she cried her eyes out at a bar one night when she saw me canoodling with a French supermodel.

I had a shit history of hurting women. This was karma. I had it coming big time. I still found it difficult to swallow; Mirabel fucking Orson.

"So, just the once?"

She nodded slowly. Tears streaked her freckled cheeks.

I wanted to hold her, to tell her everything was going to be okay. But I couldn't get her fucking *another* man out of my head. How could I be so petty? We weren't even in a committed relationship.

Vain, cringey thoughts clashed with deeper, more confused ones. I wanted to ask if his dick was bigger. Or whether he made her scream out his name while coming. *Did she come?*

I massaged my jaw. "I'm sorry about my mother. She can't help herself. She gave Theadora a hard time. I can't change that."

She pulled out a few tissues and wiped her nose. "I'd been drinking. It was awful. I pushed him off me."

My brow creased. "Did he force himself on you?" I recalled Orson's persistence at the Green Room.

"Not really. I was drunk. And maybe he *did* take advantage of me because of that. All I know is I hated it."

I gave her a sympathetic smile. "I know how that feels. I've had lots of regrettable sex." I smiled. "You're just as wild as I once was."

Her face lit up in horror. "I'm nothing like you. Before we slept together, I hadn't had sex for six months. I was sworn off it."

Comparing her to me was a bit of a stretch—up to a couple of months ago, I didn't go one night without sex. "Let's leave it there. Hey?"

She looked up at me like a girl lost. "You forgive me?"

"Look, I'd be lying if I said I wasn't a little hurt. But you're right—we weren't committed. My mother is so out of line. I'm sorry." I tapped the sofa. "Come on, sit here, and I'll massage your shoulders."

CHAPTER 19

Mirabel

"Mm... you're good at this." I closed my eyes as his soothing strokes untangled gnarls and knots. No matter how nice his hands felt on my tense muscles, he couldn't massage away the bubbling angst.

Regardless of my resentment over his mother's intrusion into my private life, now that the cat was out of the bag, Ethan asking about Orson was understandable. If Ethan didn't care, he wouldn't have questioned me. Cold comfort.

I would have wanted to know if he'd fucked someone while we'd been hooking up, despite my sleeping with Orson happening when we were no longer hooking up. My heart read this thing between me and Ethan differently than just hooking up. I wanted so much to keep hating him. That would have been easier.

Ethan was no longer that shallow, party boy I loved to tease. I could also see growth.

He wasn't just ridiculously sexy and fun to be with, he was also kind and had a deeper side. I'd been the one too quick to judge.

Despite his bad boy period, Ethan had always been a good person.

And now, *perhaps* the father of my child.

My heart sighed as his lips brushed my cheek.

"I have to tell you something," I said at last, acid exacerbated by persistent nausea burning my gut. The concern in his eyes made me dig into my palms. If my fingernails weren't so blunt from being chewed, I would have drawn blood. I puffed out a loud, steadying breath.

"What's wrong?" He opened out his hands.

I got up from the couch. I couldn't think straight while he was so close. Just the mere whiff of him was like taking a pill that airbrushed life's blemishes.

I had to tell him because I was keeping this child. I wanted to be a mother. I'd always wanted to be a mother. And thirty was a good age.

Ethan watched me pace.

"I'm pregnant," I said at last.

I stared him in the eyes, and within a breath, the blood drained from his face. His gaze filled with horror, and his mouth dropped like the joint in his jaw had broken.

"When did you find out?" he asked at last.

"This morning. I did a pregnancy test."

His face brightened a tad. "But it could be a mistake. That happened to Savvie once."

I shook my head. "I did it twice. And I've been vomiting. I feel different."

"But I thought you were on the pill."

I released a jagged breath. This wasn't an easy confession. "I sometimes forget."

"You sometimes forget?" He sounded outraged.

"Look, Ethan, you don't have to be involved at all."

His face contorted. "What? If I'm the fucking father, I think I do have to be involved. That's unless..."

"I'm having the child, Ethan, regardless."

He frowned. "I wasn't suggesting you terminate it." He rubbed his face.

How could I have made such a mess of this? Tears pricked my eyes. Here was a gorgeous man who, while pursuing me, I'd stupidly pushed away out of insecurity. Then just to add to my stupidity, I went and fucked someone I didn't even like. The more I thought about it, the more I hated myself. But then, I *wanted* to be a mother.

He remained on the sofa, elbows on his knees, cupping his cheeks like he had a sore tooth. His bewildered face rose to meet mine, as though what I'd said had finally hit him. "I might not be the father."

Our eyes locked, and I froze. My legs trembled. A welling of emotion banked up in my throat, making it hard to breathe, let alone talk.

Looking lost, he rose slowly from the couch. "I can't do this right now."

Before I could respond, he left, and I collapsed onto the couch and gripped my arms, sobbing.

CHAPTER 20

Ethan

THREE MONTHS LATER...

A GIFT bag to mark the spa's opening swung off Savanah's arm. "This is such a great place. It will be difficult to stay away."

Her sunny, contagious smile lifted my spirits. I'd worked tirelessly those three months to get that venue in good shape while running the hotel and the social warehouse project. Distraction was welcomed because while I remained busy, my mind didn't have time to wander off and be consumed by a ton of issues infiltrating my inner world.

Apart from Mirabel, whom I couldn't stop thinking about, I was barely dealing with the knowledge that my father's murderer or accidental murderer may never be found. The PI had delivered very little. Not even the name of *that* mysterious visitor.

The reception area was filled with satisfied faces. They were there for a day and night of pampering. Ambient ocean and whale sounds swished about in the perfumed air, adding to the relaxed, pleasant vibe.

Media had been invited to sample the services: from warm rocks strategically placed on spines to massages and body wraps—treatments designed to uplift and exorcise stress. Going on the sea of smiles, that promise had been delivered. Much to my business partner's delight, media and guests snapped photos of cheery A-listers.

Quality champagne always helped, and there were enough ladies and lords to keep my mother smiling. I'd made sure to invite celebrities and influencers. After receiving expensive gift bags filled with products that had them swooning, they got into the swing of things by posing for selfies—a treasure trove of happy snaps for their followers.

"This is a roaring success." Andrew accepted a glass of champagne from one of the roaming waiters. "Let's sit back and let social media weave its magic. We've already booked it out for three months."

I chuckled at his infectious exuberance.

Joining me, Savanah tipped her head towards Manon, who'd been employed to assist in the makeup department. "She's popular."

I looked over at the pretty young brunette who had Reynard Crisp frothing at the mouth. "I'm surprised he's here. He doesn't strike me as the type of man who'd go for a facial."

"He's sewn at Mummy's hip. You know that."

I watched how his eyes followed Manon around. "I hope he doesn't take advantage of her."

"He will. She's poor, beautiful, and young. She may even be a virgin. Going by Theadora's story, he's prepared to pay a fair sum for that."

I grimaced at how creepy that made him, skulking about with the calculating cunning of a vampire. "Why is Mother with such a man?"

"That's the million-dollar question." She pulled a grim smirk. "She just says he possesses valuable business contacts and insights." Savanah wiggled her fingers, showing off fingernails painted like works of modern art. "You've got an artist in the nail department. Aren't these amazing?"

"They are." I smiled.

Having joined us, Theadora also flashed her fingernails, which were just as loud and eye-catching. "This is such a gorgeous room, Ethan." She pointed at the windows that looked out onto the duck pond. "I love the color of the walls."

"Hermitage green, I think the designer called it," I said.

"After the museum?" Savanah asked.

I nodded, pleased with myself for choosing one of London's top designers.

"What are you going to do with that section at the back?" Theadora asked. "I've noticed there's a building in progress."

"Ah, something a bit radical, I'm afraid. Declan knows. Mother doesn't."

Savanah jumped in. "He's offering freebies to women in need."

Theadora's eyes popped out.

"For those who need a break but can't afford it. It was Savvie's idea. I like it, though."

She glowed with pride. "I thought it would be a nice touch. All women deserve a little pampering."

My mother walked over and gave me a nod of approval. "This will work perfectly with Elysium."

"But this is more rustic-chic," Savanah said.

"Exactly. It has a certain appealing charm, judging by this turnout." My mother turned to me, her eyes warm and supportive. I put that down to champagne. Sometimes I wished she drank more if only to soften her attitude.

"You've made me proud. Not like that silly gymnasium."

"Haven't you heard? Ethan's building a wing for women who can't afford to be here," Savanah said.

My mother's face hardened. "Not you too?"

"It's got nothing to do with you, Mum. And you won't shut this down like you did the boot camp." I pushed out my chest. I wasn't going to have her preach to me the importance of sticking with our own.

Her eyes followed Crisp, which had me again questioning whether she secretly fancied him—a horrible thought.

"Where's Will?" I asked.

"He's back at the house, working on staff rosters with Bethany."

My eyes slid to Savanah, who returned a little smile. We'd noticed how Will looked at Bethany. Our normally eagle-eyed mother seemed the last to see it, which struck me as odd.

"That's unusual for Will, isn't it?" Savanah asked.

"It's one of his many roles at Merivale. How is that design coming along?"

Savanah played with her glossy fingernails. "I'm getting there."

"You're not still seeing that hirsute hipster, are you?"

I laughed. My mother had a way with words.

"No. I'm not. I'm single," Savanah replied as though tired of this conversation.

"Good. You're too good for all those brutes."

Savanah shrugged. "Mm..."

I knew my sister well. Whenever she was between boyfriends, she got depressed. She worried me a lot. She didn't seem comfortable in her own company.

I recognized that in myself because I was once like that. After Mirabel, everything changed—for the better. I still missed her, though. I always would. I only hoped she would let me in some time, if only as a friend.

Could I do that without wanting to touch and kiss her?

Not seeing her was worse. I kept calling, but she just never returned my calls. I even went to visit her on a few occasions, but she sent me away.

Savanah's eyes followed our mother, who'd gone to join Crisp. "Don't you think that was weird? How Mummy didn't even blink about Will helping Bethany?"

"Maybe. You know Mother—she doesn't show anything. A sign of weakness, she says." A thought hit me. "Nathan's having a party to-morrow night. Why don't you come?"

I was worried about my sister. After Dusty was locked up for drug dealing, she withdrew into herself. As much as we were relieved that he was off the scene, I still wanted to see Savanah smile again. A night out in London might bring back some cheer.

"I guess they'll all be there in their boring bespoke jackets."

I shook my head. "Oh, Savvie, you've got to stop falling for the fallen."

She frowned. "I just don't get excited over our lot. You know that. And the gene pool likes variety."

I thought of Mirabel's pregnancy like I did every day.

"Have you spoken to Mirabel?" she asked.

My sister could read me well. I scratched my shadowed jaw. "I've tried. She's asked me not to contact her."

"God, that's weird. She's weird. I mean, I like her. I saw her the other night at the Mariner."

My brow creased. "Really?"

"Uh-huh. You were in London."

That wouldn't have been a healthy environment in her state. "I hope she wasn't drinking."

Theadora joined us again, and Savanah turned to her. "You were there at the Mariner. Mirabel wasn't drinking, was she?"

Theadora's decisive shake of her head made me breathe again, despite an empty feeling in my stomach.

"She's looking well," Theadora said. "And she sang brilliantly. She sold out CDs. Her new song's selling well."

I smiled. I wanted success for Mirabel. I loved her—I'd admitted that much to myself. Regardless of who the father to her child was, she would always have a deep place in my heart.

My body hadn't forgotten. I watched her constantly on YouTube.

"What about Keira?" Savanah asked after a girl I'd recently dated.

"What about her?" I asked.

"Why isn't she here?"

"Because I didn't invite her." I pulled at my hair, something I tended to do whenever an uncomfortable subject came up.

"But aren't you dating?" Savanah persisted.

My heart just wasn't in it. Neither was my body. "It's nothing. To be honest, I'm not that involved."

"She's gorgeous," Savanah said.

Yes, she was gorgeous with those long slim legs and willowy figure, but something was missing. Her beauty didn't grow every time I looked at her. Like the sky at twilight that always showed something extraordinary at every glance. Like Mirabel, who possessed so many captivating expressions that I was in a constant state of arousal.

CHAPTER 21

Mirabel

THEODORA MET ME AT the café, wearing a concerned frown. "How are you feeling?"

"I'm good. Really good. I've gotten over the morning sickness, and now I feel great."

"You look great." She gave me a supportive smile.

"I'm spending all my time here for the sake of the baby. The air's cleaner."

"The spa opened to great fanfare."

"Oh?" Although I feigned ignorance, I knew all about it. Annabel, a girl at the supermarket, had attended their opening day and told me how stunning it was.

"It's a lovely place. All the products are natural. I think Ethan had you in mind." She gave me that look of hers. Theadora liked to remind me that Ethan still cared, bringing music to my soul. That was one of the reasons I always dropped everything to catch up with Theadora.

"Is he still here or in London?"

"He's mainly in London these days. Working on a few projects." She sipped her coffee. "He's always asking after you."

Warmth rippled through me. "That's nice. So what else is happening? Did Declan get the boys back?"

She shook her head. "He's setting up an organic farm with the Newmans. He seems to like being around the land. I think he's a natural farmer." She smiled. "Strange, really."

"That doesn't surprise me. Growing up, Declan was always hanging out with the animals on our farm. He used to ask my mother lots of questions about what she was planting in the garden too."

Theadora's face filled with love, as it always did whenever I spoke of her husband as a boy. "I don't mind what he does." She exhaled. "He loves to fly. That spooks me. He's even put his hand up to volunteer in medical rescue."

"That's fantastic. Isn't it?" I studied her.

She toyed with her cup. "He's that kind of person. But it scares the crap out of me, I must admit."

"He's a very experienced pilot, Thea."

She shrugged. "He is. We went to Greece only a couple of weeks ago. He always insists on flying, and whenever he steps off that plane, he looks so blissed out."

"There. As long as planes are well maintained, not much can go wrong."

She touched my hand. "Are you really okay?"

"I'm great. 'Song of the Sea' is doing well. You know that. You did get that cheque?"

"I did." She opened her bag and passed me the note. "I don't need it, sweetie. I'm seriously rich."

"You earnt it. Please take it. I'm doing really well. Netflix picked up the song for a movie."

Her face lit up with surprise, a mirror of my reaction when that offer, thanks to Orson's managerial prowess, had come in.

"You're kidding?" Her mouth remained open.

I smiled, remembering how that news had made my day. "It's really popular. We're doing well. Your piano accompaniment made it special. So it's not just my success, but yours too."

"But you wrote it," she said, in that self-effacing way of Theadora's. For a gorgeous-looking woman, she lacked vanity. "Are you working on any other pieces?"

"I am. But I'm not going to busk or do gigs for the moment. I'm making a living from downloads. Orson's been plugging it."

"How is he?" Her lowered voice reminded me of that big question that hovered over my head.

Orson knew of my pregnancy. Unlike Ethan, he'd taken it calmly. He also suggested that if it was his, he would get me to sign something. No surprise there.

I told him I didn't want anything from him. And the look of relief on his face acted as a reminder that I didn't like him much. He was great at making music and money, but too selfish for anything else.

Mirabel waved at a pretty woman with dark hair who walked alongside a beautiful girl who could have been her younger sister. "That's Bethany. She's doing my old job at Merivale. And that's her daughter."

I noted a dark edge to Theadora's tone. "Is there something about them that you don't trust?"

"The mother's quite cagey. Her daughter served at a dinner party we were at, and Crisp looked like he was going to pounce on her."

"He sounds dangerous."

She nodded wistfully. "He's that, all right. And he's got his sleazy eyes all over Manon, Bethany's daughter, who is a serious flirt."

My brow lowered. "With Ethan and Declan, too, you mean?"

"With everyone. I'm not worried about Declan because he's so sweet to me." She smiled, wearing a starry-eyed glint.

"And Ethan?" I couldn't help myself after a little jab of jealousy.

"I haven't noticed anything there. He's off in his own world. Really distracted. I think this whole pregnancy thing has thrown him." She raised an eyebrow. "He misses you, Bel. He admitted that the other night when he came and spilled his feelings. His voice even cracked."

Having swallowed a mouthful of hot chocolate, I nearly choked. I gripped the handle of my cup "He cried?"

She shook her head. "He controlled himself, but I could see he was sad."

My heart brimmed with a mix of emotions as I sucked back the tears welling up in my eyes. "Strong and tough" had become my daily mantra. Some days, it worked. Other days, like now, after hearing all about Ethan and how he missed me, not so much.

"But really, Bel. Why don't you at least see him? Talk to him?"

I sighed. "I miss him like I would both of my arms. But I still can't erase from my mind how the blood drained from Ethan's face after learning that my baby might not be his. I can't keep seeing him, while all this doubt hangs over us."

"But what if it *is* his?"

I exhaled. "Then we will cross that bridge when we come to it, I suppose."

"Why not get a paternity test?" she asked.

"I think I'll wait until the baby's born."

"But he would have missed out on being here for you. That's what's hurting him the most."

I smiled sadly. My heart felt like it would burst. "Did he say that?" I bit my lip, which trembled.

"Not in those words, but yeah, Bel. He wants to hold your hand. Help you."

I released a deep breath. "Let's leave it for now."

She touched my hand. "Whatever you do, you know I'm here for you?"

I hugged her. "Thanks."

CHAPTER 22

Ethan

IT WAS A WEEK after the spa opened, and having worked tirelessly, I missed not pumping iron or working up a sweat. I'd developed a passion for visiting Reboot's gym, which compared to the gyms in the city with their loud, thumping music, and competitive gym junkies, Reboot was a dream.

Drake greeted me as I strolled into the sun-splashed room.

"Hey, how's Billy?" I felt for the Irish boy whose wrongful accusation at the hands of my mother sat badly with me.

"He's okay. A little down. He's got a laboring job back in London. He'd prefer to be here, though."

"I might have something for him. I'll talk to the builders working on the resort."

Drake frowned. "But won't Mrs. Lovechilde put up a fuss? Since she's convinced he robbed her? You do know he was only on the grounds because he was seeing one of the girls who works in the kitchen?"

"Declan told me." I smiled tightly.

"Good morning," Carson said as he entered the room.

"Morning," I responded. "How's the corporate boot camp scene going? Are you whipping those well-fed arses into shape?"

"Yep. They're a weak bunch. But they pay well. And there're lots of girls." He virtually winked at me.

I could imagine city chicks throwing themselves at this seriously well-built man. He was Channing Tatum's double, according to Savanah, who found it hard to string a coherent sentence around him.

"I'm moving on. I'm about to set up my own security agency," he said.

"Oh really? You're leaving Bridesmere?"

"Yep. I miss London, and there are a few girls causing issues." He scratched his sharp jaw.

Been there. Done that. I chuckled knowingly. Another ugly side to having been a player was girls heaping abuse at me, justifiably accusing me of being a first-class shithead.

Carson's girl-pulling power had become a talking piece. My sister was the only one missing out. Not for her lack of trying. But I'd heard that the burly ex-soldier, out of respect for Declan, wouldn't have a bar of it.

My sister didn't know that, and she didn't need to know. I figured a little healthy knockback now and then wouldn't hurt someone used to having everything she wanted. Not that Savanah was a petulant spoilt brat like some in our privileged scene. In many ways, she had an earthy outlook on life, which redeemed her. But then, I could have been biased, given she was my sister.

When it came to knockbacks, I'd experienced my first ever. Mirabel had taken me down a peg or two. Bruised ego or not, I still respected her for not taking advantage of this deepening attraction I'd developed for her. She could have told me that I was the actual father.

But what if the child's mine?

That persistent question lingered in the back of my mind like a pesky stalker lurking in the shadows. Whenever I allowed that question to take control of my thoughts, my heart raced. My mind and heart battled as I pondered over what to do. I knew that Mirabel was strong enough to raise the child by herself, but the thought of her going through this alone turned me into an emotional wreck. I wanted to hold her hand through it. Help her. Be there for her.

Over and above everything; I missed her. I wanted to be in her life—baby or no baby. I just wanted to see her. It was like a part of me had been sedated. Half of my body was numb. The lower half. My dick hardly moved these days.

I regarded Carson as he packed away the equipment. "So now that you've broken the hearts of all the girls in Bridesmere, you're off on a London feeding frenzy?"

He chuckled. "I'm not that bad, you know. And, look, about Savanah, I..." He scratched his jaw. "I hope she's managed to shake off that Dusty character. He's a nasty little prick, that one. I saw him pull a knife on a girl one night."

My eyes bulged. "You're fucking kidding me. Savanah had a few bruises a while back. When I asked her, she denied that he was responsible."

"He's already tasted my knuckles. I hope she's staying away from him. Because if I hear he's as much as touched her, that crooked nose of his will need reconstruction surgery."

His eyes shone with malice. I wouldn't have liked to piss him off.

"He's locked up. She's not seeing him. Which I believe because she's moping around. When I asked her to one of my mate's parties in London, she jumped at the invite. She normally stays away from my friends. They're all a bit too washed and well-behaved."

He laughed. "Your sister's got spirit—that's for sure. I'm happy to know that she's not seeing that piece of shit. She could do better."

"We've been telling her that for years."

After he left, I sweated through a one-hour workout, thanks to Drake pushing me along. He had this intuitive knack for making me go past my threshold without injuring me. If he hadn't been there, I would have left after pounding the treadmill. But he always made me put in the time, and it was paying off. Addicted to the high that followed a good workout, I'd become quite the gym junkie. Endorphins gave me that boost I needed to get out there and make up for all that time I'd lost partying.

CHAPTER 23

Mirabel

I WAS NOW EIGHT months pregnant and looked like I was going to explode. I waddled instead of walked. And as I sat there with Sheridan and Bret at the table, enjoying the roast that Bret had whipped up, I wiped my plate clean. Once the morning sickness had subsided, I'd turned into an unbothered foodaholic. Having always been disciplined when it came to food and sweets, due to my tendency to stack weight, I surrendered to my body and felt healthy for it.

There was nothing worse than guilting over food. I'd guilted over most pleasures in the past because when it came to having fun, I was a glutton. Now that I was carrying another life, I didn't miss my inner hedonist. I suddenly had time to read, write songs, go for long walks along the cliffs, or just sit for long periods, watching the ebb and flow of the ocean.

Maybe riding solo suited me after all. I didn't feel lonely. I missed Ethan, of course. How could I not? But instead of pining for him, I'd harnessed that energy into getting my life ready for the next phase of my life. It was all about my child. Art had taught me about sacrifice. And motherhood, nurturing a new little soul, would be my best work of art so far. My magnum opus.

"The gravy's delicious," I said, helping myself to another slice of beef.

"He's good for something at least," Sheridan said, poking at her boyfriend's ribs jokingly.

He smirked back. They had the strangest relationship. Five years in, and they were still together. Despite Sheridan calling him a weak so-and-so, she loved him. And although she griped about the paucity of sex, she'd admitted that she couldn't imagine her life without him.

Would treading water in a relationship be enough? The romantic in me balked at that idea. Love had to be more than just good friends with occasional boring sex.

Pete, a friend of Bret's and someone who'd flirted with me over the years, joined us for dinner. Sunday roasts had become their regular thing since Bret had taken a cooking course and decided he loved to cook, much to Sheridan's delight.

"So, how was that penalty shootout?" Bret turned to Pete.

Sheridan rolled her eyes. "No boring football talk."

Pete smiled at me. "When's it due?"

"Third week of October, I think." I wiped my lips with a napkin.

"Do you know the sex?" he asked.

I nodded. I couldn't say whether I was happy or disappointed to learn I was carrying a boy.

Sheridan, who'd been extremely supportive, had accompanied me to the fetal screening. Much to my delight, the baby looked healthy and was a healthy size.

At her insistence, I'd decided to stay the weekend. Sheridan seemed to like holding my hand. She'd even made me promise that I'd let her watch me give birth. I loved the idea of someone watching over me. I didn't know what I would have done without her.

"So what will that make him?" Pete asked.

"Star sign?" I asked.

He nodded.

"Maybe Libra or Scorpio, I suppose."

"You're into all of that, aren't you?" He accepted another slice of meat that Bret had just carved.

"When I was younger, I took an interest."

"What are you, then?" His eyes shined keenly. Pete had always liked me, and even in my big state, he still showed interest, which surprised me. I couldn't imagine being attractive to anyone while looking the way I did.

"Scorpio," I replied, hoping he wouldn't ask me to describe what that meant.

"I don't even know anything about the stars. I'm a Leo, and apparently, I'm meant to be vain and bossy." He laughed.

"You are, mate. You're always staring at yourself in the mirror, and whenever we go camping, he sits back and gives orders."

"No, I don't," he sang.

Sheridan and I laughed.

Life was good. My dream of becoming self-sufficient through music had become a reality. The stars were aligning. All I had to do was stop thinking about Ethan or, more importantly, find a place in my life for him that didn't involve my heart pounding every time we stood in the same room.

After the men went off to the pub, Sheridan and I sat back on the couch with our legs up, bingeing on *Virgin River*.

"What a way to end," Sheridan lamented. "Not knowing who the father is."

She looked at me, and her scrunched face ironed out into a smirk. "Sound familiar?"

I squirmed. "Yep."

"I can't wait for that DNA test," she said.

I thought about the look of relief on Orson's face when I'd told him I didn't want him involved. He wasn't doing a great job being a father to his two girls, so I couldn't imagine him being much help.

I was too independent anyway. I liked to run my life a certain way. Maybe I wasn't suited to pairing with anyone.

Ethan seemed to let me make the decisions. But that was with more mundane things, like what to eat, where to walk, or what movie to watch.

It was going to be just me and Cian. I'd already settled on a name. I liked the sound of Cian Storm.

"Aren't you dying to know?" Sheridan asked yet again.

Her relentless curiosity made me smile. "I think I already know."

"So it's Ethan's?" She cocked her head.

I nodded slowly. "I get the feeling it is."

"But what about if he's not?"

"Good too." I turned to face her. "Whatever happens, I'm just happy. I want to be a mother. I mean, I didn't design it this way, but I'm thrilled."

Sheridan's wistful look made me ask, "Are you okay?"

She shrugged. "I guess seeing you like this has made me all clucky. I didn't think I wanted a kid, but I'm warming to the idea. Especially seeing you bursting with health. And you've changed."

My brow rippled. "How do you mean?"

"You're more at peace with the world."

I laughed. "Unlike you, yelling at the television."

"That was you too," she defended.

Yep. We were once those angry girls protesting over corporate greed and social inequality.

"I think Ethan tamed me."

"Haha. Tamed by a billionaire."

"I used to give him such a hard time—accusing him of being a shallow womanizer."

Sheridan's mouth twisted. "Not nice. Maybe he liked it."

"I don't know." I stared down at my hands. "I'm not as angry anymore. It was too exhausting. And he's doing a lot of good in the community. He's even set up a free program for women in need at his new spa."

"Oh, like us?" she said. "We can go and get pampered for free?"

I laughed. "Probably. Only, I won't be there."

She held my stare and shook her head. "You're crazy. He's been a good influence on you, though. I can see that. I like this calmer version of you."

"Maybe I'm just getting older."

"Hardly. No, I think he has tamed you. And maybe you were too harsh on him. I mean I've met poor people who are outright arseholes. Not all filthy-rich people are rats."

"No. That's too black-and-white for sure." I adjusted my seating position to allow for my big belly. "Why don't you keep trying to have a baby?"

"I haven't used contraception for years. It's just not happening."

The struggle in her voice caught me by surprise. This was new. I'd always assumed Sheridan wished to remain childless.

"IVF?"

She grimaced. "It's expensive and, from what I hear, awfully invasive."

"I've got money pouring in with that Netflix deal, and my sales are through the roof after that video."

A proud smile filled her face. "I'm so glad you agreed to do that video. It's so great."

After learning of my pregnancy and the pain that came from leaving Ethan, I desperately needed a creative project to distract me, so I contracted a video maker. The net result was an extraordinary video of "Song of the Sea," which had a significant influence on downloads.

Sheridan touched my hand. "Thanks so much, sweetheart, but no. I'll just be an aunty to Cian."

We laced fingers and smiled.

"I hope you're going to keep staying here, whenever you're in town. Now that you're making money," she said.

"Only if you promise to take that money I gave you for bills. Now that I've got money, I can pay my own way. And what about Bret?"

"I think he appreciates you being the one to absorb my gibbering crap, leaving him off the hook."

I shook my head at their crazy relationship. All relationships had their foibles. That much, I knew.

"Hey, Pete still wants to jump your bones," she said.

I thought of Bret's blonde friend, who was attractive in that easy-going, "how's the weather" kind of way. "Hello. I'm enormous."

"No, you're not." She frowned. "It's just your tits are huge, that's all. That's probably why he's keen."

"Mm… He's sweet, but I'd get too bored. I'd prefer to be alone than in a relationship where there's not much to say."

I thought of how Ethan and I chatted effortlessly about all kinds of topics. He loved to ask me about certain causes and how I felt.

"Why don't you drop this stubborn act and let Ethan in?" Sheridan asked for the millionth time.

I sighed. He kept sending me regular texts with silly emojis, songs, and all kinds of reminders of his existence. I didn't need any, though, because Theadora kept me posted. I knew he was dating some leggy girl from London. Despite Theadora saying his heart wasn't into it, knowing that still hurt.

"When Cian's born, let's see. It just feels weird. I can't see him without wanting to have sex with him. He's an addictive man." My body prickled with heat just saying that.

"I can't blame you. The guy's hot."

"But that's the problem. When I see Ethan, I think of sex. Not a good friend I can share a cup of tea with and talk about the latest Brexit fuckup."

She laughed. "Surely you don't want to talk politics."

I shook my head. "But you know me—I need to know we can be more than just clothes-ripping lovers."

"That sounds hot, though. I wouldn't mind."

Her sad smile made me worry about my cousin's happiness. If anything, despite how close she was with Bret, being around them reminded me that I wasn't about to do anything by halves: boyfriends, life, or even art.

What Sheridan didn't know was that Ethan *did* visit me.

At the time, Audrey called out, then a knock came at the door. Instead of my neighbor at the door, however, it was Ethan wearing a sheepish smile.

"Sorry, love," she said, biting her lip and looking apologetic. Ethan kissed her on the cheek, and off she scampered, probably touching her cheek. It wasn't every day a handsome man kissed her.

I had to laugh and shake my head at the same time. "Let me guess—you bribed her?"

His head drew back in shock as though I'd accused him of hitting on my seventy-year-old neighbor. "No. I just needed to see you, and you haven't exactly been receptive."

Time stood still as we remained at the doorway, lost in each other's eyes.

I cleared my throat. "My place is a mess, and I must look awful." I tapped my belly. Close to bursting, I was seven months pregnant at the time and wearing my favorite long, loose T-shirt and nothing else.

"I'm used to your place, Bel." He smiled sweetly.

His using my diminutive reminded me of when we were kids. Since becoming intimate, he used my whole name like he was connecting to another version of me.

I stepped out of the doorway and let him in. His cologne wafted over me, and my nipples tightened.

Ethan's hair was shorter, and he'd shaved that permanent dark shadow emphasizing his chiseled jaw. What hadn't changed, however, were those body-melting, dark sultry eyes that made me forget my name.

"You've been working out," I said, going into the kitchen.

"I visit Reboot most days when I'm at Merivale." He followed me into the messy kitchen, where unwashed plates piled up at the sink.

"Oh god, please don't come in here." I pushed him out. "Tea?"

He smiled at me making a fuss, and for a minute there, I forgot we weren't together. He stood at my bookshelf and picked up a book on motherhood. "How are you feeling?"

"I'm great, thanks." I tried to sound cheery, despite sudden trembles affecting my vocal cords. As a welcomed respite from this sudden burst of emotional turbulence, I busied myself making tea.

Carrying out our cups, I joined him in the living room and passed him a cup, using all my power not to spill it. I made room for him on the sofa by pushing away my guitar and books.

"How's the music?" he asked.

"It's okay." I sat and sipped on tea, wishing it was something stronger.

"I love 'Song of the Sea.' The video's stunning." He wore genuine pride in his eyes, which made me feel teary for some reason.

I swallowed tightly. "You've looked me up?"

He nodded slowly. He seemed just as nervous as me. Normally, Ethan was the one who made everything seem easy, with that amiable, bounce-through-life approach.

We sat and drank our tea in awkward silence.

"Why are you here?" I asked at last.

"I just wanted to see you." His piercing gaze held me hostage.

I gulped back the guilt. Why had I pushed him away? Sheridan was right. I needed my head examined.

He smiled tightly. "You look beautiful. Motherhood suits you."

"I'm just fat." I laughed, looking for a way to dilute this sudden sexual tension.

His gaze burned into my face, then he moved closer on the couch and took my hand.

Sudden tingles through my body hijacked my breathing. I removed my hand. "Look, Ethan, this is too much."

"You're no longer attracted?" His brow furrowed.

"I'm more than attracted," I said, looking down at my bare feet. In need of a pedicure, I tucked my toenails under.

He rose from the couch and stood by the mantle, fiddling with a crystal. "There hasn't been one day when I haven't thought about you. I want to be part of this."

"By this, you mean my baby?"

He nodded. His unshifting gaze penetrated deeply. This was the most intense I'd ever encountered him.

Beads of sweat dripped down my arms. "But it may not be yours." I opened out my palms. I could have done a paternity test, but for the sake of sanity, I'd decided to remain in the dark. Because if the baby was Ethan's, he might have felt pressured. For the sake of my child, I preferred numbness to turmoil, known to generate toxic hormones like cortisol, potentially harmful to the baby.

He shrugged. "I miss you so much, I don't mind."

I sighed heavily. Prickling-hot tears welled in my eyes. But I quickly willed them away by summoning the strength of Hercules. My heart ached for this man. It wasn't just that I wanted sex either. Although seeing him run his tongue over those full lips had my hormones preparing fireworks for blast off.

"It feels like this is coming from your desire to do the right thing by me."

He sipped his tea and took a moment to answer. "Well, yes. But I wouldn't be here if I didn't feel something for you."

"But isn't it just sex?" I asked. "Although I can't imagine that's on your mind, seeing me look like this."

He shook his head slowly and repeatedly. "You're beautiful." His mouth curled slightly before straightening. "All I know is that I miss you. I'm not sure where this will go. But I want to be here, holding your hand. Especially if the child's mine."

"And if it isn't?"

He rubbed the back of his neck. "I don't know how I'm going to feel. But I want to be here for you. That much, I know." He looked up slowly, and his eyes held mine.

I couldn't allow myself to fall into his hooded gaze that spoke of hot sex and fun times. I breathed out my frustration in a loud huff. "I can't do this now, Ethan."

He placed down his cup and headed to the door.

I berated myself for being so fragile and cautious. I should have been jumping right in, feet first. My former wild self would have. But I had to think about my child. Passion had to take a backseat.

With all that running around in my thoughts, I tried to make sense of what he'd said or hadn't said. His words flittered around in my head. He wanted to help, but how? Would he still want me if the baby wasn't his?

I couldn't allow myself to cuddle up to him and indulge in his spicy sweetness, only to have him disappear suddenly. How could I risk my heart on him when I needed to remain strong for my child?

He ran his fingers through his hair, making that thick dark-brown mane stick up. I wanted to slap him for being so fucking handsome.

Why couldn't he be that shallow arsehole? That would have made slamming the door on his face easy.

"I'm sorry for barging in like this. I just wanted to see you."

Then I let him take my hand. That was a disaster. A beautiful disaster.

All it took was for his eyes to pierce mine for one of those soft, tender looks, and I fell into his arms. I was so dizzy from his masculinity that his strong arms had to hold me up. I closed my eyes and drifted off onto a cloud of desire.

His lips touched mine, and that was it. He had me. I let him take control. Tender and soft, his mouth caressed mine. It even quivered, or were my lips trembling on his?

It felt like we both had been wanting to steal that kiss from the moment he stepped in, like teenagers doing something wrong. From soft and explorative to fiery and hungry, his lips devoured mine. His hands traveled over my body, and I felt a hard throb against my torso. His dick had turned steel-hard, setting off a desperate ache between my legs.

"You feel hot." He spoke into my mouth. Even his breath on my tongue seemed to travel to my vagina.

Blood surged through me. My brain had shut down.

Drugged by a rush of hungry need, I surrendered to his feathery touches-turned-gropes, kisses, and nibbles.

The next minute we were on my unmade bed, where he stroked my clit and had me crying out his name.

"I need you inside of me now," I said, pulling at his hair.

My eyes rolled to the back of my head. It had been months, and the stretch was intense.

He groaned as he entered me. I lay on my side, and we rode one wave of divine heat after another, which made my toes curl.

His breath was hot in my ear as he kissed and bit at my neck. "You're beautiful."

We built and built, his dick moving in and out and his ragged breath dampening my ear. Our bodies were sticky. His hands caressed my breasts.

I released my muscles, then I was swept away in a hot wave that turned into a tsunami, tossing me under. The more muscles I released, the crazier it got. I'm not sure how long I was gone, but it was so intense, I screamed.

When my breath returned, I turned to him. "We can't do this again."

"Why?" He looked confounded like I'd knocked back entry into a world where only bliss existed.

Our world. Up to now. Babyless.

"Because I don't want to be with you like this."

"But that was hot."

"I know—it's hot for me too." I huffed.

He played with my fingers. "It's more than that for me."

My heart filled with sunshine, just hearing him admit to that, but yet, that independent me wanted to see this through alone.

"When the baby's born, we'll see how things are. By then, you might have met someone anyway."

He rose and got dressed. "You won't let me be there for you? Even holding your hand?"

I shook my head. "It's too complicated, Ethan. We're too complicated."

"Bullshit. That's just you overthinking things. I'm fine with all of this. I've had time to think about it. I prefer to be in your life than out of it."

How could I not smile at that heart-swelling admission?

I walked him to the door. "Ethan, let's just see what happens. Give me some space because I'm going to look awfully big any minute. And then after the baby's born, let's see."

He ran his fingers through his thick hair. "You know where I am."

I watched him walk off, and my heart reverted to barely beating.

CHAPTER 24

Ethan

IT WAS WILL'S BIRTHDAY, and to celebrate, my mother threw a dinner party. It was my first day back at Merivale after a week at the hotel in discussion with a renewable energy expert about lowering the hotel's carbon footprint.

I liked being back at home. I always would. And having dropped into the spa, I was buoyed by how popular it had become. Andrew, my partner, had taken over its running, and he squeezed the life out of me when we hugged.

"You came alone?" Savanah asked me as I sat.

"Yep." I unbuttoned my jacket. Thanks to my working out, my shoulders and arms had expanded. It was time to visit my favorite Italian tailor for some new clothes.

"What happened to Kiera?" she asked as the waiter poured wine into her glass.

"It was just once. I wasn't into it." I nodded as the waiter offered to fill my glass.

What Savvie didn't know was that I'd visited Mirabel more than just once. She'd made me promise not to tell anyone, which was weird, but I accepted that—for now. I didn't want to stress Mirabel in her condition.

I understood that she didn't want me offering a relationship as a good-guy act. It wasn't that for me, though. I just plain missed her. And when we were together, my body went into overdrive. I'd never craved a woman the way I did Mirabel. I also just liked being around her.

I couldn't get enough of her. But that was a few weeks ago. And despite my begging her to let me be there at the birth, she'd refused.

She'd uttered something vague about seeing a baby popping out might put me off sex with her, which was unimaginable since I had a constant erection whenever we came in close contact.

An appetizing aroma of roast lamb drifted my way as the meat was being carved. "That smells good. I'm starving."

Savanah nodded. "We have a new chef. He's great. I can't stop eating."

"How have you really been?" I asked.

"You know, the same old. I think I might go to Paris next week."

"What about your arts degree?"

She sipped and wiped her lips. "I'm doing it part-time and online."

"You sound bored, Savvie." A plate was placed in front of me, and I nodded at the offer of gravy. "I've found since working on projects and running the hotel, I haven't got time to be bored." I helped myself to salad, scooping it into a side bowl. "I've got an idea. The hotel needs new curtains and bedding. How about we meet there on Monday?"

"Why not? I'm already helping Mum with curtains and bedding for Elysium." She chewed on some food. "I will finish my arts degree."

"You should. You were always good at drawing."

She rarely stayed the course. But I was determined to be there and encourage her.

"How are you going with this new guy of yours?" I asked, enjoying the tenderness of the meat.

"Okay. Richie's nice." She chased peas around her plate. "Is Kiera still stalking you?"

I nodded. "It's frightful. I slept with her once, and now she expects marriage."

Savanah chuckled at the absurdity of my situation. "You're of age."

I rolled my eyes at her paraphrasing our mother. "I'm sure as hell not going to marry because I'm about to turn thirty."

"Mirabel's had a boy."

I nodded slowly. I'd thought of little else. Theadora, who'd become my informer where Mirabel was concerned, had told me.

"Are you going to at least ask her to have a paternity test? You've got a right you know."

"Let's see if she lets me visit first." My tight voice betrayed how emotionally unhinged I'd become since the birth of that child. I could think of little else.

She shook her head. "That's so fucking weird. She's obviously scared you'll hurt her."

I nodded pensively. There wasn't much I could add to that. Despite seeing Mirabel two weeks ago, it felt like months.

Crisp turned up and took his seat next to our mother, as always. Will sat on the other side, and when Bethany served him, it was all smiles.

"What do you think's going on there?" I slid my eyes in his direction.

Savanah shrugged. "The new maid's got the hots for him. I must say, since Will's grown his hair a little and with the permanent facial shadow, he's scrubbed up quite well with those Colin Firth looks. Especially in that velvet jacket. He's become quite the lord of the manor."

Will's effortless shift into the man-of-the-house role seemed to suit him. I'd never found a reason to dislike him, and he kept our mother happy.

"Bethany's like a younger version of Mother," she said. "She's rather good-looking."

Undoubtedly, Bethany attracted a lot of male attention. Her long dark hair, normally in a bun, was tied back in a ponytail. She wore bright-red lipstick and heavy eyeliner that emphasized her dark eyes, and she swayed her hips when she walked.

"Hey, why don't you hit on her?"

My brow scrunched. "Are you kidding?"

"Well, you fell for Mirabel. She's poor."

My neck cracked as I turned sharply to stare at her. "Why would that fucking matter?"

Savanah grinned. "You normally knock about with our crowd."

"Our crowd?" I put down my fork. "What about you and your dealers? They're not exactly our"—I hooked my fingers—"crowd."

"That's because our lot are so fucking boring. And half of them are into weird shit, like wearing girls' knickers. In any case, this is about you, not me." She dabbed her mouth with a napkin. "What I meant to say was you normally go for girls in designer. You've probably fucked every girl in this scene."

My sister had an obsession with our bedroom habits, which wasn't a subject I cared for.

"I'm not keeping count." I cracked a tight smile. "In any case, that's in the past. I've changed."

"You've become a bore, like everyone else." She took a small forkful of vegetables. Her meat was untouched.

"Aren't you eating?"

"Mm... I'm thinking of going off meat for a while. It doesn't agree with me."

"You look pale and have lost weight, Savvie." I gave her my concerned frown.

"I'm fine. What were we saying? Oh, that's right—you falling for poor girls."

"Mirabel's not poor. Her song's killing it right now."

"So you *have* been following her?" Savanah smirked.

I hadn't stopped. I watched her on YouTube all the time.

"I don't want to talk about this right now, Savvie."

AFTER DINNER, I WALKED outside with Declan for some air and a break from all the questions about my private life.

"If I hear another person asking me when I'm going to marry or where I'm hiding that special girl, I'll fucking lose it," I said. "I almost told Lavinia that I had a few hiding in the cellar and that I roll them out when I need one to iron a shirt or massage my shoulders."

Declan laughed. "Massage your shoulders?"

"Lavinia's—what? Eighty or something. I couldn't exactly be lewd. Although I was a bit more upfront with Camila. I told her that I wheeled them out when I needed pleasuring." I laughed, recalling the seventy-year-old woman's horror.

"You've only been out with that one girl, apart from Mirabel, all year," he said, as we walked around the lit-up grounds.

Those unforgettable few weeks of unbridled sex a couple of months back with Mirabel felt like a lifetime.

I missed her more than ever.

Where was that shallow prat, she'd accused me of being, when I needed him?

Drake walked over. He'd been employed as Merivale's security after more jewelry went missing.

"Hey, Drake, caught any cat burglars?" I asked.

Drake chuckled. "Nope."

"Have you heard from Billy?" Declan asked.

He nodded. "He's okay. He appreciated that job you got for him."

We walked away and sat on the bench. "Any news from the PI?"

Declan shook his head. "Only that he managed to get a hold of Luke, who's still in LA. When asked about whether Dad had a thing for hiring professionals, Luke explained that he did so occasionally."

"But why take a sleeping pill first?" I asked.

"That's the thing, he might have taken the sleeping tablet after the sex. It could have been a completely different person who happened to arrive after he'd been with whoever it was."

"In other words, two mystery visitors," I said.

He shrugged. We always hit a wall.

The sensor lights came on, and Manon, who was working in the kitchen during functions, stepped outside. Crisp followed her out. They must not have seen us because we sat a few feet away in the dark.

"*Manon, c'est un joli nom français pour une belle fille.*"

She pulled a face. "I haven't got a clue what you're saying." She popped a cigarette in her mouth.

He lit it and his cigar. "I said that's a pretty French name and for a pretty girl."

She shrugged. "Don't know. My mum came up with it."

"You've never been to France?"

"Nope. This is my first time out of London."

"Do you like Merivale?" he asked, puffing out smoke.

"Not sure. It's a bit posh, I guess."

She leaned against a wall, sucking on her cigarette, and blew the odd smoke ring.

I tipped my head in their direction. "She's rather precocious for an eighteen-year-old." I referred to her short skirt and skin-tight top. She was a younger version of her mother. They both wore heavy makeup and made the most of their feminine gifts. I wasn't attracted, however.

Declan nodded. "He's hitting on her. That's fucking plain to see."

"She's not exactly pushing him away."

"No." Declan didn't hide his hatred for my mother's business partner.

I shared my brother's dislike. Deep down, I suspected he was our father's killer. He and Mother stood the most to gain. It was an uncomfortable theory I tried to quash, though, despite it floating back to the surface like a cadaver dumped at sea.

Manon screamed, "Don't!"

Within a second, Drake raced over and grabbed Crisp by the scruff of his neck, shoving him away.

The older man stumbled back and fell on his bum. He got up, smoothed himself down, then pointed his finger into Drake's face. "How dare you! I'll have you sacked."

We ran over to see what was happening.

"Did he try to touch you?" Declan asked Manon.

She seemed more interested in Drake, gazing starry-eyed at the security guard who, in a matter of seconds, had gone from tough guy to mouse as he returned a shy smile.

"Are you okay?" Declan asked her.

Looking unconcerned, she stubbed out her cigarette on the ground. "We were just playing."

Crisp combed back his hair with his hands and lit another cigar.

Manon swanned off, and the older man's eyes shone with contempt. "You have no right charging over here like a thug."

Drake raised his palms in defense. "Hey, I was only doing my job. She screamed."

He adjusted his collar. "I'll have a word with the lady of the house over this."

"No you won't," Declan said. "We saw what happened. You were hitting on her."

Crisp's lips strained into a cold smile. "She was very encouraging." His eyes traveled to Drake's as a form of challenge.

"If I hear even a hint of you trying it on with the young staff, I'll wipe that constipated smirk off your face." Declan stood intimidatingly close to Crisp.

V-shaping my fingers towards my eyes, I added, "We're watching you."

He puffed out smoke and returned an ugly smile. Thick-skinned as always, he didn't ruffle easily. If at all.

His background was a mystery—a self-made man, we'd heard. He was also well-educated. Or was that a ruse too? He could have just been one of those well-read types who could wax lyrically about war history, politics, and art as fluidly as my mates spoke about the latest money-making fads and football club takeovers. We'd once joked that Crisp had probably arrived at his wealth through drug trafficking or some equally nefarious activity.

Drake watched Crisp skulk off. "He was hitting on her for sure."

Manon's response *had* sent out all kinds of wrong messages. Was she enjoying the much-older man's attention or protecting her job?

Declan patted Drake's strong shoulder. "You did the right thing."

The boy rubbed his neck. "I might have just lost my job. He's in thick with your mum, isn't he?"

"Don't worry. I'll make sure nothing comes out of it. You did the right thing," Declan repeated.

CHAPTER 25

Mirabel

CIAN SMILED, AND MY eyes pooled with warmth and love—the kind of love I didn't even know I possessed. I showered my son with so much affection, I had to watch I didn't smother his little soft body when cuddling him.

"He's gorgeous," Theadora crooned. "He's so big."

"I know. He's only one month old. He was such a big baby from the get-go."

Sheridan was with me in Bridesmere. I couldn't get rid of her. She'd set up a working-from-home portal, enabling her to transfer her clients online. I didn't mind. In fact, her support had proved invaluable. She was the one with the manuals, scrolling her laptop for anything to do with caring for a newborn.

Theadora dropped in often too. We'd become extremely close, and without these two fabulous women, I would have struggled. Not that Cian kept me awake. He was an angel. I felt really blessed.

The actual delivery had been difficult, though. In the end, I'd needed to have a c-section. But with Sheridan there at the hospital around the clock, I was well and truly supported.

"He really wants to see you." Theadora's begging tone had me gulping for air.

Vanity and fear had stopped me from seeing Ethan after the birth.

I ran and hid just as he came towards me that one time I saw him in the village. This childish behavior was pure protection. I couldn't have him committing to me because of the child. But then, I couldn't also revert to casual sex, either, despite my body burning for him.

"She's being stupid," Sheridan told Theadora. "I keep telling her. And what if he's the father? He's got a right, you know."

I nodded. I knew that. It would happen. I hoped he would forgive me for not allowing him to see his son born, despite the fact I was on an operating table and not the standard delivery. That made me feel a little inadequate too. Sheridan kept reminding me that it didn't matter how it happened, as long as the mother and child were well. And that, we were.

"Cian might not be his."

"When's the paternity test happening?" Sheridan asked.

I scratched at my oily scalp. I'd let myself go. I felt like a cavewoman. "Soon." I'd thought of little else. I knew I needed to call Ethan.

IT WAS SUCH A lovely sunny afternoon, we decided on a walk down to the pier. I covered Cian with a blanket in his stroller, and Sheridan and I ambled along. Every now and then, I paused to look at my son's little face, which was filled with wonder at the passing parade of life.

I felt loose and alive. My body was healing, in spite of a flabby stomach, which now came with a scar. I had taken up Pilates and was determined to get myself back into shape.

We were just about to cross the road over to the pier when I came face-to-face with Caroline Lovechilde. I'd never seen her in the village before. Dressed in a green sheath dress with gold dripping off her, she looked like she belonged in Mayfair or Northbridge. Not our sleepy little fishing village.

Ethan's mother possessed the type of ageless beauty that only a good cosmetic surgeon could produce. Caroline Lovechilde's dark eyes wore an unshifting stony expression.

I thought she would ignore me, and look over my head like she had the last time we'd met. Instead, she stopped and stared me in the face.

TAMED BY A BILLIONAIRE

Without speaking she looked inside the stroller and straight at Cian. Her face went pale, as though she were seeing something extraordinary.

She looked at me then at Cian again. "You've become a mother, I see."

"Good afternoon, Mrs. Lovechilde." I kept my tone cool. After all, she'd treated me like shit the last time we'd crossed paths.

"How old?"

"Cian's two months."

"That's his name?" Her brows moved slightly. She had an opinion, it seemed as if she were laying claim on him.

Ethan had called. We'd spoken. I'd promised him we would meet so that I could arrange the paternity test. He wanted to drive down from London, where he'd been working. That was two days after I'd returned from the hospital. I'd promised him I would call when the time was right. I still hadn't called. I didn't want him to see me like this.

Caroline's focus remained glued on my baby as though she were looking for a flaw or a mark.

"If you can excuse us," I said, then we left her standing there.

The following day, I received a call from her. Despite the private number on my screen, I'd taken the call, and when she announced herself, I nearly dropped the phone.

When she asked if she could visit me, I replied, "I have nothing to say to you."

"I know that I was rather unpleasant when you performed at our soiree, and for that, I owe you an apology."

She sounded almost human, which startled me.

"I'd like to see Cian," she said.

"Why?" My cold response echoed her cool tone.

"He's my grandson, I believe."

"That's unofficial."

"Please." She sounded needy. It wasn't something I would have expected from the tough matriarch.

"I can meet you at Milly's at one." I put down the phone, wondering why I'd agreed.

It was for Cian. If anything were to happen to me, I needed to know he would be protected if he was, in fact, a Lovechilde. I was too frightened to find out. That tiny glimmer of possibility that he wasn't Ethan's had me on tenterhooks, despite my heart telling me otherwise. A heavy weight followed me. I knew I had to find out soon, for everyone's sake.

But for now, I'd fallen into a novice-mother rabbit hole, where time didn't matter or was forgotten entirely. Lost in this maternal haze, I walked around with my brain in a fog. All I could think about was breastfeeding, staring endlessly at my son, or changing nappies.

Caroline Lovechilde was already there when I arrived. From a distance, I could have been meeting a glamorous actress at a Parisian café. There was something cinematic about the way she looked in a cream silk shirt, sunglasses, and a wide-brim hat, sipping tea.

I put the brakes on the stroller and took a seat. The waitress came over, and I ordered juice. Cian slept soundly. That boy seemed to suck on my nipples and sleep.

Caroline kept staring at him. "He's the spitting image of Ethan when he was that age." Her voice cracked as if she were about to cry.

How could she tell? Babies all looked the same at two months.

I allowed a little time for her to watch him. When Cian opened his eyes and smiled, her mouth curled warmly. That was the first smile from her I'd ever seen.

"Can I hold him?"

I nodded.

A few of the villagers who knew me walked by and waved. With raised brows, they paused to smile at Cian, and I think they were taken aback by Caroline Lovechilde's presence.

"By now, everyone knows, you realize?"

She only had eyes for Cian. Nothing else existed. "Probably."

"You don't mind?"

She looked up at me. "It's happened. And he's beautiful." Her voice cracked again.

"Look, Mrs. Lovechilde, I can see he's affected you. I can't and won't share him with you."

She stared at me without blinking. "He'll have everything and more."

I shook my head slowly. "I don't want him to be indulged. And I have my own money. More than enough for me and my son."

"Did you do this on purpose? Use my son to get pregnant?"

"Does he know you're here?"

"No. He's in London. Due back tomorrow."

"I haven't even had a paternity test."

A faint line appeared between her perfectly tweezered brows. "You were sleeping with other men at the same time as my son?"

I nearly laughed at how shocked that concept seemed. It shocked me too. How could anyone sleep around while seeing Ethan?

"We'd broken up at the time."

"He's Ethan's son. I can see that without that test."

We locked eyes, and neither of us blinked.

CHAPTER 26

Ethan

I JOINED DECLAN AS he chatted with a family friend. Everyone who was anyone had been invited to the opening of Elysium. My mother's dream had finally been realized, and despite Declan's initial reservation, the resort blended in organically with the natural surroundings. Boasting ocean views, a golf course, a state-of-the-art gym, and fine dining, the hotel would be a magnet for the super-rich seeking a quick escape.

Once upon a time, Mirabel would have brought her army of comrades and marched around shouting. I conjured up an image of her carrying a banner protesting about a heritage village building about to be developed. Assaulted by a piston of angry words, I would chuckle as she pointed her finger at me, accusing me of sleeping with the Tories.

Mirabel the firebrand was just as appealing as her mature creative version. She'd mellowed, but not enough to allow me into her life. This time, however, she wasn't protecting the natural order of things, but her heart. Or so Theadora reminded me after I'd poured out my own heart on more than one occasion since the baby's birth.

On the night of my son's birth, a dream told me he'd arrived. I'd been getting around with my head in a cloud since. That was on my good days. On my bad days, I pummelled the punching bad at Reboot or drank to excess and yelled like someone in need of a counselor.

I'd had enough. I'd decided to burst Mirabel's protective bubble and insist on seeing Cian, despite not knowing one hundred percent if he was mine. The fact that paternity still had to be established made it hard to breathe some days. There were even days when I hated her for shutting me out. Although I'd always considered Mirabel gutsy and respected her independence, my patience with her over-sensitivity had worn thin.

We milled about the shimmering Olympic-sized pool as waiters walked around with trays of canapes and champagne. The turquoise pool with its natural rock pool cascade was a perfect setting for that warm afternoon. Even the wind had stayed away.

I peered through the glass doors of the main entrance, where paintings of nudes frolicking through the forest graced the walls in a nod to that region's folklore.

"We seem to be doing a lot of this lately," Declan said, sipping beer.

I took a swig from my bottle and wiped my mouth with the back of my hand. "I'm not in the mood, to be honest."

I'd made a big decision that morning, prompted by my mother, of all people. Normally, I would walk away and shake off whatever demand she'd made, but this time, I sat up and listened.

My brother gave me one of his sympathetic half-smiles. Without me saying anything, he understood how profoundly affected I was by this birth. "How are you traveling? Have you at least tried to see him? Theadora says he's a beautiful boy and that he looks just like you."

My mouth went dry, and my face flushed at the mention of Mirabel's baby. I could hardly breathe, let alone respond because of the rush of emotions. I just stared down at my new leather boots with grass scattered on them from walking along the freshly mown grounds.

"You need to visit her," he added. "I'm sure she'll be reasonable about this."

I stared out to sea, which had teal ripples under the afternoon sun. "His name's Cian. I'm going there today. I thought I'd better make a show here first. I haven't been able to think of anything else these last two months." I circled my toe on the ground. "Mother's seen him. She insists he's mine. She's suggesting I get a lawyer."

Declan studied me for a minute. "Do you still have feelings for Mirabel?"

I nodded. "I know that's crazy."

"It's not crazy. If feelings remain strong during a space of time, then she must be special. *That* special one."

My brows pinched. "I'm not sure if I'm ready to marry. I do miss Mirabel for sure, though. Over and above everything, I want to be part of my son's life." I puffed. "That's if he is my son."

"She *still* hasn't done a test?"

"No. Unless she's got some of my DNA tucked away."

"Well then, you better go and talk to her, I think." He smiled at Theadora, who was giggling with some of the guests.

I'd seen my mother earlier; she'd looked pale while describing her meeting with Mirabel. She'd recounted how seeing my son brought back memories of me at that tender age. Her eyes had misted over in a rare display of emotion.

"On another pressing subject," Declan said, "we need to talk to Will."

"Why?" I took a deep breath, sensing more drama.

"You know how they plan to marry next week?"

As I nodded, Savanah, teetering along in super-high heels, joined us. I pointed at her hot-pink shoes. "How did you get here in those?"

"They're great, aren't they? They're new Manolo's. Love them. I might have to get that hot security guard to piggyback me home." She giggled. "Speaking of muscular males, where's Carson?" She looked at Declan.

"He's gone back to London."

Her mouth turned down. "That's not much fun. Is he still going to visit us?"

Declan shrugged. "He's set up a security agency."

"Mm... I might need to use him." Savanah stared at her feet. Her toes were painted in the same color as her open-toe shoes.

"Not another brute boyfriend?" My tone was cutting. I was growing tired of my sister's inability to date anyone but troubled men.

"I don't want to talk about it."

I looked at Declan and rolled my eyes.

"What has Mother told you about marrying Will?" Declan asked her.

"They're getting married next week. Like a really small affair. They didn't even want to have a party, which is weird for Mummy. You know her—any excuse to entertain."

Savanah turned to me. "I hear I'm an aunty. Mummy's beside herself. She wants the baby here. I know I'd like to see him."

"Yep." I puffed. "I know. I'm going to see Mirabel today."

"He's your son." She opened out her hands. "What's the issue anyway?"

Brilliant fucking question.

"It's not confirmed, by the way." I scratched my jaw. "In answer to your question, I think she's frightened of me."

Savanah laughed. "Scared of you?" She thought about it for a moment. "Oh. Like that. You mean, she's frightened you'll break her heart?"

"Maybe." I huffed. "She's the one that ran off with another guy straight after pushing me away," I muttered.

"Oh my god. She hurt you." Savanah's eyes widened, as though something unexpected had taken place.

"Let's not talk about this." I hated myself for opening that Pandora's box. My sister loved talking about relationships. She could go on all day about it.

Suddenly, a jazz trio cranked up, and a couple of family friends swung by and gushed in incoherent babble common at these functions. They seemed to think my mother was a superbeing who breathed gold dust. I returned a well-practiced, robotic smile, having adopted it from an early age, thanks to the endless functions I'd attended.

My mother called it networking. For me, it was tedious, and my neck and face always ached from smiling and nodding. But there I was, the dutiful son, doing what was expected, and at the end of the day, the resort would fill the spa with more guests.

After they walked off, Savanah turned to me. "Are you going to marry her?"

"I don't fucking know." My voice had a rough edge. I was sick of all this speculation. I just wanted to see my son.

It frightened me how hot-headed I'd become. I was unrecognizable even to myself. After my mother spoke to me about her encounter with Mirabel and seeing Cian, I sprang out of the hole I'd dug for myself—a bunker where I buried hard-to-process issues.

Adrenaline churned away in my gut. I'd lost my appetite, and I couldn't sleep. This child had taken possession of my sanity. After my father's death, I was like an onion unraveling. The outgoing, skip-through-life version of me had peeled away first, and the more layers I stripped, the grittier I got.

Declan placed his hand on my arm. "I'm sure you'll sort this out."

My mouth twitched into a weak smile.

He leaned in. "There's something I need to tell you."

A loud exhale made my chest rise and collapse. "Not more shit, please."

He wore a troubled smile. "You know this family."

"Does Savvie need to know?" My sister had baled up a man with a tattooed neck, dressed in a designer suit. He was probably a drug trafficker rubbing shoulders with old money to legitimize his ill-gained fortune.

"She's likely to make a fuss. Let's not spoil the day."

My brow furrowed "Is it that bad?"

"I think so. Let's get away from the crowd."

Taking heavy strides, I followed him to a bench under an ancient willow.

I patted the thick trunk. "Glad they didn't get rid of Wilfred."

My brother laughed at our childhood name of the tree we'd once thought possessed magical powers. Especially when the sun flickered gold on its droopy branches. Whenever I visited that spot, a cascade of warm memories always drifted over me like an easy breeze on a summery day.

On the edge of the pond rested the little red boat we'd paddled about in as boys. Now, it housed moss and an ecosystem of molds that only added to its decadent charm.

"Okay, so, what's all this about?" I asked.

"Earlier on, while climbing the track to the cliffs, I spied Will with Bethany, hidden behind a tree."

I frowned so hard, my head hurt. "Like kissing?"

He nodded.

"Did they see you?"

"No. I hurried off."

"Fuck. We've noticed the looks between them."

Declan nodded. "I have to tell Mum."

"Holy shit." I massaged my neck as sympathy for my mother intensified. "Should we talk to him first?" I tossed a pebble into the pond, trying to make it skip.

"I'm not sure. But they're to marry next week."

"They haven't exactly hidden it. How has Mum not seen it? She doesn't normally miss a bloody thing. And why's he still going ahead with the marriage?"

Declan puffed. "Watch out for the quiet ones, they say."

We walked back through the iron gates with Elysium scrolled in filigree.

Theadora walked over to Declan. "Shouldn't we make that announcement?"

"Announce what?" I asked.

"We're having a baby." Declan's eyes shone with emotion.

My mouth fell open. "Wow. And you're telling me now?"

Declan shrugged. "With everything going on in your life, I thought it best left to my darling wife." He kissed her hair and draped his arm over her shoulder.

If ever anyone needed an image of what a loved-up couple looked like, my brother and his wife were that marriage-venerating poster couple. Only they were real. Very real. And it warmed my very existence to be part of their lives.

I kissed Theadora's cheek. "That's great news."

Declan's eyes had a mist over them. Yep, us Lovechilde boys had forgotten about that stiff-upper-lip rule drummed into us as boys via expensive and dated education.

I hugged Declan. "I'm happy for you."

He looked at me with sympathy. "You're okay? Really? I wasn't sure whether to tell you yet."

"I'm elated. Really." I set my bottle on the glass tabletop. "I have to leave now, though."

"Really, but this is only just started," he said. "And what about that other matter?"

"Let's talk a little more later." I'd almost forgotten about my mother's new problem. All I could think of was seeing Mirabel and my *possible* son.

CHAPTER 27

Mirabel

CIAN BIT ON MY nipple, and I flinched. "Ouch." His big brown eyes looked up at me, and I wagged my finger at him. "You're like your father. You've got a thing for my nipples."

I laughed at myself. Was that sick of me to think of that while my baby fed on my breast? Probably.

Just as I was putting Cian back into his crib, a knock came at the door.

Assuming it was Audrey popping in for a cup of tea and to hold Cian, I opened the door without thinking. I nearly fell over. My knees came close to buckling. Before me stood Ethan, his arm above his head, leaning against the doorframe. The sleeve of his pale blue shirt looked like it would burst.

I shouldn't have been surprised—I'd been expecting him since that meeting with his mother. And I was about to call him anyway. I was just trying to summon the courage to ask him for a hair sample. Not that I actually believed it necessary as I was now convinced Cian was Ethan's son. And for that alone, I knew I had a lot of apologizing to do.

My throat tightened from nerves.

His gaze pierced mine, and my lips strained into a trembly curve.

"I've come to see my son." He looked serious. No softly spoken, caressing words that could make me give everything. Just a demand.

Like a lump of wood, I remained at the doorway. Not because I wished to block him, but because he captivated me.

I felt his breath. Even worse, I caught a whiff of his libido-teasing scent. I still had a t-shirt he'd left behind, which I couldn't bring myself to wash.

I stepped out of the way. "You better come in. I've been expecting you." I rolled my lips into a tight smile to curb the quiver. "Excuse the mess."

He followed me. "I don't care." His edginess made my shoulders tense.

"I suppose your mother told you?"

He raked his hands through his hair, almost tugging at it. His thick hair stuck up in all the right places. "She did. But she didn't have to. I've thought about nothing else since hearing about the birth." His thumb stroked his plump lower lip. "I would have liked to have been there." His eyes drilled into mine, and I had to lean against the couch to steady my balance. "To hold your hand."

"But you didn't know whether he was yours. I didn't know."

"I don't care."

Our eyes locked. His frown seemed etched on his handsome face. I could see he'd been seriously affected, and guilt sliced through me for denying him that much.

A basket of freshly laundered nappies cluttered the couch. I moved them out of the way, even though he headed straight to the white cane crib. The same crib that I'd slept in.

My aunt Hermione, my late mother's sister, took everything I didn't think I would ever need. It was the closest my son would come to connecting to his grandparents. It pained me to think my parents wouldn't get to see their grandchild.

As always after a feed, Cian was off deep in a peaceful sleep, totally oblivious to the emotional maelstrom around him. Ethan's eyes lit up with wonder. That had been me, too, because my beautiful boy felt like a miracle.

"He's a big baby," he whispered. "Cian."

"Yes. Cian Storm."

His brow twitched slightly. He looked at me. "Sounds a bit dark."

"No. It's poetic."

"My mother says he looks exactly like I did as a newborn." Ethan tipped his head to the side to study the little cherub lost in sleep. "He's beautiful." I noticed his Adam's apple wobble as he took a gulp.

His large, dark eyes had gone glassy. It took all my inner strength not to fall into his arms.

Like being reminded of hunger while eating a meal, seeing him again, close up, made waves of desire prickle across my skin. My heart grumbled at me for being such an imbecile by not allowing Ethan into my life. I had this overwhelming urge to get down on my knees and beg his forgiveness. Tears pricked my eyes as Ethan stood absorbed by his son. He looked like he was going to cry.

If only I could rewrite the last twelve months.

I went to speak, then Cian opened his eyes. He looked at his father, and they had a staring competition. Ethan's smile, the first since he'd arrived, filled that room with sunshine, and then my son smiled back.

I lost it. Collapsing onto the sofa, I buried my face in my hands and bawled. The struggle to contain myself intensified when Ethan sat beside me and wrapped his arm around my shoulders.

My eyes stung, and my throat burned as uncontrollable sobs burst out, like a water main had sprung a leak. The more I fought it, the louder I sobbed. The dam I'd built to hold back my grief burst, and the tears flowed like polluted rivers down my cheeks.

It wasn't just how my irrational and suffocating paranoia had pushed Ethan away, but that I'd robbed him of the birth of his son. As all my bad choices tumbled before me in one endless, unforgiving reel, I asked myself if this was what a nervous breakdown looked like.

Or is it an epiphany? If so, what's my lesson?

I knew the answer within a breath: stop wrapping myself in cotton wool, embrace that free spirit I'd always identified as, and join the everchanging dance of life with a brave heart.

I broke away from him and rubbed my eyes while muttering an apology. Ethan returned a sad smile and passed me the box of tissues.

I wiped my eyes and nose and ran my hands over my face. "I'm sorry. I didn't know what to do. I shouldn't have shut you out, but you weren't ready for this."

His brow creased. "How do you know that? How is anyone ready for anything as dramatically life-changing? We just somehow manage." He took a breath. "I've spent the past few months missing you. Theadora kept me informed on your health. I would've been there at the hospital, holding your hand."

I gazed into his eyes, and my whole body seemed to shake. I took a stilling breath and cast my eyes on my chipped fingernails instead of his beautiful eyes.

He opened out his hands. "Why would that surprise you? Was I the only one that felt our connection?"

I shook my head slowly and repeatedly. "I felt it. From the first night." I ran my hands through my knotty mane that hadn't seen a brush for a day. "That's why I kept pushing you away. I was overwhelmed by passion. I couldn't stop wanting to be with you. It was so intense, I lost myself."

"So you slept with Orson instead." That sober remark made me feel like he'd just dipped my head in a bucket of cold water.

"We weren't seeing each other."

"I know that. But shit, so soon? It fucking hurt, to be honest."

I nodded. "I regret it more than you can imagine. It was one of those drunken, silly mistakes."

Cian started to make his gurgling sounds, and I turned to him and smiled. My angst dissolved in an instant. It was like my son had decided to intervene on this merry-go-round of issues that I'd created and steer us onto another course.

Ethan watched his son, and like me, his mouth stretched into a big loving smile. "Can I hold him?"

I stood up. "Of course."

Ethan went to the crib, lifted the baby, and held him in his arms. Fresh tears welled up in my eyes. This time not from frustration, but from pure love. Father and son. It was a perfect sight.

"You're good at that." My voice thickened with emotion.

He made those silly baby sounds that we all do, and my son smiled at him. Warm, heart-swelling tears splashed down my cheeks. It looked like mutual love at first sight as Ethan rocked Cian and kissed his soft little cheek. I pulled out a tissue and wiped my eyes. I was drowning in emotion.

Nevertheless, I sucked it back, knowing that we'd turned a new corner. Ethan would be my son's father. Cian had a right to know him. Seeing how gentle and loving Ethan was sealed that deal.

"I'd like to introduce him to my family. Officially. Would you allow that? Can he be part of our family too?"

Ethan's urging gaze searched mine. I couldn't be so mean to keep my son from his father and family.

"You're convinced he's yours?" I tangled my fingers and had to look away because I couldn't even think straight with Ethan looking so fucking beautiful, especially when he was all raw with emotion.

His glassy gaze rose to meet mine. "I don't doubt it for one minute." He buried his nose in his son's little face. "He smells so fresh. So perfect."

"Not when he needs changing." The switch in the subject was needed.

"I'm happy to change him if you want." His face softened into a panty-melting, boyish grin. That same expression had made me a swooning wreck back when we were teenagers.

How is this going to work? How can I be around him without wanting to claw at those ripped jeans?

CHAPTER 28

Ethan

MY SON WAS BEAUTIFUL. As I played with his tiny fingers, I never wanted to let him go. I kept gulping down the lumps in my throat. My heart was doing things to me I'd never experienced before.

Looking rattled, Mirabel stood by and watched. Whenever our eyes met, she looked like she was trying to solve a puzzle. Then she would look at our son, and her face would break into a sunny smile.

I placed him down in his crib, and Mirabel helped adjust his blankets.

"He sleeps all the time."

"That's a good thing, I imagine." I kept looking at Cian, tilting my head and smiling or making silly sounds I'd never heard myself make before.

"Yep. He sleeps through the night. My aunt Hermione tells me that I'm blessed."

Mirabel became that childhood friend that I used to knock around. It must have been the mention of her eccentric aunt. As children, we'd sometimes visited her quaint little cottage, mainly for her delicious gingerbread men and women. She told us she didn't want to appear sexist. Not that I'd understood what that meant at seven.

"Is your aunt still stirring that cauldron?"

She chuckled. "Yeah, she's still making her herbal concoctions."

"She scared the shit out of me that time she turned up dressed as a witch at my tenth birthday party."

Mirabel giggled. "You did have a witches-and-warlocks theme, and she needed the money, so your parents gave her the gig."

I laughed at that amusing childhood memory. We had plenty of those, and it was nice sharing them with her.

Right now, however, it was Mirabel, the woman who had me in her thrall. She was so stunning, I couldn't take my eyes away from her. She wasn't wearing makeup, and her porcelain skin looked radiant. She'd put on a little bit of weight but in all the right places.

"Why are you looking at me like that?" She smoothed down her waist-long, wavy hair. "I know I look a fright."

I shook my head slowly. "You've grown even more beautiful, Mirabel. Motherhood suits you."

She smiled tightly and resumed looking downwards. She rose. "I'm sorry I haven't offered you anything."

"I'm good. I don't need anything. I'm just happy to be here."

She tangled her fingers, then those big, limpid eyes rose to meet mine. "I'm sorry for shutting you out."

"I wasn't going anywhere." I placed my hand on hers.

She withdrew her hand abruptly as though my palm were a glass shard.

"Why?" It wasn't easy getting Mirabel to talk about her feelings. I found that odd. Most girls I'd dated loved to talk about their feelings.

She paused at the crib and tipped her head for another look at Cian, her frown dissolving into a smile. Settling on a stool by the crib, Mirabel started to fold nappies from a washing basket.

"Do you want me to go? Am I being a nuisance?" I asked.

She shook her head and then stared deeply into my eyes, mesmerizing me again. "You know how we kissed at Jasmine's party that time?"

"That was one kiss I remember very well."

"And as you know, I bolted." She folded the square in a desultory fashion and picked up another. "You were fucking everyone by that stage."

Apologizing for overactive adolescent hormones wasn't an easy conversation. I cleared my throat. "Testosterone will do that to a teenager."

"I get that. And had we, or had you taken my virginity, I would not have expected marriage." Her eyebrow rose.

"Right." I rubbed my neck. "I would have loved to have been your first. But shit, I was only sixteen."

She fumbled with the cloth absently. "Anyway, I liked you. Like everyone did. You dick."

I laughed. "You were being chased, too, from memory. You were gorgeous then. Now even more so."

Her cheeks reddened. Mirabel, for all her experience, still had this adorable tendency to blush whenever complimented.

"That's why I didn't let you go all the way—because I liked you too much. I sensed you'd break my heart. And then lo and behold, next minute, you're on with Mariah. I mean the same fucking night."

I grimaced. "Ouch. Not my finest hour. But hey, Mariah? Everyone had fucked Mariah." I studied her for a moment. "So, let me get this straight—you're still punishing me for that?" A lightbulb went off in my head. "Oh, is that why you fucked Orson? To get back at me? To test me?"

She dropped her head and picked at her fingernails. "I was drunk and trying to get over you. I fucking regret it."

"Don't worry. I've had a few regrettable fucks myself."

Her eyes fired up. "That's what I mean."

"What?" I opened out my palms.

"Just that. You think of sex as a sport."

"Well, it once was." I pulled at a leather band on my wrist. "In any case, what I had with you wasn't just physical." I looked into her eyes, which returned a wide, glassy stare. "Didn't you feel that?"

She shrugged. "I did. But I thought all those cuddles, sweet words, and soft kisses were part of your act."

My brows squeezed tight. "What? Do you think I'm that fucking fake? Hell, Mirabel." I shook my head. "I did treat sex as sport. But not with you. I can't believe you thought I was making that up." Fire bit my belly. My emotions started to play havoc with my mood again.

I walked over to the crib, and seeing that beautiful baby calmed me down. "I've hardly slept with anyone. Just one girl since we were together." I exhaled. "I've grown tired of sex as sport."

Her lips curled into a half-smile. "Yeah. I know what you mean. Although for me, it wasn't sport as much as..." She shrugged. "I guess I was asserting my right to do what men have been doing all my life."

"Here's to feminism," I said dryly.

"Sexual freedom has led to a lot of confusion too," she added. "Anyway, to get back to what we were saying earlier, about my insecurity." She cleared her throat. "I saw the girls and how they all looked at you."

"And was I flirting with them?" I asked.

She shook her head. "No. You were the model gentleman while we dated for that short time."

"Short time? For me, it was the longest I'd ever dated one woman."

"Your inexperience with relationships also made me doubt this. Us." A half smile came and went. "Especially with me growing attached and losing myself in you."

"But I loved you losing yourself in me." I took a breath. "I felt pretty fucking jealous when I learned of you and Orson."

She pulled a face, as though she'd tasted something bad. "He was awful. I mean, he's a talented producer, and even more so as a manager, but he's not very good in other ways."

"Oh? Please tell me his dick was smaller." I winced. "Sorry, that must make me sound shallow."

She sniffed. "You've got nothing to worry about there."

"Let's just bury all that, will we?" I rose to visit my son's crib again.

We stood by the crib, where I felt the warmth of her body. I could feel her energy. Like sparks were coming off her. I wanted so much to hold her. But I read hesitancy. One step at a time. And what was I wanting here?

"Can I get a photo of him?" I asked.

She smiled sweetly. "Of course. And I'll send you some pictures from when he was born if you like."

"Oh, please do." I dragged out my phone and clicked photos. His eyes opened and I smiled at my son. His rosebud lips curled, and my universe turned into bright technicolor.

I clicked away. "He's a natural actor. He's aware that we're going all melty over him."

Her head pushed back. "Melty?" She chuckled. "You're a prat."

"And so are you."

Mirabel followed me to the door, and we stood there again. I leaned in and kissed her cheeks, lingering on her soft skin. My lips wanted to do more than taste that cheek.

"Can I come again?" I asked. "Can we have a day at Merivale? You come over for lunch with Cian."

She nodded slowly.

"Why don't you let me treat you to a day at the spa? You and your cousin or your aunty. I can mind Cian."

Her eyes fell into mine again. "You know, I might just take you up on that."

CHAPTER 29

Mirabel

AFTER AN INTENSE WEEK, I finally did what I should have done after my son's birth. I got a paternity test. I had to know. It might have just been a fluke that Cian resembled Ethan. Although Caroline Lovechilde almost fainting on the pavement confirmed the bloodline, I still needed one hundred percent certainty.

After Ethan's visit, I picked up the cup that Ethan had used and decided to have it tested. Asking him for a strand of hair felt weird. As though not trusting my instincts was some vital flaw.

When the email arrived with the results, my fingers trembled on the keyboard. I opened the document, and after scanning through scientific jargon, I landed on what I needed to know. Finally, the air that had been trapped in my lungs whooshed out.

It was a match. My shoulders sagged in relief. Reality finally seeped in—Ethan Lovechilde was the father of my son.

I'D DECIDED TO TAKE Ethan's offer of a day at the Pond. The invite had also been extended to Sheridan, who bubbled with excitement. After being handed a bag of complimentary goodies, she poked her head in the cotton bag stamped with an insignia of the Pond. "Oh my god, *Le Mer* cream." Her shouty whisper made me smile. "And an essential oil collection with a plug-in diffuser."

We'd been allocated a room where we could change and call our own for that day. I looked out at the duck pond I'd zealously tried to protect, and the building with its mudbrick façade harmonized perfectly with its surrounding environment.

Unobtrusive but calming ambient sounds filtered through the room, and just being there made me feel light.

"They must have that essential oil in the air conditioning ducts," Sheridan said, stripping down to her underwear.

We were to start the session with a massage, then a facial, and anything else that took our fancy.

"So Cian is having a taste of the billionaire's life." Sheridan chuckled.

I went to bite my fingernail. It was the first time I'd been parted from my son, and anxiety invaded my body.

"You look worried." She slipped into a white bathrobe.

"I am a little concerned about him being spoiled and treated like royalty."

Sheridan frowned. "I think it's great. Love from any corner is positive."

I thought about how Caroline's tight face had softened immediately when she knelt to look at her grandson. Yes, my son would be loved.

"It's important. You're right," I said at last. I tied the dressing gown sash and slid my bare feet into cotton-lined slippers.

"And Ethan?" she asked.

I took the glass of green juice and sipped the earthy-tasting liquid. "He's in love with Cian. I mean, he's goo-gaaing and pulling silly faces." Warmth gushed through me as I thought of Ethan's sweet affection for Cian. He doted on him. And the love I saw in his eyes mirrored the feelings I had for our son.

Sheridan inclined her head. "You look like you're going to cry."

My breath stuttered. I sank onto the comfortable armchair and buried my head.

"What's wrong, love?"

"It's difficult being around him. I still have feelings for him. I've never stopped having feelings for him. And I think he might feel the same, going on how he looks at me."

"Then what's the fucking problem? Sleep with him. Fuck him senseless."

I sniffed. "If only it was that simple. We've got a child. What does that then make us? Casual lovers who happen to have a kid?"

She shrugged. "You're overthinking again, sweetie."

I sighed. "He'll break my heart."

"So what? At least you'll have some great sex."

I laughed at how flippant that sounded.

"Lighten up, Bel. What's the worst thing that could happen?"

I went to bite a nail but stopped, thinking of the manicure I was about to have. "He runs off with a gorgeous supermodel..." I held up my finger. "Or he tries to get total custody."

It just tumbled out. That's what had been worrying me from the moment Caroline saw me in the village. I'd seen it in her eyes. She wanted my son for her own.

"He won't try to do that. Will he?" Her brow furrowed.

"Ethan wouldn't. But his mother. I don't know. She seems crazy about my son. Theadora's pregnant. Maybe once she has another grandchild, that might defuse the situation."

"Don't worry. You're the mother. Unless you do something stupid like get caught sniffing glue with a bunch of losers, then they can't just take the child."

I chuckled at that sad scenario. "I won't be doing that. I've even gone off booze. At least, I finally kicked the ciggies."

A knock came at the door, and our facilitator arrived. In caressing tones, she ran through our program of pampering, and from then on, paranoia gave way to pleasure. By late afternoon, I felt so clean and relaxed that I couldn't stop smiling as we floated out of that beautiful place.

"It's like we've had an E—without the thumping rave music and come down," Sheridan said as we ambled along, our bag of goodies swinging along with us. "This reminds me of a setting for *The Wind in the Willows*. I'm expecting Mr. Toad to come strutting out of that pond any minute."

I chuckled. "You can stay the night if you like. I'm sure they wouldn't mind. Merivale has twenty bedrooms, I'm told."

"Wow." Her eyebrows rose. "As tempting as that sounds, I think I'll drive back. Bret's invited a couple from work. I should be there."

I accompanied my cousin to her car. "I'm so glad you came. It was fun to have someone to share this with."

"Thanks for inviting me. I loved it. I think I ingested a ton of essential oil because it's still up my nose." She hugged me. "Hey, go with the flow, Bel. Think about Cian's future. It can't be too bad having money around, can it? Especially these days. It's tough out there."

I couldn't disagree.

"Are you going to tell him about the paternity test?" She squinted from the late afternoon sun.

"Maybe not tonight, but I will."

My cousin didn't miss a thing, not least the hesitant note in my response.

"They won't try to take Cian away. I don't know why you keep thinking that."

"Look at how I live," I said.

"You've got the money to move. Why don't you?"

"I am looking. I'm just attached to my little flat. I like my neighbors, and it's a quick walk to the shops."

"Then renovate."

"Do you think they could fix that place?"

"Yeah," she sang. "They can do anything these days."

I hugged her again. "I love you, cousin of mine."

I walked slowly to the hall, wondering whether Cian would be aware of the opulence around him.

Being late afternoon, the sun sprinkled its golden light over the endless garden of colorful blooms. I might have been walking into a picture book. Would there be a witch hidden under a designer dress with a shining apple?

I had to laugh at my silly imagination. I'd always been a little para‑ noid. Since giving birth, I'd become a complete worrywart. That had to stop. My cousin was right.

I took tentative steps up to the entrance and rang the bell. A moment later, an attractive woman opened the door. She was in her thirties, with dark hair. Her stare was cold and remote.

Mm… This is going to be fun. Even the staff look and act like Caroline Lovechilde.

Ethan came to meet me in that astounding room that reminded me of the Tate Gallery.

"There you are. How was it?" Wearing a long‑sleeve polo and black jeans, he looked as handsome as ever.

"It was great. Thanks so much. Sheridan was extremely grateful and sends you her thanks."

"Any time. The place is yours to enjoy." He smiled brightly.

"How was Cian?" I asked.

"He's great." The look of wonder in his eyes was the same as when he'd first seen his son. He crooked his finger. "Come."

I followed him into a yellow room filled with large vases of flowers, a burgundy velvet Chesterfield couch, a wall covered in art, and bay windows looking out to sea.

My son slept in a different crib.

"That's new," I said, stroking the woven cane.

"It's one I slept in. We've got a nursery with all kinds of kiddies' things." He chuckled, sounding like a kid himself. Adorably so. "Rock‑ ing horses and all those bits and pieces."

"A bit creepy, I reckon," Savanah said, entering the room.

Ethan laughed. "She says it reminds her of one of those haunted stories. You know, where the horse rocks on its own."

"Ew." Savanah crossed her arms and shivered. "Scary." She looked at me and smiled. "I hear you had a session at the Pond."

I nodded. "It was fantastic. A gorgeous place. You've done it well," I said, giving Ethan a timid smile.

He grinned. "See, no farmers were harmed in the process."

I went to poke my tongue at him when Caroline Lovechilde entered.

For a moment, we remained in silence by the crib, gazing lovingly at Cian. If anything, that child would be well and truly loved.

"He's a very calm child," Caroline said. "He's hardly stirred."

"We fed him. He was so cute," Savanah said.

"Speaking of which, he's probably due for a feed," I said.

They all looked at each other and nodded. "Right. Best leave you to it."

They walked out, but Ethan remained, looking a little uncertain for a moment. I went to unbutton my shirt, and he turned away.

Bizarre.

"It's okay. I don't mind. You've seen it all before."

He chuckled nervously. "I'll go and get us some tea. Yes?"

I nodded. "Sure."

"You're going to stay for dinner, aren't you?" His gaze lingered.

It took me a moment to respond. "That's if it's okay with your mother."

"She's fine. I mean, there's some drama going on. But it's got nothing to do with you."

I wiped my brow. "Phew." I chuckled. "Nothing too intense, I hope."

"Oh, it's intense, all right. I'll fill you in later."

Despite that negative subject matter, I felt welcomed, like a part of his life. A rush of warmth flooded my spirit as I allowed that comforting thought to percolate.

"Hey, Declan and Theadora will be here soon. You've heard that I'm going to be an uncle?" He was almost bouncing on the spot, and his infectious ebullience swept me along.

"I'm so happy for them. It will be nice to see them."

He rubbed his hands together. "Right back soon with that tea. Make yourself at home."

CHAPTER 30

Ethan

My son's presence had restored the cheer and brightness missing from Merivale since my dad's death. Even my mother smiled. Savanah had made a special trip back from London to meet Cian, and we were all besotted by my chubby little son. Everyone held him like a prize and cooed sweetly.

Mirabel looked cautiously amused by all the fuss. I went out of my way to make her feel welcomed and comfortable. After all, I planned to make this a habit. Not only for the sake of my son but I wanted her around me.

I sat across from her at dinner and couldn't take my eyes off her.

Our gazes lingered on each other for a few seconds. My lips curled, and we shared a flirty moment. Mirabel's intelligent eyes shone with a mix of sassy guardedness and amusement. With Savanah chatting about clothes and London, and Theadora about her children's music program, Mirabel soon loosened up.

"Cian is such a stunning baby," Declan said. "I hope you're going to make this work."

He reminded me of that big brother steering me onto a sensible path. This time, though, he didn't need to lead me by the hand. I was already there—humming along to my favorite tune with my arm around Mirabel while pushing Cian's stroller. A perfect image of domestic harmony. I only hoped Mirabel would buy into it.

"That's the plan." I smiled.

I was more than ready for a relationship. Seeing our family together at the large oval table where we'd shared so much more than just dinner cemented that desire.

After dinner, I left Mirabel and Theadora alone with Cian. My mother kept hovering about too. Declan flicked his head for me to join him outside.

We went down to the labyrinth, which over the years had become our setting for private discussions. Savanah had stepped out for a cigarette at the same time and joined us. She'd likely sensed that we were about to talk about our mother and Will's marriage. The fact that they'd married away from the family, in what looked like a hurried affair, bothered us all.

"Where's Will?" Declan asked.

"He's in London, I believe," I said. "Visiting a sick relative. Or something vague like that."

"They married," Savanah said. "After everything."

"Mother doesn't know," I said.

"We should have told her." As Savanah smoked, I fought off the urge to ask for a puff.

After we'd cornered him, Will had explained that he'd comforted Bethany while she was upset and that she was the one who'd kissed him. He'd been walking alone when they met. He'd sworn it would never happen again and begged us not to tell our mother. He'd also mentioned that he'd tolerated her relationship with Reynard Crisp all these years and that her unbreakable bond with Crisp had at times placed a wedge between him and our mother.

"We need to get rid of Bethany," Savanah said.

I nodded. "I don't know why she's still here."

"Then there's Manon. She's become an object of desire for that sleazy Crisp," Savanah said.

My brows pinched. "What? He's now fucking her?"

"I'm not sure. But I've seen how he looks at her."

"We've all seen that," Declan said dryly.

"I just think Mother needs to know," Savanah said, stubbing out her cigarette.

"I agree with Savvie." I looked at Declan. "Does anyone know Will's story?"

"I've had him checked out. He's come up pretty clean. He studied astrophysics at Oxford on a scholarship. From a middle-class upbringing in Brixton. Dad employed him to run hedge funds on behalf of Lovechilde's investing arm, after which they became partners, due to Will's brilliance with numbers and reliable results. There's not a lot more than that."

"Then maybe he's telling the truth. In a moment of weakness, he succumbed to Bethany's charms. She is very attractive," I said.

Declan nodded. "I'm with Savvie. I think we should encourage Mother to sack her."

That idea left a bad taste in my mouth. "She's a single mother."

"Then offer her a gig at the hotel in London. A job for both mother and daughter."

I nodded. "That's a good solution. At least it will remove the temptation."

I left them and went back to join Mirabel.

After dinner, I suggested she and Cian stay the weekend. Apart from finding it hard to separate from Cian, I had ulterior motives: I wanted Mirabel in my bed.

As I'd suspected, she wasn't keen. My mother still spooked her. I offered to drive her home instead.

As I carried Cian's bassinet inside her little flat, I shivered at the thought of my son living there. Mirabel placed him in his crib and wrapped another blanket around him as I watched. It was only nine o'clock, and I stood there, unsure what to do with myself. Mirabel seemed just as uncertain. Her eyes went from Cian's to mine and everywhere else.

"Can I offer you something?" she asked.

Yep. Your body and mouth.

I shrugged. "Sure, whatever."

"I've got some beer." She gave me one of her tight smiles. "Sheridan left some of hers behind."

"That will be great. And, hey"—I followed her into the tiny kitchen that could barely fit two people—"I'm sure you can drink if you express. Isn't that how it works?"

She sniffed. "You're up with all the latest mummy stuff, I see."

I grinned. "I looked it up." I rubbed my neck. It had become a daily habit—googling newborns and best practices.

"I've given up everything for now. I feel good for it, to be honest."

I nodded slowly, my eyes falling into hers again.

As she handed me a bottle of beer, our fingers touched, sending a spark through me. She must have sensed something, too, because her eyes met mine with a knowing look. I unscrewed the top and took a swallow.

As I followed her to the sofa, I couldn't help but ogle her sexy arse as her hips swayed. Her tiny waist only emphasized her curves. "Have you been doing yoga or something?" I had to ask.

"Yep, along with other stretches. I've become a bit of a fitness junkie." She smiled. "Why?"

"I'm just wondering how a woman who has only just given birth can look so sumptuous?"

"Sumptuous? You make me sound like a meal." Her mouth twisted into a smirk.

As I landed on her lumpy sofa, the spring dug into my butt, and I adjusted my body. "Would you let me buy you a flat?"

"No" shot out of her lips, making me wince.

"I just thought..." How could I tell her I didn't want my son growing up in that tiny, damp space? It didn't even have natural light during the day. How was he to grow up in that hovel?

She looked at me as though I'd asked her to move into a cave.

I sucked back some air. Mirabel was independent to a fault. Maybe that was why I admired her. The fact she wasn't on the take. But this was taking it too far. Our son needed a warm, comfortable environment to grow into a happy, healthy being.

"I'm going to renovate. I like the neighborhood. I can afford another place, you realize. 'Song of the Sea' is earning me a living." She flicked a wavy tendril away from her face, drawing my attention to her very plump chest.

"It's a great song. I love the video."

Her eyes lit up. "You've seen it?"

"Of course, I've seen it. Like lots of times." *And I've also wanked to it. You sexy fox in that tight little dress, gyrating provocatively.*

As she went about picking items from the floor, I wanted to suggest I get her some help—a cleaner or a cook or anything to make her life easier. I didn't, though. That suggestion would have fired her up, making me have to reach for the lube back at home.

Who would have thought a fiery redhead could be the equivalent of Viagra?

She paused. "I've got money. Cian's going to have the best of everything. Not public school, though."

That came crashing down like a ton of bricks. I didn't mind. My mother, UK's biggest snob, would go nuts, however. "Oh well, there's a few years for that yet."

Her eyes narrowed. I could see that she'd made up her mind about our son's future. "I want Cian to have a family, and I've only got Sheridan and her mother, my aunt Hermione. They're great and will love Cian like their own, but I want him to know his father too." She tangled her fingers. "But I will be the one to decide where he's going to live, his diet, and his education."

I sprang up. I couldn't just sit and wear it. My balls needed to make a show. Not literally, despite them throbbing that little more after I imagined unclasping her bra.

"I have a right to some say, you know. I am his father."

Her eyes widened. She looked stunned by this sudden heated challenge. I also noticed how she looked away when I uttered *father*.

"I *am* his father, aren't I?"

She looked down at a piece of paper that sat among used cups, plates, and baby paraphernalia.

"You've had a paternity test?" I didn't know why that should shock me, but it did. Cian was indisputably my son. He had to be. I'd become attached.

She went to bite a fingernail but resisted. "I had to know one way or the other."

I opened out my hands. "Well?"

"Would it matter if he wasn't?"

"Shit, Mirabel, stop talking in fucking riddles. Is he my son?"

She flinched at my raised voice. "Yes" shot out of her mouth. "He is your son. Just as we all suspected. But I needed to know for sure. I'm about to go to a solicitor and look into my rights as his mother."

My brow scrunched. "Why? What do you think I'll do?"

"Well for one, you want us to move into a posh house. And I noticed that flinch at the mention of schooling."

"I have a right. And if you go to a solicitor, so will I. I wasn't going to. But if you don't give me a say, then I'll have to."

Cian started to cry for the first time, and we both turned sharply toward his crib at the same time.

Mirabel lifted him and cradled Cian in her arms. "He's not used to heated discussions."

"No." I finished my drink in one gulp. "I guess it's normally just you."

I went to him, and as he cried, so did my heart. I wanted to hold him. To calm him.

Then he suddenly stopped. His wide-eyed, searching stare darted from me to his mother. I pulled a silly face and warbled, which made him smile, and sunshine poured in again.

Cian was back in his cradle with a blanket wrapped around him when Mirabel looked up at me and said, "You should go."

Although she pushed me towards the door, I stood still. "I don't want us to be like this."

Her eyes were wide and filled with fire. "How do you want us to be?"

Standing close, I caught a whiff of the Pond's signature fragrance, which had been massaged all over her and lost all sense of reality.

Desire swallowed my brain as I struggled to find the words. I took her into my arms, and although she tried to wiggle out of my grip, I held her close to me. Our hearts hammered together, as I buried my nose in her hair and breathed her in.

While holding her, I pulled away to gaze into her eyes, and her body softened in my arms. Like magnets, our lips touched. Her luscious mouth on mine brought out the beast in me. I went in hard. Devouring those lips like someone starved. Lust flooded my body.

She pushed me against the wall, and while I smothered her tits with my hands, she was undoing my zip. The next half an hour was an orgasmic blur. We clawed at each other's clothes. My dick was so hard and dripping for action that I knew it wouldn't take long to come.

My heart pumped like crazy, as I smoothed over her warm, soft curves.

She went to stroke my throbbing dick. "Careful. I haven't fucked for a long time."

We both seemed to need this badly—like we'd been starved, and the entrée was too delicious not to wolf down.

I parted her legs. She was soaking wet. She flinched.

"Okay?"

"Mm... please. Fuck me."

I placed my tongue between her legs and sucked, licked, and lapped her up until she was pulling at my hair and moaning.

I entered her in one desperate thrust, and my eyes rolled to the back of my head. The hair stood up at my neck, and the rush of sheer hot pleasure threatened to make me lose it. I tried to take it slowly, but I was too hot and aroused.

Her hips tilted up to take me in deep. We both moved together in a smooth, passionate dance. Her arse in my hands, I pounded into her. She was hot and slick. My dick seemed to grow bigger inside her.

It didn't take many thrusts before I surrendered to a rush so intense, I had to bite my lip to avoid yelling. We both came and cried out at the same time. Her fingernails dug into my arms. I'd missed that pain.

I'd missed everything about her—especially how she made me see stars and the way her tits rubbed against my chest. Her sensuous lips parted. Her eyes were hooded.

Cian started to make gurgling sounds as I held her tight while panting.

"He probably thinks you're murdering me."

"What?" I untangled from her arms. My mouth dropped open, and she giggled. "But he can't see us, can he?"

Mirabel brushed her hair away from her face as she got up from the couch and went to see our baby. "I'm sure he can't."

She was so gloriously naked, I couldn't stop ogling her.

"What just happened?" she asked, crossing her arms over her tits.

I took her hand and made her sit down next to me. "We just had hungry sex."

She cracked a smile. "It doesn't mean that I forgive you, though."

"Yeah, yeah." I drew her close. "Come here."

CHAPTER 31

Mirabel

THEADORA ROCKED CIAN IN her arms. "He's such a lovely baby." Her face lit up with a big smile as she stared at his tiny face.

"Isn't it he? I'm so blessed." I lounged back on a leather couch, admiring the stained-glass windows splashing a rainbow of light throughout that large room. I took a bite of moist orange tea cake, delighting at its tangy flavor. "How far are you?"

"I'm around three months now. Cian will have a little cousin around the same age. That's so nice." She tickled his nose, making him smile.

I remained quiet.

Theadora's eyes narrowed slightly. "You are going to stick around Bridesmere, I hope?"

"For sure. This is my heritage. Cian needs to be here."

"It's a perfect place for children." She inclined her head. "What about Ethan?"

It had been a week since we connected, and while my body cried out for more, my heart had decided to let my mind call the shots. "He's too unsteady to be a permanent fixture."

She jerked her head back. "You make him sound like a piece of furniture."

"You know what I mean." I sighed.

"You've got it all wrong, Bel. He's into this."

"By this, you mean fatherhood?"

"More than that." She brushed a strand from her face. "He was gutted when you cut him out of your life. You should give him a chance."

I looked down at my freshly painted toenails. After that afternoon at the Pond, I'd started to take more interest in my appearance. "Has he told you we got together the other night?"

"He did tell us." She wore a delicate smile. "But only because he was confused about you and how you keep shutting him out."

I sighed. After not responding to his invitation to dinner, there was no doubt I was being tough on him. "I'm just trying to protect myself and Cian. I mean, what happens when Ethan tires of me and Cian's gotten used to having him around?"

Theadora gave me a sad smile. "Oh, Mirabel, you're worse than me. I was very guarded too. But I slowly allowed Declan in, and he's turned out to be the light of my life."

"But that's Declan. He's always been the reliable one." I recalled Declan holding down an injured cow while the vet tried to sedate the poor creature when my father had broken his arm.

"Ethan's crazy about you, Bel. Just go with the flow."

Warmth radiated out of every pore in my body.

"Why don't you let him buy you a home? For you and Cian. He showed me a gorgeous cottage. It's so lovely. He can afford it. It's actually at the end of the laneway. Why don't we go for a walk? I can show you."

After that conversation with Ethan, I'd finally accepted that my tiny, dark flat was not a good place to bring up a child. I decided against renovating and chose to move instead.

But him buying us a home?

I started to hate this trenchant independence that had become a heavy weight on my shoulders. Why couldn't I just say, "Yes, buy us the biggest, prettiest house you can find"?

My grandmother had drummed into me the importance of us women having our own money and control. That view was largely informed by my grandfather leaving when she was pregnant with my mother. She never trusted men after that and called them heartbreakers. My father wasn't like that, I'd always reminded her. She claimed he was simply that rare exception.

Perhaps my granny's persistent distrust towards men had seeped into my DNA. And now here I was, not only fighting with my heart but also knocking back money that Ethan could well afford to give our son a secure future.

Theadora gestured for me to follow her. "Come on, Bel. It's a nice day. What harm can it do to have a peek?"

I smiled. "I could use a walk."

"Mary's here." Theadora wore a guilty smile. "I've got a maid. Gives me time to teach. There's a school concert coming up. I have ten children performing Mozart."

"It's a great idea. I'm rubbish at domestics. I'm often lost in my music, reading, or going on cliff walks. There are so many other things that fill my day. I'd get help if I had the spare cash."

That was a guilty admission, given the hard time I gave Ethan after he suggested doing just that. At his expense, of course.

"It's fantastic." Theadora shrugged into a cardigan. "I'm not great either. I get caught up in what I'm doing. I love having a clean space, though. And she cooks too. I'm so lucky."

Her contagious smile swept me along.

Yes. That could be me.

We left Cian with Mary. A mother in her forties, she filled me with confidence, and this wasn't a first. Audrey had also done the odd spot of babysitting for me.

It was a lovely summery afternoon as we ambled along. The sun shimmered through wispy, golden-green branches. An addictive earthy scent seemed to rise from the ground, and the salty breeze slapped my skin with a healthy glow.

We arrived at a honey-colored cottage. The garden alone made me sigh as lavender, roses, and violets perfumed the air, while a heart-warming picture of me reading a book on the lace iron bench fired my imagination.

The house's façade made from local rocks must have been at least two hundred years old. Sunlight glistened on the red door, like some omen hinting at an enchanted cottage. I wanted to hide the For Sale sign so that no one else would buy it.

"How much is it?" I asked.

Theadora pulled out her phone and typed. A second later, it beeped back.

"Who are you texting?" I already knew the answer, but weakened by my love of that house, I remained in quiet suspense.

While we walked down that sleepy lane, Theadora's positivity had rubbed off on me. I'd decided to call Ethan and have him ravage me first, then we could come to some arrangement—like him fucking me senseless on a regular basis in return for us sharing our son. But I couldn't imagine going without Cian for two nights.

Maybe Ethan could stay with us for those two nights? My heart liked that idea. A lot. My head, however, was another story. A lobotomy maybe? I chuckled at myself.

"Why are you laughing?" Theadora asked.

"I'm just trying to talk myself into believing I can experience domestic bliss."

"But you can. From one woman who's married to a seriously handsome billionaire, let me say it's worth it. And Ethan's a good person."

"I know he is." I smiled. "I just keep confusing him with that sex-addict teenager he once was."

"Yep. I get it. I would have hated to have known Declan while he was getting around with lots of girls."

I loved Theadora. She was such a good friend.

"So, the price?" I asked.

Her stretched mouth told me it wasn't cheap. "One million pounds."

"Wow. It's not very big."

"But it is." She gave me her phone, and I stood under the giant peppercorn tree that graced the front garden.

The back extended into a large yard. The kitchen looked modern. The bathroom was cheery and spacious. And a staircase led to another floor hidden from the front view.

Just as I visualized Cian playing in a tree house in the back garden, an older woman greeted us. "Are you interested in my home?" she asked.

I nodded, despite the unaffordable price tag.

She stretched out her arm. "Come in. Let me show you around."

An uplifting aroma of baked sweets welcomed us in as we stepped into the living room. French doors opened onto a garden with a pond surrounded by blooms and sleepy trees, just like a Monet. I envisioned sitting there, sipping coffee.

A large open fireplace sat in the middle of the room that had retained its original etched detail, making the space warm and welcoming. Light flooded in from everywhere, and the view into the back garden made that room seem much larger.

The bedroom with its turquoise wall took my breath away, as did the bathroom that came with a checked floor, a pale-pink bathtub with clawed feet, and mid-tone pink walls giving it romantic appeal.

I floated off in love.

"Oh my god, Mirabel. You've got to buy it."

Theadora's gushing enthusiasm summed up how I felt.

"I haven't got that kind of money."

She stopped walking. "Then let me lend it to you."

My jaw dropped. "I couldn't. My flat would sell for about one-eighth of that."

"Then let me buy it as an investment. You can pay me rent. Only what you could afford, of course."

As we headed back, my head swam with all kinds of domestic fantasies. I saw Cian playing in the backyard. I saw him on the piano that I planned to get, with Theadora as his teacher.

When we arrived back at her house, Ethan met us at the door, looking like a sex god in jeans and a checked sports jacket. He held Cian in his arms.

I was tempted to snap that beautiful image on my phone. Ethan, with his dark hair tussled and those chiseled good looks, holding our equally handsome little boy, made for a stunning photo.

CHAPTER 32

Ethan

"I HEAR YOU BOUGHT a house," my mother said as we were finishing dinner.

"In Winchelsea Lane. Close to Declan's place."

Her eyes narrowed slightly. When I was a boy, I recalled her looking at me with that same suspicious look whenever we played with the neighbors' kids.

"Why not live in Merivale? There are so many rooms. It will be just me soon."

I held her stare. Was she telling me she'd discovered Will with Bethany and was about to boot him out?

I gazed over at Savanah, who shrugged.

"Savvie's still here most of the time. I plan to live with Mirabel and my son. You can barely string one civil line whenever you're in her company, so how could you expect her to live here?"

"It's different now that you've coupled."

Was that what we'd done? It still felt surreal.

Mirabel had finally agreed to let me buy the house, after conceding that a nurturing and airy environment for our son superseded her need to remain independent. She also hastily reminded me that she wasn't on the take, to which I just as quickly retorted that I'd bought the house for our son. We stared into each other's eyes in silence, then I let her push me against the wall and call the shots. By that, I mean her groping my arse and pushing her naked pussy onto my very willing dick. That had become our dynamic—her asserting her independence before fiery sex that left me speechless.

She'd often send me photos of Cian. I was at a board meeting when she sent an image of Cian in the bath looking so cute, I smiled like a proud dad. I kept scrolling, and there was Mirabel in a black lacy negligee, and I nearly dropped the phone. I had to adjust my pants. In many ways, especially while going through this ravenous period, I preferred us having our own space. Mirabel was a screamer.

As Bethany served the table, Savanah asked my mother. "Where's Will?"

"He's in London. He's got a sick uncle." My mother's cool tone made me wonder if something had happened or whether that was just her being her naturally reserved self.

"Are you going to marry Mirabel?" Savanah asked.

"Let's see how things go."

"Oh, darling." My mother shook her head, looking like she'd just run over a family pet. "How did you let this happen?"

I rolled my eyes. "It's life, Mother. Babies are born this way all the time."

"When are you moving?" Savanah asked.

"On the weekend."

"Mirabel strikes me as her own woman."

My sister got that right. "That's one of her best features." *Apart from being drop-dead gorgeous and irresistibly sexy.*

"I do admire an independent woman. But she's not one of us." My mother put down her cutlery. "Why not support her and be there for Cian, but also give yourself time to meet a woman that will one day be equal to all of this?"

"At least the carols will be sung in tune." My sister chuckled.

I laughed at that ridiculous image of us playing happy families at Christmas. "We've never sung carols before. That will be a first. But I'm willing. If only for Cian's sake. I want to give him a normal life."

"We're billionaires, darling. We're far from normal."

"I plan to start giving my son a normal and happy life. Don't you want to see happy grandchildren running around?"

"Of course." She tented her sharp fingernails and tapped them. "But I also expect some input into their education and diet."

I sucked back a breath. "Mirabel doesn't take kindly to being told what to do."

My mother rose from the table. "We'll see. What about a christening? Will you at least christen my grandchild?"

"Let me discuss that with Mirabel."

"We need a party. Merivale is kind of somber these days. Since Daddy..." Savanah's voice cracked. "I still miss him."

I put my arm around her. "So do I."

On that solemn note, my mother rose from her chair. "I've got some business to attend to. I got a call earlier. They've found my necklace."

This piqued my interest. "Where?"

"Someone was selling it online. I'm about to find out the name of the seller."

Both equally curious, we followed our mother into the library.

My mother opened the laptop on her leather-covered desk, and a few moments later, she went pale.

"What is it?" I asked.

She rose abruptly and pulled on the servants' cord. A few seconds later, Janet appeared.

"Yes, Mrs. Lovechilde?"

"Call Bethany. This minute." My mother's voice trembled.

I looked at Savanah, and her eyes widened.

I thumbed through a book on Venice, while Savanah sat down on the sofa, uncharacteristically quiet. My mother, meanwhile, stood at the window, staring out. The sky showed a storm brewing, just like the mood in that room.

Bethany slid in, and my mother turned sharply to face her. She pointed at the chair. "Sit."

My mother walked to the printer, removed a sheet, and returned to her desk, while Bethany remained blank-faced.

I slid my eyes over to Savanah, who flicked through the pages of a magazine that was upside down.

"Your daughter isn't terribly bright, is she?" my mother said.

Bethany shrugged.

My mother tapped the paper she was holding. "It seems she sold my ruby necklace. It's here. She didn't even change her name. Manon Swaye. The same name she signed for those casual shifts we were kind enough to give her." She paused for a response, but Bethany's silence spoke louder than words. "That might explain why I haven't seen her lately. I suppose she's busy spending the spoils of her crime."

"I'm not responsible for her actions," Bethany said.

My mother's brow furrowed. "She's your daughter. You brought her here. We gave her board and lodgings. We employed her."

"So?"

"I don't like your tone," my mother said. "I'm about to lay charges. That won't bode well for her future. Will it?"

Bethany leaned over my mother's desk. "Then you'll be laying charges on your granddaughter."

I swear I heard Savanah's neck crack as she whipped her head toward me. My mother, meanwhile, went pale. Although her mouth opened, she remained speechless.

CHAPTER 33

Mirabel

WE MOVED INTO OUR new home, and Cian, now five months, was crawling and threatening to destroy the pretty antiques and artifacts that Ethan kept bringing home daily.

Having just arrived home after a day in London, Ethan wrapped his arms around me, giving me one of his lingering, steamy kisses that always fired me up.

He'd practically moved in. He even had his clothes in the wardrobe. It was his house, after all.

I'd sent my inner nag packing. Life was too short for paranoia. Besides, expecting the worst from a situation only promoted an unhealthy heart. I loved my new life. I couldn't have asked for a better outcome.

As Ethan unclasped my bra, he said, "I've got to meet Declan and Savvie. Something dramatic has happened."

He rubbed my tits, and I instantly forgot what he'd said. This man was insatiable. He pulled down my yoga pants, and within a moment, his head was buried between my thighs.

"Hey, I haven't showered."

"Mm... nice."

"You're fucking sick." I pulled at his hair as he licked me to the point of madness.

In the adjoining room, our son played in his "little cage," as Ethan called it, with enough toys to fill a department store shelf. We had him on loudspeaker so that his cute babble echoed throughout the house like an avant-garde soundtrack.

I lowered my boyfriend's zip to release his huge, engorged cock and devoured it like a delicious confectionary.

"I need to be inside you," he rasped like we hadn't made love for ages, although we'd had sex that morning.

How long this insatiable period would last was anyone's guess, but for now, we couldn't stop touching each other. After Ethan fucked me senseless, I lay limply on my back, basking under a cascade of euphoria. Talk about drowning in a delirium of orgasms.

"Do you think Cian thinks my screechy orgasms are me being harmed?"

"Not sure. But I love the way you sound when you come."

He gazed back at me tenderly as I brushed his hair from his forehead, then we cuddled and kissed tenderly like we did each time. Fiery sex followed by gentle, sweet affection.

"This is a first for me," I admitted, enjoying his muscular arms wrapped around me. My head was nestled against his firm mounded chest. His feathery-soft strokes caused goose pimples on my skin.

"What is?" he asked.

"Just lying here with you showering me with affection."

He kissed my hair. "I've never felt like doing this before you."

Yes, we'd evolved. Ethan's genuine expression of affection and deep friendship had allowed me to open my heart.

I rose and grabbed a towel. Going to the fridge for some water, I finally asked, "So, what's the drama at Merivale?"

Ethan nodded as I handed him a bottle. "I have a niece, it would appear, who's responsible for stealing the ruby necklace."

"But wasn't that robbery months ago?"

"Yep. Before my new half-sister arrived. It's one of many mysteries surrounding our mother. Somehow the jewelry has ended up in her possession. And that's all we know at this stage."

Just as I was about to ask for more details, a knock at the door made me jump.

Ethan rose. "That's probably Dec now."

Declan entered and kissed me on the cheek before heading into the nursery to visit Cian. He picked him up, swirled him gently, then kissed him. That son of mine was going to be well and truly loved. That thought made my heart sing.

Once Declan had his cup of tea and settled down at the table, the brothers looked at each other and shook their heads, wearing the same stunned expression.

I had to ask, "Who's this half-sister?"

"Bethany." Ethan's sober response took me a moment to think of who he was talking about.

"The maid?" My brow crinkled. "The one who Declan spied kissing Will?"

They both nodded simultaneously.

"Holy shit." My jaw dropped. "Did you know your mum had another daughter?"

Declan exhaled. "No. We haven't gotten to the bottom of it yet. Mother's got a migraine and has refused to see anyone."

"Still?" Ethan asked.

"What about Will?" I asked.

"He's still in London," Declan responded.

Ethan turned to his brother. "Has he returned your call?"

Declan shook his head and then took a sip of his tea. "He's mysteriously disappeared."

"Shit. Just like that." Ethan bit his lip, looking lost in thought. "Do you think Will knew about Bethany all along?"

"Who knows? It's a question worth asking," Declan responded.

Ethan looked at me and smiled sadly. He laced his fingers through mine. The little gesture of affection made my soul smile. It was as if he were reminding me that he was there for me.

Declan paced our kitchen, pausing now and then to stare out the window, which looked out to an ancient elm. "They all look alike. How did we not see it?"

Ethan nodded. "Even though Bethany does bear a resemblance, it's Manon who's the spitting image. And now that I come to think about it, she even holds herself the same, and I noticed the same steely expression in her eyes as our mum."

Declan nodded reflectively. "I've noticed that too." He rubbed his face. "There are so many questions still."

"Do you think Dad knew?" I asked.

Declan shrugged. "Savvie asked that same question, but then Mum told us to leave. She wasn't up for any discussion. You know how she's always been evasive about her past?"

"Well, she's going to have to tell us. We have a right to know. And what's Bethany's story? I've never seen her smile. Ever."

I sniffed. "Then she's her mother's daughter."

"They are all very similar in personality for sure, even Manon," Declan said.

Ethan's eyes widened as though slapped by a sudden thought. "Shit. Crisp."

"What do you mean?" Declan frowned. His face always turned dark whenever that ginger-haired man came up in conversation.

"Crisp was all over Manon. Remember?"

Declan nodded. "How can I forget?"

"Mother needs to know, considering Manon's her granddaughter."

Declan paced our kitchen, wringing his hands. "Will revealed that Crisp had a connection with our mother when she was around Manon's age."

"You don't think Bethany's Crisp's daughter. Do you?" I asked suddenly.

Ethan's head nearly snapped off as he turned sharply to eyeball his brother.

Declan rubbed his neck, looking understandably frazzled. "Mum dated Crisp when she was eighteen. How old's Bethany?"

Ethan's jaw dropped. "Shit. She could be Crisp's daughter, and here he is hitting on his potential granddaughter." He grimaced.

Declan returned a pained smile. "Then we must tell him if that's the case. He obviously doesn't know. He can't be that twisted. Can he?"

"Who fucking knows with him. Maybe he's aware of the kinship and that explains his interest in Manon at the dinner. Maybe he wasn't hitting on her, after all," Ethan said.

Declan puffed. "From where I stood, it looked like he was sleazing onto her."

Silence prevailed, which offered a break from all this mind-boggling speculation.

CHAPTER 34

Ethan

OUR RELATIONSHIP WAS NOW official. I'd moved into our lovely new cottage, which was more like a large house. It felt easy and natural being there. Mirabel plucked away at her guitar and sang to our son, while I lounged back with a beer.

I'd been busy arranging my life so that money kept pouring in. Booked out all year, the spa had proved popular with the wearied rich, and I'd finally included a smaller version that was purely not-for-profit, servicing local women who needed pampering.

The hotel had now gone carbon neutral, and the low-cost housing development, my passion, not-for-profit, project, had been delivered with great results.

Wealth meant I could invest in projects that made a difference in people's lives. I had more to give. And with Mirabel cheering me on, I'd decided to pursue as many philanthropic ventures as possible to fit into my busy calendar.

I spent at least one night a week in London dealing with the hotel, and even that time away had me pining for my new family. I'd never been more certain of anything in my life. I wanted this.

Cian giggled as I pulled another silly face, and my heart grew each day.

I stared down at my watch. "I'm off to Merivale. This is it."

Mirabel placed down her guitar and notepad. She'd offered to work in another room, but I insisted she stay there in our favorite room with the windowed wall overlooking a garden I could never tire of looking at.

Had it been a drum kit, saxophone, or even a violin, I might have balked, but the soothing strains of acoustic guitar were far from offensive. And soon, a piano would arrive. When our son could walk, he would learn to play the piano, we'd both decided. Learning an instrument was good for brain development, and we had our own piano teacher in Theadora.

"The big showdown." Mirabel chuckled.

"You don't mind not coming?"

She stood up and stretched her arms. "Your mother's already struggling to open up. She doesn't need a stranger around."

I wrapped my arm around her waist and drew her in close. "You're not a stranger. You're part of my family now. You know that, don't you?" I kissed her tenderly.

Wearing her usual half smile, she nodded ever so slightly. It hadn't been easy to convince Mirabel that she was the only girl I'd ever loved. And yes, I *really did* love her.

All those lonely, frustrating months when she shut me out had shown me how much I loved her. I just hadn't uttered it. I'd never uttered it before.

That loaded word felt foreign. Maybe on a deeper level, I thought it might make her run. I sensed Mirabel also found *that* word difficult to say.

MY MOTHER SAT AT the head of the table in the recently painted pink room, situated in the west wing of the house. Considering the dark nature of this meeting, that cheerful space struck me as incongruous. In equally sharp contrast to that bright room was my mother's remote mood, which came as no surprise. And despite her impeccable appearance, she looked like she hadn't slept.

Savanah arrived at the same time as me. She'd met someone and had been spending more time in London. When she told me that, I must have shown concern because she quickly added he was nice and one of *us*. Not that such information gave me cause for optimism. I'd met lots of seriously rich dickheads in my time.

Declan began by asking, "Where's Will?"

My mother looked at all of us, one by one. "He's not coming back. We're annulling the marriage."

"Oh really?" I asked. "You've been together for a while now. He has some legal rights, I suppose."

She nodded. "As I've just been reminded by his lawyer."

"Will's already sent a legal rep?" Savanah's surprise matched my own, casting a shadow over a man I'd thought to be trustworthy and loyal.

"Tell us about our half-sister," Declan said, cutting to the chase. "And is she that?"

My mother rose from the large oval table and walked to the windowed doors that looked out to the shimmering pool. With a storm coming, the darkened sky itself seemed to droop as if weighed down by this sudden tension gripping our family.

She turned and scanned our faces before returning her attention downwards. Her hands trembled slightly. I'd never seen her so hesitant and downcast.

"I had a daughter when I was seventeen. That daughter is Bethany, and she's somehow tracked me down."

"Tracked you down? You sound like a criminal," Savanah said with a dark chuckle.

Ignoring Savanah's weak attempt at levity, my mother took a breath. "I was young. I wasn't ready to be a mother, so I had her adopted."

"You didn't look for her?" Declan asked tightly.

She shook her head. "I wanted to wash my hands of it, to be honest."

"Is Crisp the father?" I asked.

Savanah's eyes nearly popped out of her head. "Oh my god, Mum. He's the father?"

My mother's face distorted into a look of confusion as though she hadn't understood.

"Weren't you an item?" Savanah persisted.

My mother knitted her fingers and nodded ever so slightly. Once again, she couldn't look us in the eyes, like she was ashamed.

"If it's Crisp, you can tell us. He's hitting on Manon, you realize? That's potential incest," Savanah said.

My mother turned around abruptly. "What do you mean?" Her face lit up in alarm. I looked at Declan, noticing how pale he looked suddenly.

"He was spotted sleazing onto her. Apparently, Drake pushed him away, and Rey fell to the ground. It was quite the scene. Wish I was there." Savanah sniffed.

"So Crisp is the father?" Declan's impatient tone was justified.

"What?" It was like my mother had lost consciousness and had only just realized the question. She shook her head repeatedly. "He is *not* the father." She grimaced as though we'd suggested she'd had an affair with a devil. A very appropriate analogy, given Reynard Crisp was the subject.

"Then who's the father?" Declan asked.

"Was," she replied soberly. "He's dead, and hopefully rotting in hell." Her icy tone sent a chilly shiver through me.

Savanah's face crumpled into shock. "Did he force you?"

Wringing her hands, my mother nodded slowly as though admitting to a crime.

"Did you report him?" Declan's voice quivered.

"Out of respect to my foster mother, I didn't."

We turned to look at each other. Blood had drained from all of our faces.

"Foster mother?"

She went to the window again and turned her back to us, as though facing us was too painful.

"I never knew my real mother," she said. "At five, I was fostered out to the Lambs. They didn't have any children. My foster mother couldn't conceive."

"Is she still alive?" I asked.

She nodded. "I'm still in contact. She knows to stay away. She's well supported."

"Did she know what he did?" Declan's voice had a steely edge. I knew about Theadora's past. He even confided, after a few drinks, that he'd thought of arranging a hit on his wife's stepfather. Hair-raising admission as that was, I still sympathized. Had that happened to Mirabel, I wouldn't have hesitated to do just that. Sometimes crimes of passion, as the Italians called it, blurred the moral line.

"My foster mother knew." Looking haunted, she turned to face us again. "She begged me not to press charges. He was a weak man. But when he drank, he turned into a monster. At least he's dead." She took a deep breath. "After I discovered I was pregnant, I decided to have the child adopted rather than a termination." Her mouth hung as she tried to form words.

Seeing our normally stoic mother crack with emotion made my heart weep. I wanted to hold her. But instead, I remained a frozen lump, trying to process this devastating and tragic insight into her early life. I had this impatient need to know her full story. The real story that we'd been denied up to now. I wanted to understand minute details, like whether they were poor or middle class and what their home was like. All those kinds of trivial, but yet important, questions.

"My god, so you don't know anything about your real mother?" Savanah asked.

She shook her head. "Finding her became an obsession of mine, especially after I married and had the resources and necessary means to search for her."

"Your foster mother doesn't know who your real mother was?" Declan asked.

"No. My birth mother stipulated that she remain a secret. A secret that has imprisoned me all my life." Her voice trembled.

Savanah stood by our mother at the window and placed her arm around her. Welcome silence filled the room. Giving us time to digest and reflect on this heart-wrenching revelation.

I looked at Declan, who looked like I felt: wide-eyed and lost for words. In my case, I knew if I tried to speak, I might sob. My heart ached for my mother so badly, a clenching lump settled in my chest.

My mother returned to the table and sat down. "That's why I'm so protective of all of you." Her voice cracked again, and my eyes burned, pricking with emotion.

"How were you able to keep supporting yourself at that age? I mean you ran away after that, didn't you?" I asked.

She nodded. I could see the struggle of all those years in her eyes. "I worked as a waitress and managed to keep my studies alive. I got a scholarship, and when I met Reynard, he helped."

"So you *were* lovers?" Savanah asked.

She nodded. "For a while. I mean, I was very much besotted." Her mouth flickered into the makings of a shy smile. This was a new woman I was looking at. My normally tough mother had turned into a lost child. She played with her fingers. "He wasn't into long-term relationships. But he paid for me to go to Oxford."

"Considering everything you went through, that was so brilliant of you to finish your studies, Mummy. In flying colors too." Savanah spoke for me because, beneath this heavy blanket of deep pathos, a swelling of respect and pride grew for my mother. Many would have buckled under the weight of such horror, but she still managed to focus and move ahead in her life. For that alone, my mother deserved more than just respect. She deserved a fucking medal.

"Knowledge is power," my mother said with a flicker of a smile.

There was something to be admired of anyone who gets to realize their ambition while struggling to survive—a battle I'd never fought. It had all been too easy. Perhaps that was why I didn't respect the knowledge that had been offered at the time.

She continued to fiddle with her fingernails then added, "I met your father when I was nineteen and in my first year at Oxford. When I fell pregnant, he married me."

"So do you think Dad only married you because of your pregnancy, knowing that he was gay?"

Great question. I appreciated my sister's straight-to-the-point approach.

"No. We *did* love each other. He had a girlfriend before me." She hesitated for a moment.

"That's Alice. He told us about her," Savanah said.

My mother's frown deepened, and she turned pale. Declan sat up as I glanced over at him. Tense silence followed. There were still too many questions.

CHAPTER 35

Mirabel

ETHAN AND I WERE in Antibes, enjoying a three-day break. We'd left Cian at Merivale in the arms of his doting grandmother and a legion of staff. As I placed my son in her hands, she'd given me a faint smile, the warmest she'd ever been.

As someone who was also guarded, I recognized that choking trait well enough. As Sheridan often reminded me, early traumas tended to stalk us into adulthood and, when ignored, robbed us of happiness. I still had some work to do. Not that I'd suffered as badly as Caroline Lovechilde. But I'd had enough bad relationships to collect a few scars along the way. Thanks to Ethan and his sweet, loving ways, the armor I once wore now rattled in a box of useless memories.

For now, I just hoped Ethan's mother wouldn't turn into a monster-in-law. Ethan kept reassuring me that could never happen under his watch. I just had to go with the flow and not expect the worst. In any case, trying to control the future was tantamount to not leaving the house in case of an accident. Losing my parents when I was a teenager had probably shaped this, at times, paralyzing fear of the unexpected.

Ethan surprised me every day. He always came through the door bearing flowers, expensive wine, handmade chocolates, and toys for our son. He loved to spoil us, even though I didn't need anything but us there together.

He would sit and watch me practice, which was weird but nice. After spending a lot of time alone, I had to get used to that. We also couldn't take our hands off each other. All the time. Hot, hungry sex followed by tender, heart-swelling affection.

I hardly recognized this new light and boundless me. Not only had I found my soulmate, but I no longer felt the need to save the world. What a huge, unsolvable burden that proved to be. Like I was running a marathon without a finish line.

Hand in hand, we strolled along the shore. Despite joggers, dog walkers, excitable children splashing about, and people lounging back on canvas chairs, it felt like we were in our own little universe.

"This is like an advert for a dating site." I gazed at Ethan, the consummate sexy leading man in loose drawstring pants rolled up to his knees. His blue shirt was half undone and flapping in the breeze.

I wore a white summery dress that Ethan had paid a fortune for.

"We're just a happy couple on holiday." He stopped walking and stared into my eyes. "Have I told you how you grow more beautiful each day?"

I smiled. "Only just this morning when I was looking yuck, after our big night." My raised eyebrow referred to a risqué moment we'd shared at a ritzy restaurant.

"It was a great night. And memorable. A first." His eyes shone with sinful pleasure.

"Oh really? So you've never fingered anyone in public before?"

"Well, not at *that* restaurant."

I rolled my eyes.

He took my hand. "Hey, remember we promised to leave our past behind?"

"Yes. I guess. But you were the one that said it was your first. You started it." I made a circle in the sand with my toe.

He wrapped his arm around me and pressed his firm chest against my ear. "In any case, you're the one that went all commando on me. I couldn't resist. And this is the land of love."

I laughed at his French accent, sounding more like Inspector Clouseau than a man of style.

"And you should know, right?" I slanted my head and smirked.

"What did I just say?" He gave me his "I'm going to spank you" look, which fired me up. "Let's just accept that we were both equally wild."

I persisted, nevertheless. "But it was still a first?"

"Yes. It was." He picked up a shell and tossed it into the water.

"What? Fingering someone in a restaurant?" I wanted to know that we'd shared something fun and unique—and dangerous, recalling how I had to smile through an orgasm, instead of my normal shrill.

"A first in a Michelin-star restaurant." His lips curved into a smile, then he chuckled as I hit him on the arm.

"You're fucking wicked."

"And so are you."

Ethan was right: we needed to draw a line to our past.

We stood and looked out at the horizon. The afternoon was perfect—sunny with a light breeze. The rippling sea had gone a mood-lifting turquoise, and the air smelt of salt and oily food.

As we remained in quiet contemplation, he took my hand and squeezed it gently. I turned to face him, and he scratched his jaw while gazing into my eyes as though he had something important to say. He continued to stare at me without blinking.

I shook my head. "What?"

"Will you marry me?"

Now that, I hadn't expected. I took a moment to respond as I searched his face for hesitancy. He smiled shyly.

Hadn't I sworn off marriage? I'd also sworn off living with a man, and that was exactly what we'd been doing that past couple of months—effortlessly.

"You can think about it if you like," he said after a long gap had passed. He bit his lip and scratched his cheek, something he did when challenged.

"You don't have to, you know. We're doing well as we are. Aren't we?" I asked. My heart wanted to punch me in the nose for that wishy-washy response.

"You don't want it?" He squinted in the late-afternoon sun. With that dark tan, he reminded me of a hot Mediterranean hunk.

"You told me you didn't believe in marriage. Remember?"

"That was me, the irresponsible party boy."

I laughed. "And what's this latest you, then?"

He moved his head from side to side to stretch his neck. "I love being a father. I take that role seriously. I worry about him. I'm even missing him right now. As I miss you when I'm away in London."

Tears pricked my eyes. The earnest shine in his gaze mirrored my feelings about our son. "Me too."

He kissed me sweetly on the lips. "I just like being with you. I like hanging out with you."

"Oh? And that's all?"

He ran his hands up my thigh and under my skirt.

"Can I answer you later?" I asked.

"Sure. You're right, though. We are together. Aren't we?"

"I'm not going anywhere. A house in Antibes. Overlooking the ocean. I can't wait for Cian to come here."

"Is that all? Just all the nice things."

"No. I'd be hot for you if you were homeless, Ethan. It's nice to have these pretty things, but deep down inside, they are meaningless without this." I ran my hand over his lips and caressed his cheek lovingly. We locked eyes and smiled sweetly.

It was all getting too saccharine for me, and I ran my hands down his six-pack towards his dick. "And this. I love your dick."

"And I love your pussy." He ran his hands over my breasts. "And I love your tits." Then he looked into my eyes. "But your eyes are your best feature."

I smiled.

Yep, we were pretty loved up.

We walked back hand-in-hand.

"What's for dinner?" I asked.

"Mm... something starting with a sixty-nine."

I laughed. "You're a genitalphile."

Swinging my arm, he chuckled. "More like a pussyphile."

"Okay. I'll give you that."

"So does that mean you're a phallusphile?"

I stopped walking. "The answer is yes."

His head lurched back. "To being a dick lover?"

I giggled at how silly we'd become. It was what we always did, even as kids, play these stupid word games.

"That. But also, yes, to marrying you."

We exchanged a smile and kissed while massaged by a soft, undulating breeze.

CHAPTER 36

Ethan

DECLAN WAITED FOR ME in the lobby of Lovechilde Holdings. The last time we'd attended a board meeting was when our father was alive.

A woman in a power suit charged along, reading her phone, and I stepped aside to avoid a collision.

"This should be a fun affair," I said.

"You're telling me." He rubbed his neck. "I asked Will to meet us before the others were due."

"By 'others' you mean our mother and the solicitor? What about Savvie?"

"I believe she'll be here. I just wanted us to meet Will alone, without Savvie, who's likely to get all emotional."

"Can't say I blame her. I won't be giving him a chummy slap on the back."

Declan's tight smile faded. "I got a call from the police." He spoke quietly. The bare lobby with its hard surfaces acted as an echo chamber. "The last man to see our father alive has come forward."

We stepped out of the way of a team of executives lost in conversation.

"Why don't we step outside for a minute." He inclined his head towards the pavement.

As the rotating door shunted us outside, Will arrived with Bethany. I had to look twice. Dressed in a green fitted dress, she resembled a younger version of our mother, especially with her hair scooped up in a bun, and wearing the exact spiked heels our mother wore.

I shot Declan a quizzing look.

"What's she doing here?" Declan's frosty tone beat me to it.

I couldn't believe the cheek of my late father's apparently loyal partner.

"It's her business too. She's your half-sister," Will said. "And soon to be my wife."

An assertive, sharp edge replaced his usual quiet, understated tone. *Who is this man?*

Declan pointed at a small café. "Let's go there and talk."

Will frowned. "Aren't we meeting with Caroline in the board room?"

"They're not arriving for another hour. I wanted to see you first," Declan said.

Will regarded Bethany, who I imagined called the shots. Just like our mother. Only our mother wasn't evil.

Evil might have been too strong a word, but Bethany's obvious malice left me cold.

We settled down at a table and, after our drinks were delivered, I started the conversation by asking, "So you're to be married?"

Will poured a sachet of sugar into his tea, then slowly stirred his tea, taking his time to answer. The gap of time seemed to stretch while he sipped tea in his typical unhurried fashion before nodding with loving eyes at his bride-to-be.

"That was quick," Declan said. "Unless..." His eyes slid over to me, and my spine stiffened. Had they met before her employment at Merivale?

"We go back." Bethany's self-satisfied smirk was like that of a cat rolling on her back after devouring some endangered bird or two.

"How far back are we talking?" My arm tendons tightened.

"Fifteen years." Will didn't even blink as he took Bethany's hand.

He was clearly besotted. Whereas the only vibe I got from Bethany sat in the realm of sinister and conniving. I couldn't imagine her capable of loving anyone.

"You worked with our father for—what? Twenty years?" Declan asked.

He nodded. "I met Beth afterward."

"I found him." She twisted her red-painted lips, the same lipstick shade as our mother's.

"You can imagine my shock when I met her. I was staring at a younger version of your mother." He sniffed.

That chuckle went straight to my clenching fists, and I shot up from my chair. Declan pushed me down gently and gave me a subtle shake of his head.

Grappling with a sudden itch to knock out Will's recently whitened teeth, I had to suck back a breath.

"I tracked him down, and we connected." Bethany's unsatisfying abridged account unleashed a barrage of questions.

"Why did you track him down?" I already sensed the answer.

"Because I knew he was affiliated with your family." She tapped her long fingernails together, just like our mother. "When I discovered Will and *my* mother were conducting a clandestine affair, I decided to unleash my revenge by taking what was hers. I would have seduced your dad, but he was a raging poof, so I went for the next best thing."

I rose sharply. "Now look you. Don't speak disrespectfully of our father."

Declan touched my shoulder, and I sat down again, fuming.

"Continue." Despite his frosty tone, Declan remained calm and collected. Maybe the army had trained that into him, even when faced with scheming monsters like our half-sister and two-faced Will.

Bethany took Will's hand. "It helps that he's also easy on the eye."

I turned to him. "You knew of her plot to get back at our mother?"

"Not initially. I was just smitten." He smiled at Bethany.

"I convinced him. And look how well it's turned out." She paused to scan our faces. I'd decided to take Declan's lead and remain cold and detached.

"Now that my witch of a mother's broken-hearted, she might understand what it's like to be abandoned. Although she'll never know what being sent from one house to another—to fucked-up foster parents only after government handouts—was like. Not to mention pedophile scum parading as foster fathers." Her dark, haunted eyes slid from mine to Declan's. "Yep, you can look shocked. But I've had a fucking rough ride. Caroline turned her back on me. Didn't want to even fucking know me. So now I've come for what's rightfully mine."

"Money, you mean?" Declan asked, his voice shaky. There was this sudden recurring theme in our lives, recalling how our mother had suffered at the hands of an evil foster father.

"What else matters?" Her mouth curved into a dark smile.

"Well, love, for one. I can see that Will seems to be in love," Declan added.

She stroked Will's cheek. "He's been a nice surprise." Bethany's tenderness faded within a breath, and her face hardened again. "I would've done this even if he was ugly and decrepit. Just to get back at *her*."

The poisonous 'her' exited her lips like an evil spell.

After that climax, and that's how it felt because we'd finally arrived at the how and why, we sat in silence sipping tea, like a bunch of awkward people with nothing in common.

I gritted my teeth. Simmering anger now included a conflict of pity and sadness for Bethany. Finding good in her would be like rummaging through a dumpster for something of value.

"So now you're both to marry and file for a cut of the family fortune?" Declan stared down at his Rolex.

Will stirred in his seat. "It's not that black-and-white. I loved your mother, but she's too attached to Crisp."

"What do you mean by that?" Declan asked.

He shrugged. "That's something you need to ask her. Crisp has a hold on her. All of her."

Steering the conversation away from that loaded claim, despite curiosity bubbling over, I turned to Bethany. "What about Manon?"

I knew that my mother had refused to lay charges and even requested that the girl come to Merivale for a talk.

"Don't know. Don't care. Her grandmother seems to have taken an interest. I can't control the little bitch." A wicked smile tugged at one corner of her mouth. "From what I hear, Reynard Crisp's circling. She could do worse."

I felt so sick in the stomach that it came as a relief when Declan stood up and beckoned for us to leave.

We left that tearoom frozen, as though we'd visited the devil and his consort.

"Hell, she's fucking sick."

Declan nodded. "She's seriously damaged. Just like our mother. Only our mother married our father and has had a better life because of it."

I stopped walking. "Are you telling me you feel sorry for Bethany?"

His decisive shake of head released the sucked-back breath in my lungs. "No. But evil is not always born. A lack of love and abuse can turn a person into a monster."

"But wasn't being given life enough? Our mother could have terminated that pregnancy, considering the brutal way she'd conceived Bethany."

He released a jagged breath. I could see he'd been just as affected by this session as me. "It's not just nurture. There's always nature."

I frowned. "You mean that she's got some of her father in her?"

He shrugged. "Maybe."

"Bethany seems to show very little interest in Manon," I said.

"Our niece strikes me just as damaged."

"But she's young. Maybe with the right influences, she might change."

Declan nodded wistfully. "Let's see. We can only try to help."

The ride up to the boardroom had done little to get blood flowing. With rigid steps, I made my way into the large room with its view of sky-piercing spires and sun-refracting glass buildings, shining like cheap costume jewelry.

My mother sat next to the family solicitor at the large oval table, where, during happier times, we'd meet to discuss the hotel, money markets, and cryptic hedge fund investments.

A few moments after we'd settled into our seats, Will and Bethany arrived, arm in arm, and my mother averted her gaze to the floor as if she'd seen something offensive.

Savanah, who'd been staring down at her phone, looked up, and her face turned dark. "What the fuck is she doing here?"

"And hello to you, too, sis." Bethany faked a smile.

"I'm not your fucking sister."

"Language," my mother returned with a bite. "Let's just get on with it. Shall we?"

Declan's phone beeped. After reading the message, he rose. "I have to take this. One minute."

I gathered from Declan's perplexed expression that the call had something to do with the police, regarding our father's visitor. I'd been so buried in Will and Bethany's story, I'd almost forgotten about that.

Will's solicitor, who had just arrived, rattled off a whole lot of claims, finishing with "Two billion."

Savanah sprang up like she'd sat on a needle. "That's bullshit." She appealed to our mother. "You can't give him that much. He lied to you."

My mother ignored my sister's outburst and whispered something to our lawyer, who then gave Will's solicitor a faint nod.

"You can't be serious, Mummy," Savanah protested.

"I want this over and done with. Give them the money."

Declan, who'd just joined us again, touched Savanah's hand, and she sat down again. I got it. That was our mother's guilt money to Bethany.

A knock came at the door, and we all looked at each other. Declan rose soberly and opened the door to uniformed police.

Declan pointed at Will. "He's over there."

The policeman went to Will and uttered, "You're under arrest for the murder of Henry Winston Lovechilde. You have the right to remain silent..."

Bethany, who screamed as the police continued to read Will his rights, was handcuffed.

Bewildered, we all remained wide-eyed as though we'd been visited by aliens.

"I didn't do it. This is bullshit." Will looked at us all, face scrunched, pleading for help.

His lawyer rose and followed. "Don't say anything."

After they dragged Will out, Bethany, wearing a blood-freezing scowl, cast daggers at us.

The policeman returned. "You're to come with us."

She shrugged out of his hand. "You've got nothing on me, pig."

The incongruity of her parading as a woman of taste while spewing vitriol like someone from the rough side of town was severely jarring.

"Don't fucking touch me," she yelled.

The lines on my mother's forehead deepened. "Was she involved?"

The stern, middle-aged officer replied, "This is a police matter, madam."

As he dragged her off, she yelled, "You haven't seen the end of me."

The shrill in her voice penetrated my ribcage, turning my heart into a lump of ice.

After they left, we remained speechless. I stared out the window at a helicopter hovering above.

Declan broke the silence. "At least we now know."

"We know what exactly?" Savanah asked.

Great question.

I rose. "This calls for a drink. Any takers?"

Everyone, including our old solicitor, nodded.

CHAPTER 37

Mirabel

IT WAS THE DAY of my wedding. I'd agreed to have it at Merivale after Ethan virtually begged me. He needn't have, though. As a self-proclaimed aesthete, I was deeply taken by the breathtaking beauty of that estate. It was my soon-to-be mother-in-law who freaked me out.

Theadora reassured me she would be there by my side. I also had other supportive friends to help cushion me from Caroline Lovechilde's chilly vibe.

Ethan laughed at how I shivered at the mention of his mother. "Don't worry about her. A wedding is just what Merivale needs to cheer us all up."

From what I'd heard, Caroline wasn't exactly dressing in designer growing up. Ethan had filled me in on his mother's sad and tragic upbringing, which was why her cold-shoulder treatment towards me and others born below her, seemed even more unjust.

In any case, I was marrying Ethan and not his mother. I would just have to learn to tolerate her frostiness.

I woke up in Ethan's childhood bedroom with him spooning me. Cian was in the nursery, being cared for by Janet, who was to be his weekend nanny for our two-day party.

My breasts were sensitive from not just Ethan's constant fondling, but from expressing enough milk to feed Cian for a few days.

"Good morning, sweetheart. This is your last day as a Storm."

"Is that why you're marrying me? So that our son becomes a Lovechilde and not a Storm?"

He smiled sheepishly. "Partly." He stroked my cheek affectionately. "His mother's a nice bonus."

I pretend punched him, and he grimaced in exaggerated pain. We wrestled some more, and feeling his morning wood, I rubbed myself against him.

"Isn't there a rule about not fucking on the wedding day?" He wore a lazy smile.

"There's no rule that says I can't suck your dick, though."

His sleepy eyes came alive. "When you put it so eloquently, I guess not."

I tossed back the covers and took him in my mouth, enjoying how his dick grew rock hard and stretched my jaw.

I sucked, licked, and teased his veiny shaft with my tongue. His growing moans told me I'd found the right pleasure points, which weren't difficult. Ethan loved having his dick sucked, just as much as I loved having my clit ravaged.

I moved my mouth up and down his thick shaft, working up a pace until his veins popped and danced on my tongue. A tormented groan followed, and he shot deep into the back of my throat.

I licked my lips clean, and he fell on his back, breathing loudly before laughing. "What a nice way to wake up."

I glanced up at the elaborate brass clock on the mantle. It was eleven, which was normal for us. I'd discovered that Ethan also favored late nights. Just like me. My music flowed better at midnight. And Ethan liked to work on his many ventures or read a Lee Childs or John Le Carré novel. He loved to read—one of many traits that had surprised me about him. I'd often suspected he suffered from ADHD, but he admitted that was probably to do with his former cocaine use.

He stretched his arms and yawned. "Let's shower. That way, I can have a little appetizer."

Mm... An orgasm before the ceremony would help ease the sudden bout of nerves invading me.

I padded barefooted on those warm floorboards, which Ethan had also recently installed in our house. Billionaire luxury had an addictive quality about it.

After being devoured in the shower, and me nearly drawing blood from my lips as I tried to stifle a scream, I was ready for what was to be my special day—a day I never thought would happen. Not just with Ethan, but with anyone.

I'd arranged to meet Theadora and Sheridan at the Pond for a pampering session first. The late-afternoon ceremony was to be held in the front room with its mind-blowing domed ceiling fresco of the Three Graces, and quirky modern art that fought for space—an eclectic mix of old meeting new that worked miracles on the eye and was a perfect setting for my wedding.

Shopping for my wedding gown had been fun. I'd met Sheridan a few days earlier in London, where I'd gone on a spending splurge.

Despite her "you shouldn't" appeals, I not only bought Sheridan a gown for the wedding but also replaced half of her wardrobe. Bret didn't miss out either. I bought him all kinds of ugly clothing items related to his beloved football team.

"We're the ones that should be buying the gifts," Sheridan said as we bounced along Oxford Street.

When we popped into a vintage designer store, she said, "Why not buy new?" Sheridan stroked a floaty silk gown by Givenchy. "Wow, this is exquisite. Shit, and the price tag is what?"

"Vintage is not necessarily cheaper," I returned. "Savanah told me about this place. She's got style dripping off her, that girl."

"That's your sister-in-law?" Sheridan asked, eyeing a green Pierre Cardin shirt.

"Yep. She's very stylish in her wild ways."

"Aah, the rich, spoiled heiress." Sheridan smiled. "How exciting. Your life is fucking interesting."

I'd filled Sheridan in on all the happenings at Merivale, and she'd become a fan like someone reading a serial, hungry for the next installment.

"Even Bret's fascinated. He asked me about what happened with the father's ex-partner who's bedding the mother's long-lost daughter."

"I'll tell you all about it over a coffee. Let's just get my little dress first."

We walked around until I fell in love with a flouncy-hemmed 60s Chanel in pearl-shaded silk.

"That is stunning," Sheridan crooned.

I tried it on, and much to my delight, it was a perfect fit. Turning around to study my back, I stood before a mirror. "What do you think?"

Sheridan shook her head in wonder. "It's perfect. Like it was made for you."

I had to agree. Envisioning that lush red room, I saw myself in this gown fitting nicely.

"Are you wearing your hair up?" She moved her head from side to side to study me.

"Maybe. I'll see what the hair stylist suggests."

We'd found my ideal dress, and I was floating on cloud nine.

Chapter 38

Ethan

My mother entered my room and adjusted my tie. That gesture, although small, was her way of supporting my decision to wed outside her wealthy clique. We'd all noticed the change in her. Since she had unveiled her past, she'd become softer, more caring.

"You look handsome." She watched me in the mirror.

"Thanks, Mum." I smiled.

When Janet walked in with Cian, my mother looked at her grandson, and her eyes lit up.

"He's an angel," Janet said.

I took my son from her hands and cradled him while warbling something ridiculous, which always brought a heart-swelling smile to his little face.

"Thanks so much for doing this. If you're looking for a new job"—I smirked at my mother—"we're on the hunt for a live-in nanny."

"Janet's going nowhere." My mother looked warmly at her oldest staff member and gave her a subtle wink. She turned to me and opened her arms. "Here, let me hold him."

Janet left us, and my mother rocked Cian in her arms.

"You will make an effort to be nice to Mirabel, I hope."

She stared at her grandson and smiled. "You're doing the right thing. This darling child needs his mother and father. I would have preferred someone from our circle, as you know." She glanced up at me. "However, I believe a child needs its blood parents."

As she cuddled my son, I sensed the pain of her abusive childhood. Now that I knew about her upbringing, I was finally able to understand those remote looks she wore at times. I wanted to reach out and hug her, but I knew she wouldn't want me to see her weakness. Despite the pinching in my heart, I smiled tightly and kept my distance.

Gradually, we would learn to show physical affection. As her children, we'd already forgiven our mother for her tough attitude toward our choices. At times, they were justified, especially in Savanah's case. But this outdated prejudice of people unlike us had grown stale.

"You will treat Mirabel as family, I hope," I reiterated. "It's not just for Cian's sake, but also for his future brothers and sisters."

"His brothers and sisters?" Her eyebrows rose.

"I'm planning on a big family. Are you ready for that?"

She nodded slowly, and her smile grew. With Cian in her arms, she leaned in and kissed me. "I'm happy for you, Ethan. Mirabel's a healthy woman. She's strong. She'll make a good mother, I believe." A line appeared between her eyes. "Is she still creating music?"

"And what if she is? Theadora's become a music teacher."

"Well, there's no need, is there? You're a billionaire in your own right."

"So?" I splayed my palms. "Art's not about money."

"No. I suppose it isn't." She was about to leave with Cian.

"Where are you taking him?"

"We're off to the courtyard for lunch." She spoke in a baby voice, and my heart expanded for both grandmother and child.

I kissed my mother and son goodbye then went back to getting ready for the biggest day of my life. I loved our celebrating it at Merivale because this was where my soul lived.

I even saw us living there one day. It was a huge estate. I loved our new home, but Merivale was where I wanted to raise my children.

A pang of regret that the farms had moved away nipped at my nostalgic muscle. Declan had been right to oppose Elysium, which had become a thriving hub of wealth and glamour. The odd designer-clad guest occasionally joined my mother at Merivale for a drink, which made me wonder if this was her way of having her wealthy cohort milling around her. She was still that ambitious woman, after all.

Declan knocked and entered. He hugged me. "You're doing the right thing."

I frowned. "Why does everyone keep saying that? Savanah said the same thing earlier."

He smirked. "You were always the bad boy of the lot."

"I wasn't *that* bad. I recall you having your wild times too."

"Before the army, I had my moments." He played with a trophy on my shelf of boyhood mementos. "I've never been happier. Marriage is great with the right woman. My love for Theadora grows each day."

"Now you're going all soppy on me." I laughed.

He grinned. "Mirabel's great. She's already like family. She's from here. One of us."

"She is. Mother wouldn't see it that way. But she was just here and, much to my delight, gave me her blessing."

He shook his head in wonder. "She never gave us her blessing."

"But she's grown fond of Theadora, hasn't she? I've noticed that little by little. Like the time they played two-handed piano on your birthday. And they seem to chat about music a lot."

"That's true. Mother's slowly coming around, which makes things more comfortable for Theadora. That's what matters to me." He picked up my football signed by David Beckham and tossed it from hand to hand.

"So did you read the statement?" I asked about Will's arrest.

He nodded solemnly. It wasn't a great subject for my wedding day, but I was way too curious to wait.

"Do you wish to discuss this now, or later, with Savvie present? She doesn't know yet either."

"Now, for God's sake. I'm dying to know. It's been eating away at me." I paused at the window. It was a sunny day. A good omen for a wedding.

"So this is what Colin, the professional…" He dragged his hands over his face. Like me, Declan hated discussing our father's private life. "He was one of Father's regulars who made the full confession."

"So this prostitute strangled our father?" I grimaced.

He shook his head. "This is the story so far. I mean, Will's still denying parts of it. But it seems two billion dollars, which was transferred that same night, the police tech unit discovered, was the major motive for the crime."

"Will got that cash? And he still wanted more from the family?"

Declan flipped the ball in the air. "Once the private account where the funds were transferred is located, he'll no longer have it, I hope. That's the problem—it came from a hidden Swiss account, and Will, who's denying having the money, has obviously managed to hide it."

I nodded. "Okay. So Will killed Father?"

"Not according to Will. There was one other involved. Will recruited Colin and this mysterious assailant, who was employed to hack our father's Swiss account. Both Will and Colin suggested that this hacker must have murdered our father."

"Was Will there?" I asked.

"Apparently not. Will knew of Colin's professional arrangement with our father and that Colin was in debt to his eyeballs. So he offered him two million pounds to be part of this elaborate plot to rob our father. Colin's conscience got the better of him, and during a night of heavy drinking, he told a stranger at a bar what he'd done. That person then immediately informed the police. Now, Will's behind bars for the manslaughter of our father."

"Only manslaughter?" I asked.

He shrugged. "They're yet to find this mysterious second person. Will is the mastermind of a crime that resulted in our father's death."

"Then he's a murderer."

"There's no DNA linking him to the crime scene. And all records with the professional hit man have been scrubbed."

"But he arranged the hit."

"According to Will, that was never the plan. This hacker was meant to get into the computer while our father slept. But he needed our father's thumbprint. That's where the drug came into it."

I nodded slowly.

"Colin was instructed to drug our father. Will must have known of our dad's prescription, or it could have just been a fluke that he drugged him with Rohypnol."

He paused for a breath. "Anyway, Colin treated it like a normal visit—hence the sex—then drugged him and left the door unlatched. From there, entered the assailant. If it had gone to plan, our father would have woken to discover he'd been hacked. Being a hidden account, he couldn't have done anything about it. That was the wisdom. However, Father must have woken while having his thumbprint taken and struggled with the assailant, and well, you know the rest. The transaction still took place after that."

I scratched my jaw. "But wouldn't there be CCTV footage of the hacker?"

"The cameras in the hallway and at the entrance were turned off at that time."

"Then the cops should be able to find this hacker-stroke-murderer via Will's computer."

"Like the police already suspected, he's not going to be easy to find. According to Will, he never met the hacker in person. The job was arranged via the dark web."

I shook my head. "Shit. What's Bethany's part in this?"

"They have her communicating with Will. She didn't cover her tracks, and via phone records, they were able to learn about the plot. In parts."

"So she'll be charged with conspiring?" I asked.

He nodded slowly. "Probably."

He rose. "Enough for now. It's your wedding day. Let's not talk about this again until another time when hopefully more will come to light."

"I'm not sure I like the idea of Manon being here."

"I just ran into her. She was bossing Janet around. She's moved in."

"You're kidding. I didn't know that. That means she'll be at my wedding."

"She's our niece," Declan said.

I added some product to my hair and combed it up high. "Why do you think Mother's asked her to stay?"

"Maybe out of guilt. Or because she recognizes something familiar in Manon. They are identical in features."

I sighed. "We're in for an interesting time. Again. Never a dull moment here at Merivale."

"No." He patted me on the arm. "See you out there. Theadora's performing your wedding march."

"Can't wait." We hugged.

MIRABEL LOOKED LIKE A goddess as she walked, or I should say floated gracefully towards me in a gown that complimented her sexy curves. I smiled like a man about to sail off on a journey that promised endless possibilities, which included a healthy, happy life with a ton of giggling children playing at my feet, and a beautiful, creative woman to hold, make love to, and share my life with.

Cian had brought so much joy into my life that I loved the idea of more children. Mirabel seemed quite happy with that idea too. We were both on the same page about many things—something I could never have predicted at the start of this on-and-off relationship.

Alex stood by my side, sporting the same bewildered grin he'd walked in with. He hadn't quite come to terms with me getting hitched. As the last of us wild party boys, he had yet to settle down. I supposed it was kind of ironic that I'd asked this self-proclaimed libertine to be my best man.

On piano, Theadora performed Satie in all its languid beauty. An ideal choice for that romantic red room that had seen its fair share of celebrations.

"*And the moonbeams kiss the sea.*" One of a few graceful lines from a Shelley poem was recited by the female celebrant.

Mirabel whispered. "That is so beautiful. And you chose it?" She looked stunned—a common expression for her, when, on those odd occasions, I showed remnants of my expensive education.

Her lips tasted like honey as we kissed, amid cheering guests. Theadora then switched from classical to twentieth-century pop with a rendition of "All You Need is Love" by the Beatles.

I left my stunning new wife with her girlfriends, purring over the emerald ring I'd given her—something I'd chosen from the family collection because the green jewel reminded me of her eyes.

I headed over to greet the many guests, which included Kelvin and Jarrad, the hobby farmers who had their property next to Elysium. I'd insisted on inviting the farmers that both Mirabel and I'd grown up with. They stood out with their ill-fitting suits, but I loved them being there.

"You're looking gorgeous," Kelvin said. "Love the suit. This cream satin-embossed waistcoat is simply stunning. Let me guess—Savile Row?"

I had to smile at the local farmer, who planted lettuces dressed like he was heading off to a London club.

"Yes. I was fitted by the Westmancott himself." I touched the fabric of my blue-grey silk suit.

"Oh my. It fits you like a glove," Kelvin purred.

"Talking of designer, Elysium is turning out to be quite the place to be," Jarrad said.

"I haven't had time to visit since the opening. I hope it's not too noisy."

"There's the golf course between us. The only annoying thing is the occasional flying ball. But there's another wing being built, we've noticed. A casino, I believe." He looked concerned.

"You'll have to talk to my mother. I haven't heard of any talk of a casino."

He leaned in and whispered conspiratorially, "I've heard that Reynard Crisp is behind it."

My brow pinched. "That's news to me."

Kelvin nodded solemnly. "You can imagine it will bring all sorts of happenings late into the night."

"I'll have to talk to my mother."

I left them with a strange feeling in my gut. The last thing any of us wanted was a casino at Merivale's doorstep.

Savanah kissed me. "That was such a sweet service. And Mirabel looks stunning. Like one of our own in that vintage Chanel."

"She is one of our own. We all grew up together."

"Say, who's that guy circling Mummy?"

"That's Mirabel's producer, Orson."

"Oh, that's the guy?" Savanah frowned. "And you're okay with her inviting him?"

I shrugged. "I'm not a complete stranger to some of the girls here."

Savanah laughed. "That's right—you had a thing for farmers' daughters. They're all here. It's quite a turnout. When's the band arriving?"

I glanced at my watch. "At eight. Dinner first. A string quartet. All nice and quaint, and then the party."

"Should be a hoot. I would have preferred a DJ, though."

I waved at an old friend who'd caught my eye. "I'm told the band covers all the favorite dance tunes."

Savanah kept gawking at Orson. Wearing an outlandish burgundy suit, he looked like he'd fallen out of a 70s *Rolling Stones* article.

"Hey, he's flirting with her, I think. And Mummy's smiling. I think she likes him. He is kinda hot in that sexy-daddy kinda way."

I shook my head. My sister and her labels. "Well, at least he wasn't Cian's daddy. That's what counts."

"But it would be too weird if he hooked up with Mother, wouldn't it?"

"They're only chatting, Sav."

"Mm... but he's got stars in his eyes."

"Our mother's a stunning woman."

"She's also filthy rich and very single," Savanah said.

We glanced over, and some younger men, who'd obviously heard about our mother's newfound solo status, hovered about her.

"And the wolves are circling." Savanah chuckled.

"More like pups," I added.

"She's the veritable cougar. But Orson looks around her age."

"Mm..." I didn't like the idea of him flirting with my mother, knowing that he normally went for girls half his age.

Savanah tipped her head towards Manon. "She seems to have settled in."

Manon wore a short, tight little number more suited to clubbing than a wedding.

"Mummy let her keep the money. I thought that was wrong."

"Why am I getting the feeling you're being all territorial all of a sudden?"

"I'm not," Savanah appealed. "It's just weird that she's let her into our inner sanctum so easily."

"At least, Mum didn't invite Crisp," I said.

"He'll be back for his prize, I bet."

"You really think Mother would sit back and allow him to seduce her granddaughter?"

Savanah shrugged. "Maybe not."

Declan joined us with Theadora.

"Hey, you look like you're about to pop," Savanah said to Theadora.

"Any day now." She smiled looking lovingly at our brother.

"Thank you for playing. It sounded fantastic," I said.

She leaned in and kissed my cheek. "Congrats. Mirabel looks gorgeous."

"Doesn't she?" Savanah said.

"Where's this new boy of yours?" Declan asked our sister.

"There he is." She waved at her new boyfriend, who was skinnier than her usual muscle guy.

"Another tosser?" My brother uttered under his breath.

"I heard that," Savanah said. "He's from the peerage, I'll have you know. He's Lord Featherby's son."

"He's got a loud dress style. A little like Orson," I said, regarding the embossed off-white suit that reminded me of furniture covering.

"Ollie's got an interesting approach to his wardrobe. That happens to be Versace," Savanah said.

Her new boyfriend joined us, and my sister introduced him to us.

"So Ollie's short for?" I asked my sister's new boyfriend, who seemed to bounce on the spot. I could only assume he'd sniffed a line or two.

"Olivier. My parents named me after some famous actor."

"Laurence Olivier, you mean?" Declan asked.

"I think so." He looked at Savanah and pulled a smirk.

I glanced at Declan, who remained cool. Yep, our sister had attracted another tosser.

I went to find my beautiful wife and spied her chatting with some of the farmers we'd grown up with.

John Newman patted me on the arm. "I always knew you two had a thing."

I looked at Mirabel and smiled. I wasn't going to deny that I'd always found my new wife hot and desirable.

"How's the new house going?" I asked him.

"Marvellous. The missus couldn't be happier. We've got a new grandchild, and it's a lovely bright house. Such an improvement. The farm's doing well. We're now producing organic dairy products. And we are making a killing, thanks to you. I might have resisted, but, boy, that change has done us the world of good."

"Change can be a great thing." I smiled.

I pardoned myself and led Mirabel to a quiet corner. "Are you having a good time, Wife?"

"Yes, Husband, it's a hoot."

I ran my hand over her silk-covered hip. "This is beautiful. You are beautiful."

She stroked my lapel. "And you in a tux look good enough to eat."

"Mm... I am feeling a little hungry myself." I hooked my arm. "Can I accompany you to dinner, madam?"

Arm in arm, we went to join the guests in the ballroom, smiling and giggling at anything and everything.

EPILOGUE

Savanah

FROM A DISTANCE, MY friend Jacinta looked bored as a guy with a paunch hanging over his pants chatted her up.

"Hey there." I kissed her on the cheek before giving the man an "off you go" flick of the hand.

Jacinta giggled. "How do you that?"

"I just tell them to piss off."

She laughed. "They might take offense at that."

"Nuh. They love it." I chuckled.

Thumping with loud music, the trendy Soho bar was normally fun after a few drinks, but I wasn't in the mood. "Hey, do you mind if we go somewhere not so loud?"

Jacinta gulped her white wine, rose from her stool, and smoothed down her bodycon dress. "Show the way."

She linked her arm in mine, and we stepped onto the pavement. It was nine o'clock, and the street smelled of cologne, car fumes, and greasy fast food.

As we dodged groups of strutting revelers coming from every direction, she asked, "Where to?"

I wasn't in the mood to dance or flirt or anything too social. I just needed a chat.

"How about there?" I pointed at a small, dimly lit bar called the Red Place. "I've been there before. It's a little eccentric, and mainly gay from memory, which suits my mood. Do you mind?"

She shook her head.

We walked into the red-walled bar crammed with black-and-white images of Paris and famous people. A sign advertising Friday night poetry made me pause.

"What night is it?"

"Thursday." Jacinta frowned. "You really are off with the fairies."

I exhaled. "Yep. I'm having one of those weeks."

We settled for a small table with a flickering candle in a leadlight jar. The waiter sashayed over, and against the sound of ethereal lounge music, we made our orders.

"What's up, Savvie?" Jacinta's blue eyes shone with sympathy. Her dependable and unwavering support made her the go-to girlfriend for that deep and meaningful talk.

"Oh, you know, another quarter-life crisis."

"Let me guess, you've given Olivier the flick." She ran her hands down her blonde hair so that it remained a smooth sheet. Jacinta went out of her way to maintain an impeccable appearance. She was like a walking cosmetic counter, always up on the latest products, promising to pump her lips, make her lashes longer, and remove wrinkles that hadn't even started to show on her porcelain-smooth face.

She was that girl who sprang out of bed while her lover slept so he would wake to see her perfectly made-up.

Having grown up with me, Jacinta was that sister I never had. Her parents owned a chain of high-tech franchises and were super rich. We'd shared our first cigarette and even lost our virginity on the same night to a couple boys we met at Glastonbury festival, in a droopy tent of all places. We often laughed about the experience whenever we visited our wild teenage years.

It wasn't just wild adolescent fun we'd shared. Like me, Jacinta changed her boys as often as our hairstyles, which was often, given our restless need to experiment with hair colors and new looks. Due to this colorful sex life, we had plenty to share when we met up for drinks, which was every few days. In between, we would chat on the phone.

Sienna was another close friend, but we'd lost her for now. She'd fallen for a guy she'd met in Morocco.

That was what we did. We would fall for someone, disappear for a few weeks or so, and return either laughing or crying.

And now my body and soul screamed for change. But I had this alarming inability to focus on anything long enough to finish it. I couldn't even finish a book. At college, I would pay brainy students for essays on books we were meant to study. My friends couldn't believe that I never made it past chapter three of *Fifty Shades of Grey*. That was the longest I'd stayed on any book, so it was a compliment to the author. My doctor had diagnosed me with ADHD.

"I'm still seeing Ollie." My dull tone reflected the numbness in my body, mind, and spirit. I might have appeared shallow, but something deep inside me was knocking at the door trying to bust me apart.

"You're bored with him, aren't you?" She inclined her head. "I know you, babes, you're normally bouncy and cheery when you're with a new guy."

"You've met him." I thanked the waiter as he popped down our drinks along with a bowl of crisps. "I need friction."

A slow smile grew on her puffy lips. "Mm... I know what you mean. Like eight inches of it."

"I'm not getting that." I frowned.

She looked horrified. "He's got a small willy?"

"Average size." I sipped wine to chase down the salt.

"You know what they say—size doesn't matter. It's how they use it." Her heavily drawn-on eyebrow arched.

"Yeah, well..." I played with my glass. "He's not that good in bed. He's that get-on-top-and-hump-and-pump guy. A few minutes later, it's over."

She pulled a face like I'd described an unpleasant dental procedure. "You need to give him the flick."

"I should try to stay on. He's going to be a lord one day. That would make Mother happy. Ethan and Declan have let her down. The pressure's on me to deliver some blue blood."

"Boring," she sang, taking a handful of crisps.

Jacinta was a romantic, like me. She believed that nothing other than hot sex and romantic love would induce her to utter "I do."

"Savvie, this is so not you. Can you hear yourself? You're hooking up with a guy only because of his pedigree." She studied me closely. "Does he at least make you come?"

"Nope. I end up having to finish myself, while he's snoring, mind you."

She winced. "Oh, that sounds terrible. And you want to marry this guy?"

"I just can't trust myself." I huffed in frustration. "The guys that make me hot and bothered are generally the poor ones. You know, bad boys. What the fuck's wrong with me? Even now, whenever I see an inked guy standing on the corner, probably doing a deal, I want to jump him."

She giggled. Jacinta, by her own admission, extracted much entertainment from the stories of the boys I'd hooked up with.

"There's something sexy about men who work hard."

"Work hard? Mm... like selling drugs."

"Have you heard from Dusty?"

"Nope. He's locked up. And look, he was hot in bed, but I've got to clean up my act. I'm the daughter of a billionaire, for fuck's sake. I need to get my shit together. Marry and then run Elysium."

"My parents stayed there a week ago. They loved it. The rock-pool spa was a highlight for my mother. And Dad hasn't stopped raving about the golf course and its ocean views. Mother got to ride horses. It's such a good idea for the London elite."

"They're coming from everywhere. We're getting a lot of Americans."

"It's summer. That makes sense. What about winter and those cutting winds?"

"It will slow down, I guess, but there's still lots of interest. And there's to be a casino, I'm told. That will bring people all year around."

"I know." Her blue eyes sparked as though she'd solved a complicated puzzle. "Marry Olivier and get yourself a lover."

"Mm... That sounds complicated and messy." I crunched on a crisp.

"Complicated and messy is far from boring." Her eyebrows waggled.

"For someone watching from the sidelines like you, maybe." I sniffed. "Maybe I need to take hormones that make me less horny around muscly bad boys. I mean, just saying that is making me all hot and bothered."

Jacinta laughed. "Hey, muscly, inked guys are fucking hot."

A man passing our table turned and nodded with that "Oh yeah" expression on his face.

I looked at Jacinta and giggled.

"Then just wait," she continued. "Maybe try Tinder again."

"Oh god no. That's so not me now. I'm about to turn twenty-nine."

"You're wanting children?" Jacinta looked shocked.

I fiddled with a coaster. "I'm not that clucky, to be honest. Although Theadora's just given birth to a beautiful boy. And there's my nephew Cian, who's so cute, I could eat him."

She giggled into her glass. "Just keep dating. I know—let's go to Paris for Fashion Week."

"I guess." I sighed. Perhaps I needed to see a counselor again. My mood was so low. "Most of the men there are gay. The last time, I ended up with that sexy coke dealer we met on Champs Elysees. Remember that?" I puffed. "I'll just keep seeing Olivier for now. Maybe I can teach him to go down on me or something."

"Good luck. It's not something you can force a guy. He either likes doing it or not."

"Don't I know it." I sighed. "Dusty couldn't enough of it. He was a pussy juice addict."

She laughed loudly. "That's hilarious. Really?"

I nodded with a wistful smile, recalling Dusty getting on his knees and licking me dry. "They were his words. I went from lots of orgasms to fucking nothing. As you know, I've never come with a dick before." I stared down at my fingernails painted like a Kandinsky, thanks to the excellent nail artist at the Pond.

She nodded sympathetically. "Only one person has made me come with his dick, and he broke my fucking heart."

I patted her hand. "Well, you did fall for the college Casanova."

"That's why. Hudson was a fucking god in bed."

"Better to have experienced it than not. Hey?" I inclined my head.

"I guess. But he set a huge benchmark."

"*Huge* being the operative word, hey?"

We laughed, and I felt better. A drink and having a heart-to-heart with my bestie worked wonders for my mood.

"Is there anything you like about Olivier?"

"He's one of us. We share similar stories and experiences about growing up with super rich parents."

Jacinta clicked her fingernails on her glass. "Andy's great in bed, but I could never marry him. We have absolutely nothing in common."

"But that's the thing. The ones that make us all breathless and steamy are shit to talk to, and the one's that we relate to are boring fucks."

She shrugged. "Then wait."

My phone beeped, and it was Ollie. *Where are you? Can we catch up? Like tonight?*

I released a breath. "It's him. He wants to catch up."

Jacinta's mouth turned down. "I thought we were clubbing?"

I could use a good workout, and dance clubs beat boring gyms. I wrote. *I'm out with Jacinta. Lunch tomorrow?*

He wrote back. *Sure. I'll hit the strip clubs with my mates then.*

That didn't even tweak a muscle. *Have fun. Don't drink too much.*

I finished my drink, dropped a bill on the plate, and rose. "Come on, then, let's work off some calories."

Jacinta followed me out the door. "Let's go to that place where the sexy daddies hang out."

I laughed and linked my arm to hers as we sashayed along that busy strip.

CARSON

I FLICKED THROUGH MY statements looking for a hint of good news. The security agency had gone under, and now I faced bankruptcy.

Angus stuck his head in the fridge. "There's nothin' here."

I rubbed my head. "I haven't had time to shop."

"Let's get pizza, then," he said, bouncing on the spot. My brother had never been able to sit still. How he'd lasted in that cell for three days was a miracle.

After using everything I had to bail him out, I'd started moonlighting as a bouncer.

"Are you paying?" I asked, knowing the answer. Every spare penny my brother got went either up his arm or his nose.

He scratched his arm filled with track marks from twelve years of drug abuse that had started at sixteen.

Angus opened the cupboard, where a lonely packet of crackers and can of soup stared back at him. "Shit, man, there's nothing here."

"I used up everything to get you out. My company's folded."

Responding with an unfazed grunt, he shot me a "nothing I can do about that" look. He picked up his keys and a pouch of tobacco from the table.

"Where are you going?" I asked.

"Just going to hang with some of the guys. They'll have some food."

I puffed. "You're on bail, Angus. If you're caught even puffing on a joint, you'll go back in."

Staring at me blank-faced, he went to move, then I grabbed his arm. "I fucking mean it."

He shrugged out of my clutch. "Leave me alone. I know how to look after myself."

Having to work, I couldn't exactly put a ball and chain around my younger brother's ankle. I'd promised our mum I would care for him, but Angus was beyond help, and now he'd dragged me down with him.

He would shoot up again for sure. At twenty-eight, Angus wasn't doing anything to help himself.

Our mother died when he was twelve. I was sixteen and could fend for myself, but my brother ended up in foster care with some nasty people who had him stealing, taking drugs, and doing errands by the time he was fifteen.

Now I was back to square one. I'd used up all my savings. The agency had folded, and I was about to return to Bridesmere and resume working at the boot camp for Declan. At least I had that to fall on, and the pay was generous. But I couldn't exactly take Angus with me. He would rob everyone and cause no end of issues.

I headed out and jumped into my car—an SUV Declan had kindly let me keep. It was a fuel guzzler, though. I would have preferred something small and easy to park, especially in the city.

Tapping the steering wheel and humming to John Mayall, I drove along the crowded streets of party-central Soho. Girls in skirts within an inch of their arse wobbled along in dangerously high heels, while boys sniffed around in packs.

Like it or not, without this rabble of fun seekers, I wouldn't have a job.

When did I decide to become everyone's strict father? That was how it felt some nights—me having to knock sense into hormone-drunk teenagers and young adults. They weren't always young either. The worst was the male packs in expensive suits hovering about gentlemen's clubs. They couldn't fight their way out of paper bags, despite their egos telling them otherwise.

I parked my car at the back of the dance club. As I jumped out, a heavy bass beat hit my ears, which wasn't my idea of a great night out. I was more a blues man myself, music from the deep south of America.

As I walked through the alleyway leading to the entrance, a mob of males in expensive sportswear and gold chains loitered in the shadows, peddling chemicals cooked up in some makeshift lab. Judging by the well-dressed girls and boys hovering about, I imagined the dealers were about to cash in.

I hated drugs. Never touched the stuff. I'd seen what it had done to Angus. And as a bouncer working at clubs, I'd also seen my share of overdoses and girls being carried off by some fuck-now, regret-later guy. But my job wasn't to stop that, even though I'd done that on occasion. My job was to block packs of hungry males from entering the popular dance club. Because of that, there was the odd skirmish or two, which, after Afghanistan, was like dealing with a bunch of toddlers chucking tantrums.

"Sam." I waved.

My colleague nodded. "Hey, Carson. How's it?"

I shrugged. "You know, another boring night arguing with drunken dickheads. Life could be better."

He laughed.

That pretty much described our night. Either me or Sam lifting the odd idiot by the scruff of his neck and pushing him away—gently. One had to be careful in this game. Lawyers loved to hassle heavy-handed bouncers. Regardless, that cash payment of a hundred and fifty pounds meant I could stop off at the all-nighter and get some food.

Four hours later, at three o'clock, a call came through, which I ignored. But when it buzzed again, I checked the number. Although I didn't recognize it, I thought my brother could be in trouble, so I picked up.

"Carson, help."

"Who's that?"

"It's Savvie."

"Are you injured?"

"I've been cut." She sniffled.

"Where are you?"

"Just outside Club X? Do you know it?"

"Yep. Just hold on a tick. I'm not far."

I jumped into my car and took off. Since it was Thursday, the streets were half empty, with only cabs mainly getting around.

As I parked the car, I saw Savanah sitting on the ground, holding onto her arms. People just walked past, ignoring her. That's what I hated the most about this city—no one seemed to care.

I ran over and helped her up. I undid the bloodied scarf she had around her arm and was relieved to find the cut was shallow. Helping her up, I put my arm around her waist. She'd been drinking.

When we were in the car, I passed her my water bottle before asking what happened.

She guzzled some liquid and wiped her lips. "Thanks. That's better. I'm glad I had your number."

I couldn't recall ever giving it to her. "It looks like you just need a bandage for that. It's not deep, just some antiseptic and bandage should do the trick."

She shivered. Her brown shoulder-length hair was a tussled mess, but that could have been intentional. It was her face that told the story of a big night mixed with drama. Her eyeliner had run, making her blue eyes stand out.

I started the engine. "Where are you staying?"

She shook her head. "Please take me back to your house. Or maybe you could stay at mine? I can't be alone."

I thought of Angus. I had to keep an eye on him. But on the same token, I couldn't take Savanah back to my place, not with my brother there.

"Yours it is, then," I said, telling myself I'd only need to hang around until she fell asleep.

I gave her time to chill out before asking questions.

After what had been a silent trip, we arrived at Mayfair.

I helped her out and although it looked like she could walk, I helped her up the stairs to the entrance.

She rummaged in her bag filled with so much stuff it took some time to find her keys.

Her hands trembled as she tried to fit the key into the red door's lock, so I ended up doing it for her.

"Are you here alone?" I asked.

Although she'd already mentioned that earlier, looking at the rich trappings, I expected a butler or some kind of staff, like at Merivale.

"I sent the staff away for the night." She wore a weak smile. I'd never seen her so frail before. Savanah was one of those chatty, confident girls that I imagined didn't have much to cry about. Until now it seemed.

We entered the bathroom, which was the size of my living room and smelled of expensive cologne. She sat on a fluffy chair as I dabbed ointment on the wound and then bandaged it for her.

As we stepped out of the bathroom, she asked, "Can I offer you a drink?"

"Just tonic water will do," I said.

She inclined her head. "We've got plenty of Gin."

I smiled. "I'm sure you do. But no, just tonic, thanks."

She looked disappointed. "Okay, then." She poured herself a big hit of spirit with a small amount of tonic. I already knew Savanah was a lush, so that didn't surprise me. I'd also been known to hit it hard in the past—that was why I'd become a moderate drinker.

Passing me a drink, she wore the makings of a flirty smile.

During the time that I'd known her, Savanah hadn't hidden her interest. If she weren't my best friend's sister, I would have propositioned her. She was the most beautiful girl I'd ever seen. But she seemed to think she could snap her fingers and get what she wanted. Hot body and gorgeous face aside, that kind of entitled attitude made me grumpy. Sure, I had a weakness for long-legged, slender women, and I was a sucker for big blue eyes. But I liked my women down-to-earth, and the less makeup, the better.

I waited until she sat down with her drink. "So tell me, what exactly happened?"

"We were jumped by a street gang."

"By 'we' you mean a friend?"

"I was with Ollie. My boyfriend."

"Your boyfriend?" My eyes widened. "Where's he?"

"Great fucking question." She gulped her drink. "He ran away and left me to fight them off. Can you believe it?"

"He's a piece of shit then, isn't he?" I shook my head in disgust.

"They just came out of nowhere."

"They didn't take your phone, though."

"No, they chased him instead. So I'm not sure what happened to Ollie." She flicked a dark strand away from her face. "I'm kinda worried about him. But he shouldn't have left me there."

"You got that right." I couldn't believe a man doing that to his girl-friend—or any woman, for that matter. "And then they cut you?"

She nodded as her lip quivered on the rim of the glass. "They stole my jewelry and credit cards. That's after I put up a fight, but then they flashed a knife and cut me on the arm, and I gave them everything."

"It's okay. You're safe now. This sort of thing happens all too often."

"Yeah. I know. It happened one night when I was with Dusty. Only Dusty defended me. Not like spineless Ollie."

"Introduce me one of these days, and I'll be sure to give him a lesson on where to find his balls."

Her mouth curled slightly. "There'll be no next time. I'm dropping him."

"Can't say I blame you there."

After finishing her drink, she rose and stretched her arms. "Bed, I suppose. Do you mind staying while I have a quick shower?" Her eye-brow arched.

"Okay. Sure." I reached over and picked up a Sotheby's auction cata-log and flicked through the pages, staring at pretty pictures of art and objects that were as far from my world as Ikea was for the super-rich.

She came out in a dressing gown, and I rose off the leather couch. "I best be off, then."

Her face lit up with alarm. "No, stay. Please."

I looked down at my watch. It was four o'clock. "I've just got to make a call."

"To your girlfriend?" Her coquettish smile made me frown. *Is she still distressed?*

"No. My brother." I scratched my head. "I've got to call him."

I went into the hallway and called Angus, who picked up after a few rings.

"Hey. You woke me." He sounded sleepy—or maybe drugged.

"I'm just checking you're okay. You're at home?"

"Yeah. I'm in fucking bed. Asleep."

"Good. Stay there. I'll be back by the morning with breakfast."

"Picked up a babe? Hey?"

"Nope. See you in the morning."

I put away my phone.

"You're close to your brother?" She looked quite relaxed, making me wonder why I needed to be there.

"I'm his carer for the moment."

"Oh, he's not well?" Her eyes shone with concern.

"You could say that. Anyway, where shall I crash? I'm tired."

She knitted her fingers, looking a little perplexed for some reason. "Sorry. Of course."

She directed me to the guest room, which, with its burgundy velvets and gold-framed art, could have been a room in Buckingham Palace.

I pulled back the satin cover, and after stripping down to my briefs, I slid onto the super-soft sheets that smelled like a garden of roses. I closed my eyes and stretched out my body, indulging in billionaire luxury.

My eyes had only just closed when I heard footsteps. The cover lifted, and a flutter of cool air brushed over me. The mattress dipped slightly.

I turned on the lamp. Savanah sat up in a silky, see-through night-gown that left little to the imagination.

"What are you doing?" I asked.

"Can I sleep with you?" She reminded me of a needy young girl, but she was a woman in every sense of the word.

I was too tired to argue. It was too complicated. This girl was too complicated. And while I got the feeling that it wouldn't take much to remove that silky fabric and slide into her, I wasn't about to do that.

She snuggled up behind me, and I allowed myself to enjoy the warmth of her body, telling myself that was as far as it would go.

Her hands had other ideas, though.

CHASED BY A BILLIONAIRE IS BOOK 3 OF LOVECHILDE SAGA

jjsorel.com

ALSO BY J. J. SOREL

Flourished

jjsorel.com
JOIN MY MAILING LIST BY EMAILING ME
enq@jjsorel.com

Printed in Great Britain
by Amazon

27924224R00149